"I'll do anyth[ing,]"

Melanie said fiercely. "Only help me save my son."

Teo stared at her coldly. "The price is too high for anyone to pay."

Wild hope swept through her. "Anything," she repeated. "I have money. Not much. I have a house—"

"You," he cut in harshly.

"I don't understand...."

"You said anything I want. I want you. *You* are the price."

Melanie felt as if the edges of the universe were slipping away. Teo's silver-blue gaze burned into hers, and she had the odd notion he was seeing her very soul....

Marilyn Tracy lives in Portales, New Mexico, in a ramshackle turn-of-the-century house with her son, two dogs, three cats and a poltergeist. Between remodeling the house to its original Victorian-cum-Art Deco state, writing full-time and finishing a forty-foot cement dragon in the backyard, Marilyn composes complete sound tracks to go with each of her novels.

Having lived in both Tel Aviv and Moscow in conjunction with the U.S. State Department, Marilyn enjoys writing about the cultures she's explored and the peoples she's grown to love. She likes to hear from people who find pleasure in her books and always has a pot of coffee on or a glass of wine ready for anyone dropping by, especially if they don't mind chaos and know how to wield a paintbrush.

SHARING THE DARKNESS

MARILYN TRACY

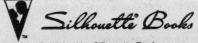

Published by Silhouette Books
America's Publisher of Contemporary Romance

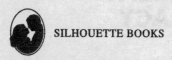

SILHOUETTE BOOKS

ISBN 0-373-51160-4

SHARING THE DARKNESS

Printed in U.S.A.

CHAPTER ONE

A man's scream and a loud metal-crunching crash echoed simultaneously through the narrow canyon valley. Both sounds, hard and desperate, seemed to come from everywhere, the cloud-heavy sky, the cold misting rain, the sodden ground beneath Melanie's feet. She whirled right, then left, as did the gas station attendant and the two old men playing checkers in front of the station.

Perhaps because of the trauma she'd been through in the last few weeks, the last few years, she immediately closed her mind to the outside influences of the world. A terrifying thought struck her. Had Chris had any part in that noise she'd heard? His talent—her curse—was growing stronger every day, partially thanks to the efforts of the scientists at the Psionic Research Institute. They had wanted to train him, and had only succeeded in frightening them both and making her life—and Chris's—a living hell.

Guilt stabbed her with sharp recrimination. How could she even think that Chris might be involved? Hadn't her three-year-old had to face enough blame and fear in his young life without his mother succumbing to anxiety about what he might have done?

But a quick look assured her that she needn't have worried; her three-year-old totally ignored the almost preternatural silence. A soft smile played on his lips, his baby face was lit with an inner contentment and, as was usual since his days at the Psionic Research Institute, his small, chubby fingers wiggled in waving motions.

A host of small items—a comb, a red ball, a comic book action figure, a plastic lid from a fast-food drive-in, even a tube of lipstick—danced around the interior of the car, hovering in the air, set to a tune only Chris could hear. And they were held in midair by his mind only, little puppets controlled by a small puppeteer.

Melanie swiftly looked around to see if anyone was watching her car but didn't relax when she saw that no one was paying her son the slightest attention. When was the last time she had relaxed? She couldn't remember. It may have been the day before young Chris was born. And she'd been in labor then.

Another scream rent the air and Melanie gasped. Chris's eyes didn't so much as flicker. His entire focus was upon his little collection of dancing objects, which whirled so effortlessly, so defiantly, in midair. He'd always had the ability to manipulate the world around him, even as early as six months old, when he'd turned the toys on the windowsill into a mobile over his bed.

But until his days at the PRI, he'd been easily distracted and the toys would drop to the ground. Whatever they'd done to him, he'd apparently found a place to escape. Now when Chris concentrated on making his toys dance, he was totally oblivious to the rest of the world.

Only violent shaking or abrupt body contact could snap him from this unusual withdrawal. This was what the scientists at the PRI had done for him. *To* him. And they would have done far more if they'd had the opportunity…an opportunity she was determined not to give them, despite their threats.

At least, Melanie thought bleakly now, Chris hadn't been the cause of whatever crash had taken place in these lonely mountains.

But something had.

In the stillness following the tremendous racket—a silence made all the more noticeable by the lack of any jays' raucous calls—one of the old men spat tobacco juice onto the muddy pathway that served as a sidewalk flanking the gas station. The dark spittle narrowly missed a wet paint-chipped sign that had long since faded into little more than a testimony of poverty and abandonment. The sign read Loco Suerte.

To Melanie, lost in the back roads of northern New Mexico, trying to escape the clutches of the PRI scientists, tired from two steady weeks of fruitless searching for the only man she thought might be able to help them, and now standing stock-still in a chill October mist, the scream still echoing in her ears, the village's name was curiously apt…Crazy Luck. It was just the kind of luck she *would* have.

The old man who'd spit spoke in a lisping Castillian Spanish that she automatically, though with some difficulty, translated. "Demo. His vehicle slipped. Demo's car fell off that *loco* jack he made." His voice was as lacking in emotion as his face, but creaked like the door the gas station attendant had pushed through only minutes earlier.

The gas station attendant, or possibly the owner, a short squat man of about fifty with at least three days' growth of jet black beard, a filthy once white T-shirt, and a thick, black mustache that fully covered his upper lip, barked several curses in Spanish and broke into a run toward the side of his station. Just as he was rounding the corner, he slithered to a muddy stop and yelled at Melanie in English, "She doesn't turn off! Close the gas, will you, *señora?*"

As if his words broke some sort of peculiar spell woven by the scream, the crash and the seeming indifference of the old men playing checkers, Melanie turned to "close" the gas, fumbling with the antiquated apparatus that passed as a gas tank. As she did so, she heard the attendant—owner?—yell from out of sight, again in that curiously lisping Castillian Spanish, "*Abuelito,* call the sheriff for an ambulance! And get me some help here. Demo's trapped under the car!''

While one of the old men, presumably the grandfather the attendant had called to, pushed his chair back and seemingly slowly reached for the telephone—a device that looked as though it had been installed by Alexander Bell himself—Melanie heard the loud curses of the attendant from the other side of the low, dilapidated building.

Even as the older man called the sheriff, the slip-slop of many feet on the mud street told Melanie that help had arrived. Six or seven men appeared from out of the forest and the nearby adobe structures she had earlier mistaken for abandoned, or, perhaps magically, from the slick, muddy street that five minutes' earlier had been totally devoid of people. They were followed rapidly by several women, most of them dressed in black, one carrying a small child.

Melanie didn't feel as if she was in the United States any longer. She had stepped back in time to some mountain village in a different country.

Again Melanie glanced at Chris, willing him in vain to halt his toys' dance. Again, her worry was in vain. No one noticed her son; all attention was focused on whatever had transpired around the side of the dilapidated garage.

''¡Uno...dos...tres!'' the attendant yelled, and on the count of three the combined voices of all the men groaned in seven-part harmony. ''Again! Try it again!''

Melanie told an unresponsive Chris to stay in the car, and followed the sound of the voices until she stood just around the pocked corner of the gas station. Then she averted her head in quick negation, closing her eyes sharply against the sight of a man lying too still, apparently crushed by the old Chevy that had lost its mooring on the jack and now was being held some two feet above the man by seven straining men.

"Throw it over," the attendant yelled.

"But Demo's Chevy—"

"Throw it over! Who cares about the car? On three.... *¡Uno...dos...tres!*"

The heavy, battered classic flipped over with a groaning shudder and slithered down a muddy embankment.

"*¡Madre de Dios!* He's alive!" a woman screamed.

Melanie opened her eyes again and tracked the line of the woman's pointing finger. The mechanic, though bloodied and covered with oil and grime, was indeed feebly moving. Melanie couldn't have said how, but he was.

"Jaime, *andale!* Fetch El Rayo!" the attendant yelled. Then, without looking to see if the young man he had clapped on the shoulder did his bidding, he bent over the hapless mechanic.

"But, Pablo..." the young man protested.

"Now, damn it! Fetch him!" the attendant snapped, again without looking at Jaime. The youth stood uncertainly for a moment, then bolted into the thick trees flanking the gas station to the north.

Pablo bent lightly, resting a hand on the injured man's brow. "Demo...Demo, boy, can you hear me? You'll be all right. *Abuelito* called for an ambulance." The attendant looked upward, as though praying, then back down as he said urgently, "And *he* comes soon."

Melanie held her breath. El Rayo—Rah-e-yoh—might be translated to mean The Man of Thunderbolts. Was her quest to be ended this easily? Or was the peculiar term, "El Rayo," some odd colloquialism for doctor or even ambulance? But the attendant had said, "*He* comes..."

He...El Rayo.

She'd spent the last nerve-racking two weeks dodging around the country, slinking in and out of seedy hotel rooms at night, spending entire days in a paid-with-cash rental Buick, accompanied only by her unusual and telekinetic son, seeking a man who was said to destroy brick buildings by a mere wave of his hands. A man who, according to the files at the PRI, was a recluse, a barbarian and a would-be killer. A man who could literally move the earth or eradicate it with a look.

Was he the man with thunderbolts in his fingertips?

Melanie realized that until this moment, hearing the odd designation, she had nearly given up hope of finding the man she sought. She had never felt foolish in her quest, that wasn't it. Anything she could possibly do now, any bizarre hope of saving Chris from the scientific experiments at The Psionic Research Institute was worth any investigation. But just an hour earlier, lost and tired, her back aching from the many miles behind the wheel of her car, and tired of dodging free-floating bits of tissue, food wrappers, or even the road map, she had been prepared to admit defeat.

If there was a powerful telekinetic hiding in these rugged, terrifying mountains, it was obvious he didn't want to be found. Up to now she'd been relying on every facet of her own telepathic abilities, her own clairvoyance, and they might have led her here, but she wasn't even sure where *here* was.

From the files, she'd illegally studied, she'd known he was reclusive. She'd known he'd be hiding. *And dangerous?* her mind offered. *Yes,* she'd also known that, both from the files and from her own chaotic and vague dreams in which a man named Teo Sandoval called her name as electricity flew from his very fingertips. Dreams that always left her shaking, a scream choked in her throat.

But at the same time, the very dangerousness that was inherent to the man she sought, dreamed about, was what made him her last hope of saving Chris from being taken from her. Her former husband, Tom, had already signed over his custody rights to the PRI...it hadn't taken them long to try to secure hers. And when she'd refused, still furious with her ex-husband for even thinking he could get away with such a thing, they had made it perfectly clear how little an obstacle they considered her. If she weren't around, they'd said, Chris would become a ward of the court. And since Chris's own father wished them to protect his only son, no court in the world would deny their petition for full custodial rights.

She had fled the institute that night, knowing full well that the PRI scientists, privately funded and not regulated by any governmental watch committees, believed themselves above any and all laws. They had no intention of letting anything get in their way, especially not a mother who didn't exhibit any sign of their coveted telekinesis. So, by fair or foul means, they planned to snatch Chris and harbor him at the Psionic Research Institute permanently, a captive subject to their bizarre experiments and brutal testings.

A woman holding a small child moaned and sagged, but was caught and shushed by the older woman nearest her. "Be quiet, Doro. Pray. El Rayo comes. One touch and your husband will live. You know. Believe it."

At this Melanie had to stifle the flood of questions that sprang to her lips. If she voiced any of them, she might be asked to leave, and she couldn't do that until she was certain this El Rayo wasn't the man she sought so desperately. To forestall the surge of hope welling inside, she reminded herself that she wasn't in the rolling countryside of Pennsylvania any more, she was in the backwoods of the Sangre de Cristo mountain range, a place where the superstitious populace still believed in curses, witches and miracles. A place where she was the only Anglo in a world of ancient Spanish; the outsider who neither fluently spoke their unusual dialect nor understood their customs.

Pablo pulled back from the mechanic and Melanie had

to cover her mouth with both hands to restrain an instinctive cry of dismay. It would take nothing less than a bolt of lightning to help this man. In fact, Melanie doubted there was much a trained physician could do, even if he carried patented miracles in his little black bag, for the mechanic was all too obviously dying. Automatically she lowered her precious mental guard to seek the mechanic's thoughts and caught them too easily.

Madre de Dios...why can't I breathe?

She slammed the gates of her mind tightly closed. She couldn't bear hearing a dying man's thoughts.

Seeing the crumbling face of the woman holding the child tightly to her shuddering breast, hearing the murmurs of the men around the dying mechanic, Melanie felt disassociated. She seemed in two places at once. Here, in the chill October afternoon rain in a lonely mountain village in northern New Mexico, carnage at her feet, and *there*, in a too bright laboratory, watching a team of white-coated men attach electrodes to her son's chubby chest while he cried at the chill of their fingers and shrank from the fear and longing in their eyes.

"The ghost clouds come," the mechanic's wife moaned, snapping Melanie back to the present. "Demo will die. See how they come for him!"

Melanie tilted her head to follow the woman's gaze, not needing to squint her eyes against the soft rain. Thin, foglike wisps of white snaked through the tall pines, slinking over the high, treeless peaks and silently creeping downward toward the village. Melanie restrained a shudder. She could see why a superstition about the clouds might be generated. They did indeed look like stalking ghosts.

A bird swooped down from a nearby tall pine and, as one, the crowd around the mechanic gasped. The mechanic's child began to cry, restively, perhaps from being held too tightly against his mother's breast.

An older woman called out, "An owl! It's an omen! Call Tierra Amarillo's church for a priest!"

Pablo growled something about "talking goats" at the woman, then fell silent, his gaze fixing in Melanie's direction. One by one, the rest of the group turned, grew quiet. For a moment Melanie thought all eyes were trained fearfully on her, then she realized their cumulative gazes were just beyond her shoulder. She felt an almost atavistic fear of turning around to discover what could hold that many voluble people so absolutely silent. Could Chris have left the car, dancing objects in his wake?

She fought the sudden attack of nerves and turned.

The youth, Jaime, stood to one side of the muddy station stalls, as though keeping a fair distance from the man who strode across the water-burdened street toward him and the garage. Melanie had the urge to do the same as the young man and couldn't resist drawing closer to the damp and chipped adobe wall.

Behind her, the crowd now gathered around the dying mechanic sighed and whispered, "El Rayo...El Rayo." The muted voices underscored the strangeness of the man approaching them.

He walked as though in no particular hurry, though his stride was steady and broad. Like a bullfighter's, Melanie thought, snared by the sighing, chanting voices behind her, or like a king's all-powerful steps.

"The car fell on Demo," Pablo called out to the silent figure, cutting through the whispers. "He lives. But only just."

"El Rayo," the mechanic's wife begged, "help my Demo, please."

Melanie turned to look at the group of townspeople and noticed they had all pulled back—like Jaime, like herself— as though contact with this stranger would be injurious to their health. She couldn't blame them. There was something so dark, so forceful, about the man that it seemed to exude from his very pores. And yet, almost as if whatever it was about him was electrical—and if he was the man she sought, it might very well be electrical in nature—she felt her skin respond to his presence.

He was of Latin descent, with a dark complexion and jet black hair that hung far below the collar of his shirt, farther still, perhaps beneath his shoulder blades. Either one of his recent ancestors had been Anglo or he was a throwback to the true Spanish that had originally settled these mountains, for the man's eyes were a glittering pale blue-gray, the color of the sky on a stormy winter's afternoon.

This imposing stranger wasn't tall, perhaps only six feet or so, but his shoulders were broad enough to strain at his rough flannel shirt. His hips were narrow, and his thighs, tightly encased in his jeans, were muscled and thick. Moisture clung to his dark hair and seemed to shimmer, creating the impression of a dark liquid halo.

This had to be *him,* Melanie thought wildly; everything about him exuded dark mystery and raw sensuality. He was more spirit than man, a wild black stallion, a lone timber wolf, a clap of thunder on a cloudless night. He gave the impression of absolute power.

She had to know if he was, indeed, Teo Sandoval, the man she'd needed so desperately. She unveiled her mind a notch and reached out to him when he paused, stopping at the side of the building. His eyes seemingly took in the entire scene at a glance.

His mind was questing so—reading all—she couldn't get through, and dropped her guard another notch.

He said nothing as most of the people tried explaining what had happened at the same time. He turned his gaze finally, and with cool appraisal, to Melanie.

She felt a moment's pure shock as her gaze linked with his, as his mind tried to probe hers. It was a rare enough occurrence, to actually lock eyes with someone, but it wasn't the rarity of it that triggered an inner quaking in Melanie. An elemental sexuality seemed to transmit from the stranger like the coldest of mountain winds and, at the same time, like the heat of a cliff's edge baked too long by a summer sun. She knew instinctively this man was like no one she had ever known before, and she couldn't seem to think clearly enough to decide whether that boded well or ill.

Lines from the files on him she'd read chased through her mind, incoherent, fleeting. After the fiasco, after his demolishing an entire wing of the PRI when they had pushed him too hard, after he had escaped their clutches, one psychiatrist had written of him: *He's a man of extreme conscience. I don't know whether Teo Sandoval should be condemned or praised. But at all costs, he should be left alone.*

If not for Chris, at that moment Melanie would gladly have turned and left the man alone, abandoned her quest for his help, because, linked with his gaze, for a single, shattering moment she had felt as though they were the only two people on earth. She shivered, feeling totally and wholly exposed. Then she felt him strengthen the probe to her mind, as though ready to rifle through her thoughts, glean every drop of knowledge about her. She swiftly clamped her mind closed, slamming the door on her thoughts, her soul. That slam seemed to echo inside her and it somehow hurt.

Though he didn't so much as flinch, some instinctive knowledge told her that she wasn't the only one affected by their exchange. Something about it had shocked him, as well. She had the oddest notion that for a single flicker of time she had been looking into the man's very soul. She had caught a glimpse of a well of anger and loneliness trapped inside him. An aloneness so extreme that it seemed far removed from any mere lack of human companionship, to the point of being another emotion altogether, one that would make others cringe in terror.

She didn't have the sensation of reading the man's thoughts, there was no tingling awareness of any sort of telepathy or mind transference; she knew that feeling all too well. This was more simply and starkly a case of knowing some facet of his innermost feelings. Nothing anyone said could have persuaded her that she was wrong at that moment. What she'd seen, what she'd *felt*, was an intimacy as strong and bonding as the marriage of night and day, as sharp and poignant as a final farewell.

Something flashed in the man's eyes and as abruptly as he'd pulled her into the depths of his gaze, she felt released, or more accurately, thrown aside. She had shut her mind to him, but now, brusquely, he was wholly closed to her, as well. He was once again a stranger, and all she could see in his unusual eyes was her own reflection. She shuddered in relief.

He turned from her then and, without having to ask anyone to clear the way, walked through the group that parted for him as they might have for a god…or a monster in their midst. He drew a deep breath, shook his hands out to the side of his body like a fighter preparing for the ring, then slowly knelt over the wheezing mechanic.

It wasn't until she saw him kneel that Melanie realized he wasn't carrying that extension of every country doctor's arm—the medical kit. He had come to aid this mechanic with no more than his bare hands. Or, Melanie thought a little wildly, with his pale, hypnotic eyes.

He was the one. He had to be. Teo Sandoval, a telekinetic whose powers had been strong enough to frighten the PRI, perhaps the only man on earth who could help her save her son from their designs.

Behind him, around him, the odd collection of assistants

and relatives made the index finger-over-thumb sign against evil despite their avid gazes. Melanie saw with some sense of irony that now that he wasn't looking directly at them, all strained to see everything this unusual man might do.

To Melanie's wonder, then consternation, he appeared to do nothing at all. Then he gently pulled away the mechanic's bloodied shirt, exposing the ravaged, lacerated chest. Melanie bit her lip to keep from groaning in horror.

El Rayo then raised both hands over the man's chest and flexed his shoulders as if steeling himself against a great ordeal. A multivoiced sigh rippled through the anxious crowd. As if that were a signal of sorts, El Rayo lowered his rock-steady hands to lay them directly on the man's bloody chest. Again Melanie had to hold in a cry of instinctive protest.

Though his back was to her, she could see a shudder seize him and shake him as violently as though he were caught in a tornado. A moan escaped the mechanic's wife and her baby whimpered once, then all were silent again. Even the winged denizens of the forest seemed to be holding their breaths.

Unconsciously, Melanie had drawn closer, and now took another step forward, as much to see better as to offer whatever assistance she might have to give. Pablo's arm shot out to restrain her. A work-roughened hand encircled her wrist.

"No, *señora*," he whispered. "Wait."

"What is he doing?" she asked, and though she had only breathed the question, she was shushed by the older woman flanking the mechanic's wife.

"Wait," the attendant said again, and turned his gaze back to the tableau at their feet.

As if rigidly locked in a battle as ancient as the mountains themselves, the stranger beneath her seemed frozen over the dying mechanic. Ignoring both rain and the people crowded near him, his concentration was solely and absolutely on the man under his hands.

Melanie had the disorienting feeling that she had experienced the merest hint of that concentration just seconds earlier when they had locked gazes. And a dim part of her wondered what his hands would feel like against her skin, and if that deliberation of mind and soul would accompany his touch. She shook her head as though the movement would rid her mind of such unusual imagery.

From the reaction of the crowd, and from the rumors she'd heard, read about, back in Pennsylvania, Melanie half expected thunderbolts to shoot from the rain-heavy sky or for the ghost clouds to come snatch the mechanic and his odd healer from their midst. But in actuality the rain only continued to fall softly and silently, the ground grew muddier, and the people standing around got wetter and colder.

Somehow, to Melanie, this seemingly prosaic attitude of Mother Nature's only strengthened the illusion of magic that was transpiring before her very eyes. A contrast, nature's indifferent energy versus that of the man at her feet. She felt as though she were watching a play that had been written in the Dark Ages, but was seeing it unfold in another country, another time.

And in watching this bizarre spectacle wholly at odds with all she had known to be true before, Melanie trembled. Could it be true? Could this man really heal with his touch? She suspected—no, she *knew*—he would, if by no other means than sheer force of will.

The thought sobered her. And made her hopeful for the first time in six months. Could Chris ever learn to harness his talents for good, for tremendous good, instead of making his toys dance, and instead of the sorts of goals the PRI had in store for him?

She dimly pondered what she was witnessing: an old-fashioned, often disputed healing. Even as she realized the implications of this "healing," she wondered, almost in anger, what, if it was true, this man was doing in the back-woods of nowhere. Why hide such a gift? If he was indeed such a healer, he should be out in the world helping millions, hundreds of millions.

She remembered the notes on his telekinetic abilities, remarks recorded when Teo Sandoval had been only some nineteen years old and as wild and furious as a trapped mountain creature. And then she remembered the detailed description of his destruction of one entire wing of the PRI. That he hadn't killed anyone had been a miracle in and of itself. The PRI scientists had termed him "untrainable," "irredeemable," a barbarian with untold powers. When he'd fled the institute, no one had tried to stop him. Nor had they done anything to stop the annuity the PRI had established for his father and his heirs when he essentially sold Teo to the PRI almost fifteen years ago. As Tom had tried doing with Chris.

But with such powers, such a tremendous gift for healing, how could Teo Sandoval remain at the edge of nowhere, allowing pain and misery to exist in the world, when by a touch he could alleviate so much?

More than that, he should be out in the world helping children like Chris learn to live with their unusual gifts. Keeping them safe from being exploited as he had been. Would she be able to persuade him to help her? To protect her son and teach him how to live with his double-edged gifts?

She felt that sense of helpless anger coalesce into determination. How dare he linger at the edge of oblivion when the PRI was threatening to take her son away, tear him from her against her will, shunt him away into some frightening institution simply because he was different…and then try to use his unusual talents for their own desires? This man, if he was indeed Teo Sandoval, had endured a similar child-hood. How dare he ignore other children like him?

Time seemed to stop and the entire universe seemed to focus on this one small portion of land, man and hope. El Rayo's beautiful hands, broad-palmed with long, narrow, tapered fingers, seemed to lay upon the mechanic's chest, or to hover above it for hours, though Melanie found out later that the entire scenario had lasted a mere quarter turn of the clock.

Suddenly she felt a difference in the quality of the air. The low clouds continued to spray a fine mist upon the silent onlookers, the still mechanic and the dark healer, but a new element had been added, or perhaps subtracted. The air all but crackled with electricity, smelled heavily of ozone—as if lightning had struck the ground they stood on.

She could feel the tension rippling through the rough hand around her wrist, and she half suspected the man who held her had forgotten he was doing so. He, like everyone else, was watching, waiting, probably crossing his fingers for a seeming miracle or, like some of the others, against evil.

Then El Rayo gave a sigh, strangely like a groan of pain, and reeled up and backward from the mechanic. His moan was echoed by the crowd, but no one moved to assist the staggering healer. He turned blindly, stumbling over some-thing, nearly falling, slipping on the sodden clay soil that comprised the earth in the New Mexico mountains.

Shocked by his pallor, by the blue rimming his full lips, Melanie ignored the now surrounded mechanic and invol-untarily cried out and tried to reach for him. Again the hand on her wrist held her back.

"No, *señora*. You must not," Pablo murmured. Not "you *should* not," but, "you *must* not."

"Let me go!" Melanie cried, snapping her arm away from her would-be rescuer. "He needs help!"

Unaware she was calling out in Spanish, she didn't understand the look of amazement the attendant turned on her. Or was it something else? Something to do with her wanting to help the "healer"?

"No one can help El Rayo, *señora*," he said. "I have tried for many years. It's no use." His voice sounded as sad as his face looked, but did he mean the man was beyond help, or that he would not allow another to lend aid?

A cry from the mechanic's wife snared everyone's attention and Melanie turned to see the mechanic slowly pulling himself up to his elbows. "Doro?" he asked in a sleepy voice. "What happened, Doro? Why—?"

Everyone pushed to answer him, to assist him, and in the brief distraction, Pablo released Melanie's wrist. Without further thought, she lunged for the strange healer before he pitched into a thick scrub oak.

Wrapping her arms around his body, she eased him back against her, though his weight pulled them both to the ground. A tremendous shudder worked through his body and he half turned, instinctively seeking the comfort of her arms.

He might be weak but his gaze was as sharp as it had been earlier. And whatever residue there was of his lightning touch seemed to ripple and eddy against her skin, making the hairs on her arms rise. She felt her heartbeat accelerating and knew by the tension on his face that he could hear it, feel it throbbing against his cheek.

She told herself she was holding him as she might a child, but knew this was a patent lie. This man inspired a riot of sensation in her, but none of it was the least motherly in nature. Her mouth felt dry, her fingers against his face trembled.

His lips parted, his eyes glittered at her, a cold distance bridging an anger she couldn't fathom.

"No one touches me," he said harshly in English, his

deep baritone rough, the words as ambiguous as the man himself. Did he mean that no one had? Or did he mean that no one *should?*

When she didn't move, didn't release him, one of his hands raised to wipe the moisture from her face. Was the moisture a product of the mist, or had she been crying? She didn't know and with his fingers lightly tracing the curve of her cheek, she couldn't have begun to guess.

Her heart all but thundered in her chest and she felt a strange languor seeping through her body. Was he hypnotizing her? Was his touch making her feel things she'd never even imagined, let alone experienced?

His silence and intensity frightened her. Dear God, she thought in desperation, what kind of a man was he?

"Don't you know, *señora,* that one touch from me can kill?"

CHAPTER TWO

When Melanie had shaken the attendant's hand from her arm, when she'd run to try to stem El Rayo's fall, she'd acted out of pure impulse. He'd needed help, she had responded. But this was no pathetic, wounded man. He was all but admitting he could kill her with a single touch. And his hand upon her cheek made the message all that much more ominous.

She wanted to say something, anything, to deflect the conflicting signals in his stormy gaze. But all she could think was, *He is the one.* She was holding a man whose single glance could destroy an entire two-story building, had her arms wrapped around a force that could maim as easily as he apparently healed.

This was the man she'd been looking for, desperate to find, and now he was not so obliquely threatening her.

But had it been a threat or a simple statement of fact? Something told her instinctively that nothing short of total exhaustion would ever have allowed him to lie so still in her arms. Everything about her first impression of him attested to that single fact. He was a man who stood alone, apart from the rest, needing and wanting no one.

The line from the psychiatrist's report teased her again. *But at all costs, he should be left alone.* Not advice, not a casual reference, but a dire warning.

However, his weight, his face against the swell of her breast, his warm breath teasing her through the thin material of her wet blouse made her certain the psychiatrist had other meanings in mind. *He should be left alone.* Oh, yes. He most certainly should be left alone. To touch him was to dance on the edge of a high cliff without a parachute. To feel his fingers on one's face was to know the searing heat of a volcano and the icy plunge into a glacier lake.

Melanie swallowed heavily. She had to ask for his help now, at this moment, while his powers were at least moderately on the wane, while his internal batteries were obviously somewhat depleted. This might be her only chance because she knew from the way the townspeople had averted his gaze, had avoided hers, that they would be unlikely to aid her in finding him again. He was *their* mystery, their El Rayo. A miracle man of this magnitude wasn't likely to be a subject of much discussion, and certainly wouldn't be offered to an outsider.

"Please..." she began, only to trail off at an increase in the volume coming from the group to their left. With a great effort, she dragged her gaze from El Rayo, the man she believed—*knew*—to be Teo Sandoval.

Over the bulk of his shoulder she could see the crowd around the mechanic. To her further shock, the young, bloodied man was being assisted to his feet. Whatever protest she might have uttered died on her lips as the man grinned crookedly and patted his own chest. At that moment all knowledge of her Spanish eluded her and she was never certain afterward what was spoken, but watched, in wonder, as the mechanic gently hugged his openly sobbing wife and baby.

Like the others, she had seen the mechanic's chest, had heard the gurgle of expiration from his damaged lungs. She'd heard the so-called death rattle often enough in her lifetime to have recognized it here. There had been no doubt that he would die. She'd felt it, had seen it in all the faces of the people anxiously crowding around.

She looked back down at the man in her arms with a combination of awe and fear. She knew now why the townspeople had stood back from him, had avoided his sky-pale eyes. She was more than a little afraid of him herself. But like the villagers in this small mountain community, she needed him.

She wished she could believe that with him so spent in her arms there was nothing to fear from him, but as if that crew of yesteryear PRI scientists surrounded her, she could sense their doubt, feel their nervousness, hear their murmurs of awe. Was it the influence of the local people, happy that their Demo lived but wary of the man who healed him, or was it something she discerned about him all on her own?

She wished she could feel empathy for him, alone with his gift, but only felt a wary sympathy instead. Something about him, locked anew in his glittering gaze, the dark liquid halo of hair touching her, made Melanie feel that she had dived into a crystal-clear lake and discovered, too late, that it was truly crystal, not water at all. There was something terribly sharp and hard about him, no matter how helpless he might now appear.

He studied her for all the world as if she were the anomaly, as if she were the cause of the commotion beyond them.

"You're very foolish, *señora*," he said.

She agreed with him absolutely. But desperation bred foolishness...and heroics. And she didn't believe he was calling her silly or inept, but was speaking from dark knowledge, from some untold need to warn her away.

She heard someone ask another how she could be touching El Rayo. Until that moment she hadn't stopped to truly consider what she'd witnessed. Not one person had touched him, most had even avoided his gaze. He had touched the mechanic, not the other way around. Was this what the attendant had meant when he'd uttered, "You must not," and held her away from the reeling Teo Sandoval?

On some dim level, not overriding the mesmerizing quality of his gaze but augmenting it somehow, she was half aware of the looks of awe the townspeople were leveling at her. Had none of them ever touched the man? She wanted to open her mind again, catch reasons, rationales, but the power of the man in her arms kept her from lowering that guard.

"Please…" she said again, but wasn't certain what she was asking of him now. She was too conscious of his warm face against her wet blouse, his hand dropping from her own overwarm cheeks.

She thought of Chris, of how his own father had shrunk away from him in fear, of how baby-sitters had fled the house in terror, of how even the scientists at the PRI had touched Chris only when wearing lead-lined gloves. She had been the only one who wasn't afraid of Chris, had been the only one to openly give him the small assurances that he was lovable and loved.

Was this man in her arms only a taller, adult version of her son? Perhaps once, long ago. But no longer. Melanie shivered in recognition of the differences. Teo Sandoval was nothing like Chris. Her son had yet to enter life, this man had slammed the door on the outside world. Her son's tiny fingers made objects dance in the air, this man's touch either cured or destroyed. Shining light or utter darkness, both sides warred inside this man's soul. Pray God, Chris never knew such contrasts.

She tried calling on whatever mild powers she herself possessed to reach into the future and see the outcome of this meeting, but with her mind so firmly closed to the man in her arms, her inner crystal ball remained cloudy, indistinct. Then his eyes narrowed in part suspicion, part confusion and she recognized him from her dreams, the same dreams that had led her to this misty mountain and to this man. She recognized his face from the PRI photographs and from her nightmares, the ones that left her choking on tears, the sound of her own screams ringing in her ears.

As if hating what he was seeing, he turned his face abruptly, pressing tightly against her breasts. His hand gripped her shoulder in a rough, nearly painful grip. As vulnerable as he might seem, drained by this unusual healing, Melanie didn't consider him an object of pity. His power, the strange magic within him, might be quiescent, but she knew it was a momentary, fleeting circumstance. It would be back. And when it came, it would be strong enough to demolish his surroundings...or save a man's life.

He opened his eyes and met hers. Again she had the fleeting impression of a lone timber wolf. And like the lone wolf, the message in his eyes was definitive. *I stand alone...that which comes near me comes in peril.*

No gratitude radiated from his eyes, no measure of relief. The only thing she could read was raw distrust. There were other things there, as well, but they were darker, rougher, too frightening to contemplate.

He shivered as if fevered, and suddenly, as if by virtue of having moved, his energy sources seemed replenished. Now his body felt overwarm against hers, making her uncomfortably aware of the intimacy of their embrace. His eyes never wavered from hers and this added to her unease. He wasn't searching her eyes or her face for answers, was instead staring at her in complete rejection.

For a moment she had the fanciful notion that he stared at her as a creature of the wild would. A creature that was trapped in the piercing beam of a pair of headlights, with an almost weary acceptance of doom, of a fate gone so far awry as to announce certain death. She wished she didn't recognize the look, but she did. She'd seen it in the mirror of yet another cheap hotel room just this morning. She'd seen it yesterday, last week, a month ago, and all too often since the first day Chris had made the toys on the windowsill dance for his dumbfounded parents.

But Teo Sandoval wasn't like Chris. Shaking her head slightly to rid herself of the mere thought, Melanie took a shaky breath. His eyelids lowered slightly, dangerously, and *any* thought she'd had of *any* similarity vanished. He didn't look trapped, only supremely cautious and prepared. *Deadly.*

He didn't move, didn't so much as shift, but she was suddenly wholly conscious of the fact that the only thing preventing him from rising to his feet were her two arms wrapped around him. But she couldn't seem to let him go. It wasn't that she didn't want to, she did; her arms were numb, as though they'd fallen asleep, though she knew that had to be impossible. What was he doing to her? Or was she doing something to herself, the need she harbored for his help making certain that she wouldn't let him slip away?

He slowly raised a dark, strong hand. The palms of his hands were broad, and the fingers long and tapered, marred by large, slightly irregular knuckles. They could have been the hands of a sculptor...or a murderer, she didn't care. All she knew was that they held the power of the universe in them. She'd seen the photographs of the destruction he'd caused with a single wave of those hands. And now she'd seen evidence of that power with her own eyes, she was captivated...and terrified of what his touch would do to her.

She willed herself to push away from him, to pull back, but couldn't seem to move. Somehow she could sense the violent emotion in him, and it frightened her. Then, just as she thought she'd cry out, his hand reached for her. But instead of touching her face again, as she'd more than half expected, he lifted a wet strand of her hair. He caressed the strand with his fingers, as if memorizing its texture, staring at it as if it were some great enigma.

Her heart was pounding so loudly, so furiously, she was certain he would be able to hear it, if not feel it.

He studied her hair, almost as though mesmerized by it, then slowly transferred his gaze to her own widely opened eyes. Then he gave a rather sharp tug to the hair in his grasp.

"You are very foolish, *señora*," he repeated. His voice was still slightly raspy, and Melanie suspected the reason why. The harshness had nothing to do with a lack of language skills but was, rather, because he seldom spoke.

Something in his tone, in his rough touch sent a spark of fire through her. Again she had the sensation that the two of them seemed to be alone on this hillside, far away from all humanity. She was suddenly and deeply aware of this strange man's sheer masculinity and, by contrast, her own femininity. Her lips parted in wonder at the feeling. How long had it been since she'd felt anything like this? More than a year? More than two or three, perhaps. Since Chris had been born probably, and possibly even before that.

Part of her wanted to reach up and cover this healer's hand with her own. Growing inside of her was a desire for affirmation, need to show him she understood a want he hadn't voiced. But before she could speak, his hand dropped her hair and came to rest on his chest. Melanie swallowed, tasting an odd disappointment. Such raw power he held in those lax fingers, yet all he'd done was touch her face, hold a single, wet lock of her hair—

"Let me go," he said. Though his voice was nearly a whisper, the command was as sharp and clear as a clarion.

Slowly, almost painfully, she unlocked her arms, setting him free. She refused to meet his eyes. To do so was to drown in his abject aloneness, that cold, crystalline rejection. To linger there was to willingly submit to what she knew was his double-edged power—the gift of life or the capability of total destruction.

But he remained motionless, didn't pull away from her. And now that she was no longer holding him, the intimacy of their positions seemed all the greater, for his head still pressed against her breasts, his body still curved against hers.

As if in rescue, she heard the distant whine of sirens. It was probably the sheriff and ambulance the *abuelito* had called earlier, which raised another set of questions. Would Teo Sandoval stay long enough to hear her request? After meeting his eyes, touching him, did she even dare ask it of him now?

"Quickly, El Rayo...you must go now," Pablo said. "The sheriff comes. People. You have to go now. Johnny's only a mile from here, maybe less. If you don't wish them to see you, you have to hurry. *¡Andale!*"

The other man motioned for Teo to rise, but made no move to help him. In fact, he kept his eyes studiously averted. Melanie saw a look of pure hatred cross Teo Sandoval's face and recoiled from it even though it wasn't directed at her but at the attendant who had spoken.

His muscles rippled and contracted and Melanie bit her lip against the visceral reaction the motion inspired in her. She saw Teo give Pablo a cold, measured look that seemed to contain some dreadful message, and shivered inwardly. She hoped she would never live to receive such a baleful glare.

"Let him go, *señora*. It's no favor to keep him here," Pablo continued. Melanie's brow furrowed. Even to her still dazed mind, the man no longer had the look of a backward, poverty-stricken gas station owner, but instead seemed to have something of Teo Sandoval's strong, potentially threatening aura about him.

"I'm not stopping him," Melanie said, and even to herself her voice sounded hoarse and taut with tension. She allowed her hands to slide away from him, to the cold, wet ground where the mud felt slimy and slick after the roughness of his shirt, the warmth of his body.

In a swift, powerful stretch, Teo silently pushed to his feet and, after a moment's hesitation and a slight sway to the right, turned as though to leave. For a dismaying moment Melanie thought he would disappear without a word, and wondered if perhaps the man was like an idiot savant, capable of incredible feats but not "fully there." The PRI files hadn't indicated anything like that, and yet the scientists *had* deemed him a barbarian. Her mind hotly denied the idiot savant possibility, and without conscious decision, she called out in protest.

"Teo!"

He stopped as if shot, and turned back to look down at her. Though she felt none of that soul-shattering connection that had gripped her earlier, she was all too aware of an inordinant amount of relief at the look of wariness, of cold intelligence, in his eyes. She found herself holding her breath.

"Who are you?" he asked. His voice was still rough and scratchy. And this, too, inexplicably served to ease her confused mind. He wasn't wholly recovered, and therefore *had* to be human, after all. His eyes darkened as he waited for her answer.

She told him her name and he nodded slowly, as if he had expected her to say Melanie Daniels.

Pablo muttered something, but trailed off when Teo turned his silver-blue gaze in his direction. The attendant shrugged and looked away uncomfortably, shoving his hands into his pockets.

Teo's eyes were narrowed as he switched his gaze back to her. "How do you know my name?"

Melanie could see a wealth of wariness on his face and

noted that his entire frame seemed a testimonial to that tension. She knew, by his question, that her earlier suspicions that he didn't wish to be found were accurate. Teo Sandoval. The one man who could possibly help her son. This was him. Until this moment she hadn't let herself truly believe it. But it was true. *She'd found him.* He *had* to help her, but instinctively she knew she would have to tread very carefully.

He was still waiting for an answer to his terse question. Melanie drew a shallow breath. Was he telepathic, as well? Her mind was closed to him, certainly—she had been able to close it at will since childhood, even though it opened alarmingly easily in sleep—so he couldn't be reading *her* thoughts. But was it possible that he could read deeper than mere surface thoughts, perhaps pluck the truth from her subconscious?

"I—I heard about you. I read about you in the f-files at the Psionic Research Institute."

If she'd expected him to look shocked or even recoil in some exaggerated rendition of horror, she would have been disappointed; he did neither. He merely stared at her with the cold flat expression she was coming to associate with him.

"I need your help," she said finally.

Something flickered in his eyes at that, but his facial features didn't shift an iota.

"My son...he..."

"I help no one," Teo rasped.

"But...the mechanic?"

Teo waved a hand dismissively, but didn't try to correct his obvious falsehood or to explain away the contradiction.

"Please..." she murmured, staring up at him, blinking away the sudden sting in her eyes. "You have to help me." She wasn't surprised that her voice sounded as hoarse as his.

"No."

"I can pay. I'll pay you anything," she said, knowing even as she said it that it wouldn't help, wouldn't matter. The amount of money he'd gained control of years ago, money in an account established by the PRI, was enough for anyone's needs. More than that, however, was the fact that anyone able to survive in the wilds of the New Mexico mountains—alone—for so long couldn't have much interest in material objects.

Something flickered in his gaze. "If you know what's good for you, *señora,* you'll leave now. Women don't travel alone in these mountains," he said softly, his tone far from kindly.

"Please...I'll pay *anything,*" she repeated desperately, hoping the words could be heard over the painful pounding of her heart. She tried pushing to her feet, but her hands only slid in the mud and she merely scooted forward an inch or two.

"*Señora,*" he said, a dangerous light now in his eyes. "Your money means nothing to me."

The silence left in the wake of his words was torn by the shrill pulse of the sirens' screams. Melanie jumped and automatically turned to watch the arrival of a brown Bronco bearing a sheriff's silver star on the side panel. It whipped into the muddy gas station lanes. Not twenty yards behind the Bronco was a large, white ambulance with red lights whirling angrily in the gathering afternoon dusk.

She turned back and was too late: Teo Sandoval—El Rayo—was gone, having disappeared as thoroughly as if he'd never been there. She frantically sought his solid figure among the shadows of the surrounding forest, but saw nothing save pine boughs, sodden scrub oak and dark, dark shimmers of raindrops winking at her as though in amusement.

The unmistakable sound of tires losing their grip in mud

called her attention and she turned just in time to see the sheriff's mud-spattered unit spin across the gas station driveway. By yet another miracle on this peculiar day, the unit avoided slamming into anything, but did serve as a sharp reminder that she'd left her son alone in the car. With a single backward glance toward the seemingly empty woods, she awkwardly pushed to her feet and made her way to Chris.

In the pandemonium that reigned upon the sheriff's arrival, and the ambulance driver's frantic attempt to avoid collision with the sheriff's Bronco, Melanie realized that Teo Sandoval had been allowed to fade from sight. Amid the explanations of why the sheriff had been called—a call Pablo now said apologetically had proved unnecessary—Melanie noticed that no one mentioned El Rayo. It was as if he didn't exist.

She listened to all the explanations and the carefully worded evasions, and with one eye on Chris—who, thankfully, was now asleep and therefore unable to maintain his dancing game—searched the woods across the road for any sign of the most powerful telekinetic on record.

She wouldn't betray El Rayo by asking the voluble townspeople about him in front of the sheriff, but she intended to stay where she was until she could ask where the healer had gone. She also preferred to be the one to approach the villagers rather than have any of them get close enough to the car that they might wake Chris and witness his amazing bag of tricks.

Wiping as much mud as possible from her clothing and hands, she waited quietly until the furor had lessened somewhat. Then, with one last reassuring glance at her son, she walked around the building.

Despite the gathering darkness, the evening shadows, Teo could see the woman clearly. He watched her round the corner and rejoin the fringe of the group surrounding Demo. She was covered in mud and her hair was sodden from the rain. But there was nothing amusing about her. Nothing at all.

His gaze remained on her, and he willed her to look his way, to find him in the shadows. He'd seen her looking before, trying, squinting her remarkable eyes against the mist, questing for him. Though he'd felt the shock of her gaze sweeping the branches beside him, around him, seemingly right *at* him, she hadn't spotted him, had stared through him as though he were invisible. Her gaze had merely traveled on, taking in the oak, the red and shriveled leaves, the wet shadows surrounding him.

Why couldn't he read her? Why couldn't he hear this woman's thoughts, feel her wants, needs, and the thousand other confused little memories, impressions and dreams that seemed to bombard him from everyone else in the world?

Without even trying, he could "hear" everyone standing around Pablo's gas station. Demo was filled with pride over being the object of everyone's attention. Tempering that pride was a heavy dose of relief, not that he had survived the car falling on him, but that he had lived through El Rayo's touch of lightning. Doro, his wife, was thinking of the pot of frijoles she'd left on the stove when the men had first called that Demo had been hurt. Were the beans burned? Did they need salt, more chili? The baby's diapers were wet and his nose itched. Jaime was wondering who the new *señora* was and if she would talk about Teo, about what she had seen. And then there was Pablo, the hardest to read of all of them. His thoughts were half closed, gifts like Teo's twisting the thoughts into chaos. Pablo was hoping, as he always did, that he would live long enough to be forgiven an afternoon's trip many, many years ago.

But Teo couldn't read her at all. Not even a glimmer of her mind was revealed to him. It both frightened and intrigued him, because, for a startlingly clear moment, he *had* been reaching for her thoughts. Then she had shut him out. He'd felt a distinctive mental slam. It still echoed inside him. Yet before she had slammed the door on his probing, for a few charged seconds he'd seen something in her that he'd never encountered before.

An intangible something, almost like a daydream. And it rocked him to his core, for that intangible something had seemed all too like a promise of hope or connection. But he knew all too well that promises only led to despair and pain—

He shook his head in anger. Damn this woman. *Who was she?* What did she want? The only other time he'd felt blocked from someone's thoughts had been at the PRI, and then only because the men in the lab coats had stood behind leaded glass and lead-lined doors. But there hadn't been any intangibles there, only fear, hatred, need and furious control.

She had *touched* him. She had held him in her arms, moved the hair on his brow, smoothed the rain from his cheeks. Her fingers had been warm and soft, not healing hands such as his were, yet oddly remedial in their very presence.

Why had she helped him? Was it because she didn't know his terrible curse? But she had to have known. She had called him by his name. His *name.* How long had it been since he had been held, even in sympathy? How long had it been since he had heard his name upon a woman's lips?

She had said something about the PRI. She seemed afraid of it. She had damn good reason to be; if the PRI wanted her, they would succeed. Or had he misunderstood...and *she* was from the PRI?

He wanted to scream out in anger, lash out in denial. *No.* It couldn't be. Yet, wasn't he weak from the healing? He might have been too weakened from the healing to recognize all the dangers today. He fought the rage building in his lungs, the pain boiling in his heart.

God, he thought, and then stopped. No amount of prayer would help him. It never had, it never would.

He cursed her silently for ever coming to Loco Suerte. She was too damn beautiful and, though he knew nothing more of her than her name, and perhaps a measure of her desperation, he was too attracted to her. She'd stripped him naked not only with her gentle embrace, but by the very fact that she'd touched him at all. He ached for more and, though he knew it was irrational, hated her for that, for making him want her...for making him remember that for him there was to be no touching, no love, no life. Ever.

A host of questions clamored in his mind like the raucous calls of piñon jays in winter, and slowly answers coalesced. She wasn't from the PRI, but she wanted him to help her son. She would pay anything, she'd said, but he'd told her to leave. And he'd meant it. It was far too dangerous for her to stay. Too dangerous for him.

His thoughts turned to her son and his gaze followed their direction. The child was no more than a babe and was asleep, dreaming of his mother and a host of simple, nothing thoughts.

As if recognizing the intrusive stranger even in his dreams, the small child sat up suddenly and, standing on tiptoe, peered through the rain-streaked rear window. Unlike his mother, the boy located Teo easily. Honey-brown eyes, totally unlike his mother's deep green, stared from a baby's rounded features. They were old beyond his years, yet the child still remained an innocent. A small hand raised and fingers waggled in Teo's direction.

Unconsciously, Teo smiled in response. The simple gesture felt foreign on his lips, crooked somehow. He felt something shift deep inside him, a shaft of pain that somehow transcended the pain he felt whenever he healed or even the joy of making the universe move to his will.

Watch.

He heard the child's clear command. The smile faded from Teo's lips as the unfamiliar touch settled in his mind, possibly in his soul. It was cool and light against his senses, but clear nonetheless, and knowing. The boy had known he could talk with him, mind to mind. How?

Watch me!

The little fingers wiggled again, but this time Teo knew it was no wave, but another command. Various objects in the car—a pen, a comb, a red ball, some kind of little man doll and other things—suddenly began to bob around the back seat.

The shaft of pain that had shot through him earlier returned, except this time it twisted, driving the hurt deeper, wrenching at him. The boy was like *him,* could have been a blond version of himself at that age. The child, her child, was another of the damned.

Then, like his mother's had before him, the child's mind suddenly closed to Teo, and a barrier he couldn't penetrate was welded across the small head.

It was then he understood exactly what the woman wanted of him. And he knew he could help her, but knew he wouldn't dare. If he spent any time at all with the child, with the mother, he would not survive. Some small, locked away part of him would finally die, because even a moment in their company and he would surely be overwhelmed by painful memories, longing for things he couldn't have. He would be reminded of far too many broken promises and shattered dreams.

He pressed a question to the boy, but the child didn't respond. Teo understood the boy like he couldn't the mother. The child was concentrating on making things "dance" and while he did so, he was blocked to all other influences. He, too, had done that once. But only as a small child.

He could remember the peace, the sense of blessed quiet that came with that kind of focused thought, and longed for it still.

Two people who could block him in one day? Yet, weren't they mother and child?

He heard her tension-stretched voice in his mind, *"I'll pay anything."* What if—

He angrily lashed out at the sodden scrub oak before him. He couldn't afford to finish the thought. Wondering was for fools and innocents. He'd made his path, and damn her for making him even doubt the certainty of his need to be alone.

She shouldn't have asked him. She shouldn't have come here with her satin-soft hair and her green eyes that brimmed with tears and pain. And she shouldn't have brought that child who even now made his world spin with no more effort than another little boy might send a small top careening across a linoleum floor.

Yet a part of him wanted to say yes to her plea. That part wanted to tell her that he would help her, would help the boy. And another part hated her for making him feel this foreign and long, long buried want.

He was right to deny her cry for help. He didn't need to add any grief to his life; he deserved his hard-won peace. He deserved the solitude he'd fought to achieve. A child such as he had once been, a woman who wasn't afraid to touch him…both would conspire to shatter that peace, to erode his fragile hold on control.

He could feel that control slipping now, could feel the electricity building in him, aching for release. His heart beat too fast, his chest rose and fell with each ragged, shallow breath he took. His fingers still felt the silk of her hair, his nostrils conjured her scent, and his body trembled with the need to hold the power inside him. Damn her.

"No," he murmured roughly, denying the need within. But the electricity didn't subside, it only gathered strength.

With a growl of rage, he turned and crashed into the woods, needing to get as far and as fast away from the woman and her son as he possibly could.

A branch struck his cheek and he cursed softly, groaning in a mixture of anger, hurt and sharp, anguished want. The sky above him exploded in lightning, answering his pain. Blue and jagged, the bolt rent the sky, suffusing his face, reflecting, he knew, the fury in his eyes.

The crack of thunder that followed nearly deafened him, but he didn't slow his raging race up the mountain. Then another streak of fire shot across the sky, followed by another deafening clap of thunder. His chest heaved and he shook with the effort to keep his emotions under control. But the storm raging around and above him was proof that he'd failed.

The sheriff, Johnny someone, turned to Melanie with an expression that told her clearly he considered her at fault for having been on the scene of an accident in his district.

"Did you see the car fall on Demo Aguilar?"

She felt rather than heard the collective holding of breaths.

"No, I was beside my car. I only heard it fall. Heard him scream. Then everything happened so fast," she said casually.

She could tell the townspeople suffered the tension of waiting for her to expose what had really happened, to reveal the presence of one healer—destroyer—named El Rayo, who carried the force of lightning in his hands. They hadn't helped him, but neither did they want the sheriff to know he had been there. She didn't have to ask why; she knew the answer. Teo wanted it that way.

"She was buying gas when the Chevy fell off her jack onto Demo," the elder of the two checker players said.

"The Chevy was on your jack?" Johnny asked, his bushy eyebrows pushing upward.

"No, no, Señor Sheriff," Pablo corrected. "It was the jack of Demo's, but she broke."

Melanie looked at the attendant with new respect. This broken, ignorant speech routine was an act. She'd heard him speaking perfectly understandable English just a few minutes' earlier.

"The car, she fell on Demo. We thought he was dead. That was when we called you. But the car, she didn't kill him. No. See for yourself. We lifted it off him. Now he is fine!"

The crowd murmured assent and pushed Demo forward to show the sheriff the faint remains of his once near-fatal wounds. Melanie was struck by how adroitly Pablo had turned the sheriff's attention from her. The townspeople obviously wanted no mention of El Rayo to reach the sheriff's ears. If it weren't for the warning she could read in almost every pair of eyes, she might have wondered if she hadn't imagined the entire episode.

But it had been real. And what she had seen in Teo's eyes and had felt in his touch had also been real. Too disturbingly real. If they didn't want her to talk about him, she would play along, but they couldn't stop her from talking *to* him.

The sheriff wrapped up his futile investigation a few minutes' later and departed into the early night amid much good-natured assistance from the men in the crowd, who helped him extricate his vehicle from the mud.

Melanie was about to ask Pablo for help regarding locating Teo Sandoval when she happened to catch a glimpse of her son in the back seat of her rented Buick. His entire entourage of movable objects was bouncing around the interior of the car like a mobile without strings, like leaves snared by a whirlwind.

She ran to the car and tried opening the back door. It was locked. She called to Chris, but he didn't hear her; he never did when he played this way. Another thing to thank the PRI for, she thought as she wrenched open the driver's door and lunged over the back seat to grab his shoulder. He started and turned, a sunny smile lighting his lips. Objects fell like heavy rain, clattering on the dash, the seats, the steering wheel.

"Chris, honey. Please don't dance anything for a minute, okay? Try very hard. Listen to me. People are here. Don't *dance*. Okay?"

Chris shook his head solemnly. "No dance."

"That's right. No dance."

She backed out of the car, keeping a finger pointed at Chris to reinforce her point. She knew the gesture was largely in vain, for like any three-year-old, memory was only a vague dream and soon he would be lured into the delight of making the items move once more. As always, she knew she could punish him to make him remember to refrain from making things dance, but that seemed the ultimate of cruelties, to punish a child for what came most naturally. It would have been like punishing Mozart for writing a symphony or Einstein for fiddling with physics.

She quickly surveyed the group rounding the gas station corner. They were looking at her curiously, but not with undue questions; they had apparently only seen her race for her car and were now watching her with anticipation for her next unusual move.

All except Pablo. He had seen Chris, had seen the bobbing objects. She recognized the fact in his wide, fearful eyes, in the hand hidden behind his back, no doubt making the finger-and-thumb sign against evil.

"No dance, Chris," she murmured, still holding her finger up in the air. "Don't you dare dance now."

Suddenly lightning rent the blackening sky, blinding her, turning the universe into a jagged gash of blue and red. A monstrous clap of thunder followed before she could even catch her breath. As if the sky itself were angry, huge drops of water pummeled the ground and the people standing numbly in the already sodden driveway of Loco Suerte's gas station.

When Melanie's eyes cleared, she saw that as one, the group had huddled together and were now swiftly clearing the area. Within seconds, for the first time since the metal-crunching crash, the place seemed as deserted as when Melanie had first arrived. Again, except for the gas station attendant.

He remained where he'd been before the lightning and thunder. His eyes were on the inside of her car. On Chris.

"You have to help me," she said urgently.

He turned his eyes toward her. She couldn't quite read the expression on his face, but instinctively knew it wasn't unpleasant or even fearful. If anything, she thought she detected sorrow there. She lowered her guard a notch and found she was right. But she didn't dare relax her protective walls long enough to probe deeply into the reasons for the sorrow. Teo Sandoval was out there somewhere, and she was all too likely to unconsciously seek and link with his mind. And this would be too dangerous now, he'd read the strange feelings she was already harboring about him.

"Just tell me where I can find him," she said. When he didn't say anything, she added, "Teo Sandoval, can help me with my—"

"He's like Teo was," Pablo interupted quietly, lifting his chin in the direction of the car, and the child inside.

"When he was a boy, Teo was like that. God, how I remember."

Whatever it was he remembered, it wasn't pleasant, nor was it a comfortable memory. As if Teo were there now, and angry over being discussed, the sky again exploded in light and sound.

"Then you can see I need his help," Melanie said. She felt tears welling in her eyes. The sudden thunderstorm was frightening and she'd come too far, been searching too long. She felt she had no reserves left. "Please, tell me how to find him. Please help me."

The attendant looked over his shoulder at the dark, rain-drenched woods, and then back to her. Even through the rain she could sense his indecision, his worry.

"I won't tell anyone about him," she said urgently.

"I wasn't thinking that, *señora*," he said.

"Please…"

"Those people that took Teo all that time ago. They hurt him badly, I think. He never talks about it."

"They are the same people that want my son," Melanie said quickly, holding back a sob.

"Are they following you?" he asked quietly.

Melanie suddenly realized where his questions were leading. "No," she said. It was a half lie. They *were* following her, but according to her prescient dreams, they hadn't found her yet.

Pablo looked at her for a long moment, perhaps attempting to weigh her words for their truth.

She added urgently, "They want my son. They want to use him, just like they did Teo." Even to herself, her voice sounded desperate, confused. She took a deep breath and added fervently, "But Chris is only a baby."

"He'll refuse you," Pablo said flatly.

"But he knows what those scientists will do to Chris,"

Melanie blurted out, as if by convincing this man, she could persuade Teo Sandoval.

"Perhaps that's *why* he'll refuse," the attendant answered obliquely. "The *niño* will remind him. Of too many things."

"But he can't just let them take Chris from me. He, of all people, knows what will happen," she protested.

Pablo looked back at the car, his dark eyes penetrating the even darker interior. He looked more miserable than ever. Melanie held her breath as he studied Chris.

Finally he sighed heavily, muttered something in Spanish beneath his breath, and said, "Go one mile down the highway—" he jutted his chin in the direction Melanie had originally been heading "—and then turn left onto the dirt road. You won't be able to go all the way in that car. You will have to walk. You and…your child."

"Thank you," she said. "Thank you so much." She swiftly strapped Chris into the back seat, and locked and shut the back door. She had turned and already started to get into the car when she remembered that she hadn't yet paid him for the gasoline. Dragging her purse over, she started to pull out some dollar bills.

The attendant waved her offering away and stepped back beneath the canting portal. *"De nada,"* he said, then added in English, "For nothing. You touched him. For that, I think *I* would pay *you.*"

"Thank you—" Melanie began, but Pablo held up one mud- and grease-stained hand.

"Trust me, *señora,* you should not thank me."

Melanie, too dazed by the day's events, the furious storm overhead, and with the end of her quest in sight, only put the car in gear and steered to the narrow highway.

When she glanced into the rearview mirror, she saw Chris and his dancing toys. And beyond him, standing in the furious rain, the gas station attendant. He was back there, watching her slow progress up the mountain.

Just before she rounded a curve that would cut him from view, she saw him cross himself and look up at the flashes of lightning zigzagging across the night sky.

Was he praying that Teo Sandoval wouldn't enact retribution on him for telling her how to find him?

Or was he praying for her?

CHAPTER THREE

The sky flared as lightning bull-whipped across the sky and the resultant thunder sounded like the drums of fate, deep and heavy, reverberating with promise…or threat.

The rental Buick slid sideways and despite Melanie's frantic attempts to correct the spin by turning the wheel in the opposite direction, it continued its revolution. She felt low brush scraping the side of the car, scratching it but also cushioning it, preventing it from going any farther afield. Almost luckily, the car died.

For a dazed moment Melanie found herself still trying to turn the wheel, still trying to see through the sheet of oppressive rain to the narrow track that made up the road to Teo Sandoval's hideaway. When she finally realized the car wasn't moving, that the only sounds she could hear were the rain, wind and total silence of the Buick, she had to fight the desire to simply sink onto the seat and cry herself to sleep.

But she couldn't allow herself that luxury. If she fell asleep now, she felt she might never wake up. Her one hope was somewhere up that road and no amount of rain, thunder or even dark, possibly animal-laden, woods was going to prevent her from attempting to enlist his aid. Surely he would turn them back out into the night, into a raging thunderstorm. Reclusive he might be, but surely not inhumane.

If she told herself that often enough, she thought, she might actually start to believe it. Especially if she ignored the utter rejection and wariness she'd read in his eyes, the tension rippling through his broad shoulders. And if she forced herself to forget the photographs of the PRI's demolished building, the stark recommendation of the PRI psychiatrist that Teo Sandoval be left alone at all costs.

Taking a deep breath, she gathered Chris from the back seat, fastening him in his waterproof coat and hood. As luck would have it, by the time she managed to drag on her own light parka, the furious rain had abated to a fine drizzle, although the sharp, angry wind whipping the tall pines to creaking protest sent what rain there was directly into her eyes.

She held Chris against her shoulder with one hand and tried focusing the flashlight on the muddy road with the other.

"Hold on to me, Chris," she said, hitching him higher.

"Dance, Mommy," Chris chirruped.

Melanie knew he meant he wanted his toys to accompany them, but she wished he could make *her* dance right then, make them both as seemingly weightless as his ever-present entourage of floating objects. Her son had never seemed heavier than at this moment with her feet slithering in the mud, her body shaking from cold and exhaustion.

But at least one of them could mentally escape the arduous trek. "Okay, honey. Dance all you want," she said wearily.

Another flash of lightning blinded her momentarily, but it seemed farther away now, higher up the mountain. Unfortunately, that was exactly where she was heading. She paused for a moment, catching her breath, and shifted Chris to her other arm.

Even in the dark, she could see his toys in the air right in front of them, unaffected by the wind or the drizzle. Chris's entire focus was on them, rendering him blissfully oblivious to the discomforts of their journey up the mountain. She reflected, not for the first time, that in many ways the PRI had given him a precious gift, that while they may have been frustrated and angered by his ability to close them out, his complete concentration was more a blessing than a detriment. It spared him what his mother couldn't escape.

She resumed her difficult hike, and soon had fallen into a shambling rhythm, thinking not of the man up ahead, not daring to hope he could be persuaded to help her son—and her. Instead she found herself remembering the early days at the PRI, the lavish meals, the hushed and awed voices of the scientists. Those days had been bright with hope, tense with anticipation. They had also been before she'd discovered the murderous intentions behind their every gift.

Then her thoughts drifted to her former husband, and she again remembered the look on Tom's face when he'd fled from her, from Chris and his unruly powers. The oddly definite final glance he'd shot her as he'd accepted the payment for revealing Chris's unusual nature to the driven scientists, for signing away his half of their custodial rights.

She had blamed him bitterly when he'd left them two years ago, had hated him when she saw that cowardly defiance in his greedy face. But she'd never despised him as much as she did at this particular moment, trudging up a muddy hillside in the dark. On the run from the men to whom he'd nearly succeeded in selling his son.

But the two weeks of desperately seeking Teo Sandoval had helped to blur Tom's features, crystallize his personality. She knew now that he'd always been a runner, fleeing at the first sign of difficulty, quitting jobs that were too demanding, leaving towns that seemed too judgmental. Though she hadn't known it until long after they'd been married he'd abandoned his first wife and daughter, so was it all that surprising that he would turn tail and run at the first sign of Chris's stringless mobile? And how could she not have expected a man who constantly sought get-rich-quick schemes to eventually try to sell his own flesh and blood for the proverbial handful of silver?

Nonetheless, she still felt the deep pain of the betrayal just as she'd felt it when Tom had left. Then, she'd only considered the abrupt cessation of sharing responsibilities, decisions. But now, thanks to him, she was trekking up a backwoods mountain road that had been turned to sliding mud by a freak prewinter rain and seeking aid from a man who could destroy as easily as he could help her, from a man who had already told her to leave, whose eyes had underscored the dangers he'd warned her about.

For a brief moment exhaustion overcame her and she stopped, considering turning back, running elsewhere, seeking asylum in some far away region. But then she smiled bitterly. *No* place was far enough from the PRI to be truly safe. If they could track her by no other means, they would use their stable of psychics to find her. Chris's mother knew too much about them. She suspected even more. They couldn't let her escape and possibly expose them. Her dreams, while perplexing, still revealed enough for her to understand that their conceived end justified any means. And those dreams told her clearly that the PRI would stop at nothing, because no one—with the possible exception of Teo Sandoval—was as powerful a telekinetic as her son. They wanted him, and would do whatever it took to get him.

She shivered, thinking of how they would pervert Chris's innocent dancing abilities. She heard a crackling rustle in the nearby trees and swiftly darted the flashlight over the brush on her left. She saw no animal, no human, but the light wildly strafing the tree branches, the low scrub oak, somehow frightened her. It clearly revealed how terribly alone she was on this muddy road, how utterly defenseless.

Startled into action, she continued her journey. Half running, trying desperately not to slip and fall in the cold mud, and clinging to Chris with all her might, Melanie staggered up the rough trail, not even bothering to try to use her flashlight as a guide.

She was almost stunned when she realized she was no longer running nearly straight uphill, but had leveled out some twenty feet ago. She had reached the apex of the mountain and now stood in a huge, broad, night-darkened clearing.

No house broke the line of her vision, and tall, imposing cliffs rose high above an inky black horizon. The black could only mean one thing: the land dropped off sharply. She and her son were standing on what felt like the very edge of the world. Beyond the clearing on her left were a series of small, craggy hills that dropped sharply, leveling out to form the cliff edge. And judging by the width of the black strip, the cliff hovered above an abyss that might cut through the very heart of these mountains.

Had the gas station attendant knowingly sent a woman and baby to a wrong location? Was he, even now, behind her on that treacherous road somewhere? Or had she taken a wrong turn, gone right instead of left? Surely he'd said take the first dirt road to her left?

Tears of frustration, fear and abject despair stung her eyes. She blinked them back determindly. If she started crying now, she might never stop.

Just then lightning arrowed across the sky and illuminated the clearing, revealing the harsh face of the rock wall beyond the abyss, and the craggy hills facing her. Incredibly, the lightning also revealed a pair of massive wooden doors set into the lowest of the rocky hills that descended to the cliff edge.

Dear God, she thought. He lives in a cave?

Small flashes of lightning continued to flicker from behind heavy clouds, lighting the clearing with red, gold and blue flares. And still Melanie stood staring at the imposing set of doors, the narrow portal that stretched in front of them.

She looked back over her shoulder at the dark, muddy road she'd traversed to get to this spot. It looked even more imposing and dangerous from this vantage point than it had coming up.

Drawing a deep breath of the misting air, she told herself that she'd come this far, she wasn't about to turn back now. She needed Teo Sandoval's help. And nothing was going to make her leave without pleading her case before him. Nothing.

She straightened her aching shoulders, ignored her icy-cold and muddy feet, and pushed her sodden hair from her face. Crossing the twenty or thirty yards leading to the set of wooden doors, she knew how Puss 'N Boots must have felt, or Beauty upon reaching the Beast's castle—utterly terrified and equally determined not to show it.

All too quickly Melanie reached the narrow portal her-alding the doors. She stepped up two wooden steps and crossed the rough planking after pausing to scrape some of the mud from her shoes. Chris's toys stayed in midair at her side, as unaffected as ever by Melanie's tension, the wind, the misting rain or the lightning. Would the sight of the toys affect Teo Sandoval's decision to help her? Or would it make him even more determined that she leave without his aid?

She hiked Chris up and closer, tucking him securely be-neath her head, cradling him, as much for her own security as his. Then she rapped on the massive doors. Her knuckles against the heavy wood made about as much noise as a whisper in a crowded room.

Using the flat edge of her fist, she pounded the door in a repeated series of three loud bangs. No one answered. Teo Sandoval didn't appear. She waited for a few seconds, then redoubled her efforts. Still no answer.

She stood irresolutely for about a minute, not knowing what to do. She had focused so thoroughly on the trek to get here that she'd never once considered what she would do if he was either not at home or refused to answer his door. If, indeed, this even proved to be his home.

On the portal was a rough, hand-hewn bench and after a few seconds spent staring blankly at it, Melanie realized she was eyeing it as a place to spend the night. Nothing on earth was going to drive her back down that road, and no matter how cold it might get during the night, at least the portal offered some protection from the rain. And she could confront Teo Sandoval by the light of day.

A creak beside her made her turn. One of the massive doors slowly, ominously, swung outward. As dark as it was outside, she would have expected light from inside to spill across the floor of the portal, but instead, in some strange optical illusion, it appeared to her that the dark from the inside snaked out, spreading across the wooden planks, seemingly defying the laws of physics and filling the already shadowed portal.

It appeared no one stood behind that open door, and Melanie found herself holding her breath. No more, she thought. She could take no more.

"What do you want?" a gruff voice asked, the tone menacing.

Melanie couldn't seem to speak. Now that the moment was at hand she felt that nothing on earth could persuade her to enter this strange and forbidding dwelling, if indeed, dwelling it was.

Chris stirred in her arms, one baby hand sliding upward to cup her lips. Automatically she pressed a kiss into that tiny palm. The simple gesture, the sheer banality, the sweet honesty of a mother's kiss for her beloved child, steadied her as nothing else could have done.

She'd come so far, so desperately, and now she was ac-

tually in the company of the one man who could possibly
make the universe spin correctly again. She couldn't leave.
Not now.

The shadows in the doorway, strengthened by flickering
lightning and elongated by the unseen mountains looming
above the house, shifted and realigned, and Melanie realized that Teo Sandoval had stepped into the open doorway
and was standing not three feet in front of her, watching
her closely.

His dark hair, long and as black as the night, blended
with the shadows, as did his swarthy face and dark clothing.
But she could easily see his odd, pale blue-gray eyes and
knew he was studying her intensely even as he didn't reveal
a single clue to his own thoughts.

She needed him so much, had sought him out for so long,
that she felt tears prick her eyes. *Don't make me do this,*
she wanted to tell him. *Don't make me beg.*

"You have to help me," she said abruptly, and only
realized—after she'd closed her mouth—that she hadn't
voiced it as a plea, but as a rough command.

She clung to his gaze as if his remarkable eyes were the
only thing between her and drowning. Again she felt that
brush of his inner self, if not his thoughts. *Alone,* he seemed
to project at her, not as a state of mind, but rather as a state
of permanent being. Searching quickly, lightly, she intuited
no hint of self-pity or despair, only fact, unequivocal and
unconditional.

She swiftly closed the tenuous bridge between them,
sealing him off, not willing to let this powerful telepathic
and telekinetic man know the full extent of her desperation,
the need that had been housed in her so long it felt perfectly
at home in her. The depth of that need had nothing to do
with Chris, nothing to do with the PRI, but she knew if she
opened to him, he would read it all.

She'd read the files on him. She knew he could pluck

any thought, any emotion, from an unblocked mind. Without leaded hood, no human being was closed to him. Except her. Her own skills made it possible to close herself off to him.

But it was tempting to let him see what the PRI would do to her son. Surely that would turn the tide in her favor. Surely he would be unable to refuse helping her if he knew.

After a timeless moment or two his expression shifted, as did his body. For a split second his image hung in the air—a dream, an unsmiling Cheshire cat, face wary, eyes shuttered—then he melted back into the shadows.

"Don't!" she called swiftly.

"Don't what, *señora?*" he asked. His tone mocked her.

"Don't send us away," she said.

"I told you not to come, that I help no one," he said.

"I had to," she said fiercely. "There isn't anyone else I can turn to."

"You came to the wrong man, *señora,*" he stated flatly, and at that moment Melanie believed him. But belief didn't dampen her need for his help, her determination to enlist it.

"The PRI is trying to take my son away from me. They mean to use him like they did you. You can't let them do this. You can't be that cruel."

"I can be anything I wish, *señora.*" His voice was as cold as the night and twice as dark. "And as 'cruel' as I choose to be. Now get out. And don't ever come back."

Then he swung the heavy door shut.

Melanie stared at that blank, imposing door for a few seconds, feeling the blood drain from her face, the determination ebb from her heart. What kind of a man was he? How could he refuse to help a baby, a child like he must have been? How could he turn her away so callously? She dropped her guard one notch, but swiftly shut it again as she felt *him* questing at *her* mind, attempting to storm it with his anger, his own determination to break through her mental barriers.

A deep rage began to seethe in her, infusing her veins with righteousness, her mind with a nearly blinding fury. How dared he.

She lifted her fist to the door and furiously pounded, no polite series of timid thuds this time, but a frenzied demand for his return. The doors remained shut. Melanie kicked at them, yelling as she did so.

"I'll stay here—" kick "—and I'll sleep on your damned bench—" kick "—until we die of starvation—" kick "—but I am not going back down that mudslide you have for a road—!" kick, *kick* "—I am *not* taking my son back out into the night, into the rain! Open this door!"

She lashed her foot out at the door for a final savage kick and met no resistance.

Pale eyes glittered at her either in extreme anger or some other equally intense emotion. Melanie tried stilling her ragged breathing, her too rapid heartbeat. She felt her own anger draining from her as swiftly as it had risen. For the first time since stepping onto his wooden portal, she felt pierced by the cold, exhausted by her journey up the mountain.

"Please," she whispered.

"How did you get here?" he asked her harshly.

She stared at him blankly. "What difference does that make?" she asked aloud, but inside she was wondering what he might do to the gas-station attendant who had directed them up this strange mountain.

A bolt of lightning razored across the clearing, bathing the portal in blue light tinged with purple. The entire world seemed infused with ozone. Melanie flinched, but didn't make a sound, didn't take her eyes from the silver-blue gaze before her. *Please*, she begged silently, but still didn't lower her guard.

"For the night only," he rasped. She couldn't fool herself enough to imagine there was anything remotely inviting in his tone or in his eyes. He melted into the shadows once again, this time leaving the door open. It seemed a yawning black maw, open and waiting for her to enter at her own peril.

A chill of apprehension rippled down her spine and for some unknown reason her limbs felt oddly languorous. Her knees shook and her heart thundered every bit as loudly as the rumble in the sky had earlier, and yet Melanie managed to force herself to cross that ebony threshold. Somehow the very crossing had taken on a significance of its own— brides were carried across thresholds; in some countries it was considered bad luck to talk across that strip separating the inside from the outside.

And now, on what seemed to her the very edge of the earth, she had crossed of her own accord, entered the dark domain of a man of rare power, of raw force. She had the prickling sensation of destiny taking over, of having willingly entered the twisted home of something—some*one*— who lived outside the laws of man, outside the governance of society.

Dear God, what was she doing here? Why had she insisted that he take her in? This was madness, insanity. This had to be worse than the PRI. But nothing could be worse than that. Could it?

The door shut behind her with a loud thud, and she knew an atavistic fear of being trapped within these thick rock walls, locked in with a stranger whose very touch granted life or could strip it away. She grasped Chris's rounded little shoulder and held him tightly against her, as if by protecting him she could ward off danger altogether.

The windowless hallway was too night-darkened to grant her vision and she felt suddenly light-headed. When he spoke, she was unable to control her start.

"You should have listened to me," he said. Disembodied, his voice no longer seemed harsh from disuse but rather as though it came from someplace deep inside him or from the very walls of his home. It was low and carried a note of warning, of promises long broken, of bitter disbelief and harsh resignation to the fates that guided him. In the dark, he seemed much less a man than a vehicle for the odd power he carried inside him.

She couldn't see him at all, but felt his eyes upon her though she knew it was impossible. Even Teo Sandoval couldn't see in the dark. Or could he? She could *feel* him, inches from her, so close she could smell his heady mountain scent, warm herself from the heat radiating off his body.

Was he waiting for her to say something? How could she speak when she couldn't see his eyes, couldn't gauge his reaction?

"You leave at first light," he said.

"My car is stuck in the mud," she replied quickly, as if this were argument enough for her to stay.

"Pablo will help you get it out. I'm sure he's the fool who sent you up here. I'll deal with him later."

"Oh, no," she said, but his silence made a mockery of her protesting lie. "I— Don't be angry with him."

"If I am, *señora,* it has nothing to do with you."

Melanie didn't know what to say to this. If he was angry at the gas station attendant, Pablo, then she'd placed the man in grave danger. For Teo Sandoval was capable of doing anything. The time he'd been angry at the PRI, an entire scientific wing of a building had been smashed to bits.

"Please," she said again, although this time she wasn't quite certain what she was asking of him.

"At first light, *señora,*" he said, somehow giving the formal title a derisive intonation that she'd never heard given it before. Suddenly it was a threat and a promise at the same time. Not only that, but the tenor of his voice had changed as he spoke. His rasped voice seemed a caress now, and there was something else, some primal question laced in it that seemed torn from him against his will.

Though her heart still hammered in her breast, the pounding now had nothing to do with fear of the night, fear of the rock cave that seemed to spill down a cliff side. Now all her fear was of the man beside her in the dark and it stole her breath and made her legs feel weak and insubstantial.

She felt the dark around her as if it were a living presence. It pressed at her back, at her face, just as his scent did, as his body warmth did. Yet another shiver that had nothing to do with cold ran across her arms, and her fingertips tingled. She fought the urge to send her free hand questing for him in the dark. She wasn't afraid of what she might find, but of what she might discover about herself.

"I...could we turn on a light?" she asked. She half wondered if he even had anything remotely resembling electricity.

"Afraid of the dark?" he asked, still not moving. His voice carried no trace of an accent and yet seemed foreign nonetheless.

"Yes," she said, but it was a lie. Before entering his home, she had never been fearful of the dark. And she wasn't now; she was scared of the tension in her chest, the trembling of her fingers, the ache his voice inspired in her. Most of all, she was terrified of Teo Sandoval.

A sudden clatter of objects striking the stone floor beneath her made her start and step back only to stop abruptly when she stepped on something. It rolled away from her feet, making her shiver in primal fear, only to realize almost instantaneously what the object was—Chris's red ball.

Somehow, incredibly, in the midst of her tension, her

fear, and in this dark hallway of an even darker man, Chris had fallen asleep. Only when trying to please his mother or when asleep, did he break the focused attention on his dancing toys.

"Give him to me," Teo's voice commanded.

Melanie shrank back from him, holding Chris fiercely with both arms. She felt Teo's large hands brush hers as he tried removing Chris from her grip.

"No," she said.

"Don't be an idiot," he said roughly, pushing her hands from their fervent hold.

With as great a reluctance as she had ever known, Melanie relinquished her hold on her son. It was utterly terrifying to stand there in the dark and hand her son to Teo Sandoval, a man who could render a scientist's mind into a vegetable. But there was no alternative. Besides, if she was to gain his help, she would have to gain his trust.

She heard the faintest of rustles, felt a hint of movement in the air and then heard him speak again, this time from a considerable distance. "Stay there."

"Wait—"

"I'll be back," he said. "For you."

Melanie called out to him, but received no answer. She stepped forward, nearly tripping over Chris's fallen toys. Moving cautiously, she stretched her hands out in front of her, but couldn't see them, could see nothing. She couldn't feel any walls.

"Where are you taking him?" she called out, but again received no answer. He had gone, taking Chris with him. This was pure torture, she thought. She was not only in a strange place in the dark, but an even stranger man had removed her son from her custody.

She stopped trying to follow when she ran into something, a table or possibly a tall chair. She wished she could feel a resurgence of that anger that had infused her veins earlier, but she didn't. All she felt was small, alone and very, very frightened.

She clung to the awareness that he said he'd be back for her, and then realized for the first time how he'd said it, not simply that he'd return for her, but that he'd return...for *her*. She had only been thinking of Chris then, but now, by herself in the blackness, she heard the curious emphasis that had been in his final words.

It seemed hours before she heard any indication of his returning, time that stretched into insanity, filling her mind with horrible visions of what he might be doing to Chris, how Chris might have wakened and been frightened to be with a stranger, away from his mother.

Straining her ears, she heard a dull thud somewhere far away, followed quickly by his light footfalls. For a large man, he moved remarkably quietly. And suddenly she knew he was in the hallway—or whatever she was in—with her. She couldn't see so much as a glimmer of him, but she felt him nonetheless.

That blessed anger she'd missed earlier returned slightly, attempting to override the terror she felt at being alone in the dark with him. She was furious with him for making her feel this way.

"Where did you take Chris?" she demanded to know.

He didn't answer her, making her wonder if she'd misunderstood her own conviction that he was even there with her.

But almost immediately his hand encircled her forearm, making her jump in galvanized reaction. She jerked herself free. "Tell me where Chris is," she commanded.

To her discomfiture, he chuckled and again took hold of her arm. His grip was gentle enough, but the heat from his fingers seemed to burn through her dripping parka, the damp blouse beneath it. She felt she might as well have been naked, the way his touch seared her skin.

She held herself perfectly still, trying not to even breathe. His chuckle deepened, but without being able to see him, only hearing that husky laughter that somehow conjured images of smoke and fire, and feeling that burning touch, Melanie didn't believe Teo Sandoval was even slightly amused. The tenor of the chuckle underscored tension, cruelty and anger, nothing so simple as humor.

Oh, God, what had she done by bringing Chris to this man?

"Come," he said, pulling her closer to him. Her hand brushed his chest, his own knuckles pressed against her breast.

"No," she said, her voice ragged with her fear of him and her intense awareness of his knuckles against her breast.

His hand tightened and he pulled her even closer. Both her hands were crushed to his chest now, and she could feel the heavy thud of his heart beating against her trembling touch. His hot breath teased her, danced across her temple.

"You came to me," he rasped, his voice the roughest of raw silk. "You're the one who begged to stay. Not the other way around."

Melanie told herself that remaining perfectly still was her best defense, though, if she were perfectly honest, she couldn't have moved. Then she tried assuring herself that she couldn't move because he held her too tightly, too forcefully. But while true, it wasn't the *whole* truth, because she liked the way he held her, relished the feel of his heart pounding against her, his fiery touch burning her.

Branding her, his free hand stroked the wet hair from her face, caressed her cheek and moved lower, trailing a delicate, sinister graze along her sensitive throat. Her breath caught and to her dismay, instead of trying to escape that touch, she found herself arching her neck, allowing him greater purchase.

With a low, evil laugh, he bent his head and followed with his lips the trail his fingers had blazed.

Melanie felt her knees buckle in reaction, though whether that reaction was due to fear of him or sharp acceptance of his scalding kiss, she didn't dare explore. But she realized her fingers weren't flat against his chest any longer, but had curled, as if by their own volition, and now clung to his flannel woolen shirt.

He pressed his lips against the hollow of her throat, against the madly throbbing pulse in her neck. His tongue slowly tasted her, making her moan in fearful acknowledgment. Blind to everything but his touch, she could only think of him as incorporeal, a phantom without substance other than his lips, his tongue, his roaming hand.

What had he said? *You came to me...not the other way around.* It was true. She had crossed the threshold of the home of the mountain king and now he was exacting his penance, claiming his due. She murmured some protest, which he silenced with his kiss, covering her mouth, invading her with his scorching tongue.

His fingers were bands of iron, strong and forceful, and he dragged her to him in harsh need. His kiss deepened even more, and his body was as solid as the earth itself, his grip as strong as the jagged rocks of the cliff they were standing upon.

The blood was pounding in her ears, and her heartbeat seemed a timpani. Part of her mind screamed at her to put a halt to this, to pull away and cry a denial of the chaos he roused in her.

His scent filled her nostrils, the firm, bold touch of his roaming hands sent shock waves of sensation through her, his ragged breathing formed an odd counterpoint to her too rapid heartbeat.

He tasted of mountain herbs and soon passed the taste to her. Their breaths mingled and fought, their tongues quested and sought, and Melanie didn't believe there had ever been a moment in her life she had felt quite as alive as this. Every pore on her body seemed to open and drink him in. The very blood in her veins felt effervescent, eager. It was as if that magic in his hands was performing a different kind of healing now, a healing that was long overdue, a curing more of her tortured senses than any overtly physical ailment.

He kneaded and caressed her body, rousing her to insanity, slipping his hands behind her, pulling her body even tighter against his, running them over her shoulders, her arms, the curve of her waist, coming forward, sinuously stroking her rain-dampened thighs, she knew she had to stop this, that he would misunderstand, that anyone would, that *she* was. But she also knew that if she stopped this now, she would never, ever, feel this deliriously alive again. She could no more have called a halt than she could have turned away from watching him perform that seeming miracle at the garage.

His hands strafed her body, cupped her buttocks and they roamed her back, beneath her parka and higher. He ruthlessly shoved her blouse aside and captured her breasts with his hands. Without stopping his kiss, he groaned, and with a dim shock, she realized he was trembling as greatly as she.

As if this awareness snapped her from a spell he'd woven around her with his tongue, his touch, she suddenly pushed at him, frantic to be free.

"No," she protested raggedly. *"No."*

Her words seemed to splash on him like acid on silver, harsh and corrosive. He pulled back his hand immediately and stepped back from her. She could hear his fast breathing, could almost feel his fierce attempt for control.

She heard other rustling in the dark corridor and, from outside, several tremendous claps of thunder.

"I told you not to come," his voice rumbled from the darkness. And with that, Melanie knew what the rasp in his voice really sounded like now—fingernails scratching velvet. Were his words an apology of sorts? An accusation? Or the simple truth?

"I had to," she whispered back.

He didn't say anything and Melanie found herself remembering all the nights she had awakened screaming from a recurring nightmare, a dream in which Teo Sandoval had figured prominently. She had a face to go with his name now. Was the terror yet in store for her? Could she expect to be so terrified soon that she wouldn't be able to control the screams of fear? Though she could never remember exactly what had transpired in the dreams, the residue of the nightmare was always the same—the taste of tears and terror on her tongue, the sense that something stalked her in the woods and the sight of a red ball lying too still on a bed of pine needles.

He touched her again, his fingers lightly grazing her lips, her throat. "Come," he said. His hand slowly lowered to take hers. When she would have pulled away, he tightened his grip, but this time, pulling her forward, he guided her down the long, stone corridor.

"There are stairs," he said, and she felt him step down.

"Why isn't there any light?" she asked, amazed at her own temerity.

He didn't answer but continued to wind his way down a curving flight of stone stairs. Gratefully, Melanie clung to his hand and pressed one shoulder against an arched wall. She knew now what it was to be truly blind, grateful for the whisper of his feet upon the stairs, the touch of his hand, the solidity of a rock wall, even as she was frightened to death of him.

It seemed like hours before he stopped, and she heard the unmistakable sound of a door opening. A crack of blessed light appeared. Melanie had never felt so glad to see anything in her entire life. She instinctively rushed toward it, only to be blocked by one his of muscled arms.

"You'll leave in the morning," he said again harshly, his voice filled with grim command.

Numbly, Melanie nodded.

"You understand me?" he asked, but it was less a question than a bald statement of truth.

Melanie wasn't certain that she did understand, or was, perhaps, afraid that she understood too much. If that kiss in the entry hall of his mountain cave was any indication, she might understand him very well indeed.

"I—yes. I'll go in the morning," Melanie said, feeling resigned to the matter now, nearly indifferent to those that would eventually come looking for her. Almost anything they did would be easier to comprehend than what she'd felt in that dark corridor.

Now, seeing that crack of light, recognizing in it a salvation of sorts, as if mere light could dispel the sensations Teo Sandoval had awakened in her, Melanie pressed forward, pushing his arm out of the way. She shoved the door open fully, crossing into the light.

And froze.

Beyond her stretched a softly lit cavernous room. It *was* a cave. And wasn't. Its rock ceiling must have stretched some thirty feet overhead, and the two walls on either side of the doorway were rough and formed from the inside of the mountain itself.

Melanie realized then that, from the forbidding wooden doors to this, they must have traveled down a tunnel, a volcanic hole perhaps, and had passed through the very mountain. Instinctively, she drew back against him, aware that this room hung over the abyss she'd sensed outside. They were, literally, on the other side of the mountain.

The far wall of the cavern didn't exist; at least, it was not made of rock and inner mountain. It was formed entirely of enormous lengths of glass encased in massive beams of wood. Windows, she thought half hysterically. They were windows. No one with vertigo or acrophobia could ever stand anywhere near those monstrous windows.

In the daylight they would probably capture every nuance of the sun's rays, but at night, like now, they had become huge, monolithic mirrors that stole the light from the kerosene lamps and reflected the room. She could see herself pressed against the dark man, two seemingly small figures in a distant doorway.

"The boy is in there," Teo said after Melanie could finally drag her gaze from that black window and her own mirrored terror. She followed his jutting chin and saw a small doorway set into the stone walls. It was on the far righthand side of the room, flanking a huge fireplace. The carved wooden door stood open. A subcave, she thought with near hysteria. Would one wall of that room also hang over the abyss cutting through the mountains? The notion made her feel ill.

She started for the doorway, more than anxious to get away from him, needing to see that Chris was all right, desperate to think, to find some rational explanation for what had happened in that dark corridor, some reason why she'd felt more regret than anger when she'd pushed him away.

"After you check on the boy, you come in there," Teo said, stopping her short. She turned and followed his pointing finger to the other doorway, the one flanking the far right of the megalithic fireplace.

"I'll be f-fine with Chris," she stammered.

"There's no room. You'll sleep in there," he said. His tone brooked no argument.

Something in his voice made her look at him in sudden, sharp suspicion. Though she knew he couldn't read her mind, he nodded slowly. A wicked, wholly unamused smile curved his lips.

"That's right, *señora*. You wanted to stay the night. Fine. But you will spend it in *my* bed."

CHAPTER FOUR

Melanie's mouth went dust dry and her heart leapt in erratic fury. She had literally demanded that he take them in, let them at least stay the night. And somewhere between his first grip of her arm and her final shoving him away, she had clung to him, returned his kiss with an intensity of her own. Now he stood touch-close to her, watching her assimilate his words, his dark message. Was it a challenge?

As they had done in the mist outside the gas station, she felt their gazes lock, sensed a great inner turmoil in him and knew it was mirrored in herself. Thank God, she was closed to him.

His words still echoed in her ears, in her frightened mind. *That's right,* señora. *But you will spend it in* my *bed.*

Dear God. He was right; she had been an idiot. To have expected anything from Teo Sandoval, to have believed that a man who lived as far apart from humanity as he did would be a perfect gentleman, was the essence of lunacy.

In those vague dreams she'd had of him, just the whisper of his name had left her shaken and trembling. And when she'd dreamed of him, she'd woken screaming…was this yet in store for her? Had she really been peering into the future as she'd done all too many times in her life? Could the future be changed, was it mutable? Or had she been dreaming her own fate?

"N-no," she said finally. She felt the light hairs on her arms rise in sharp reaction to a sudden electrical pulsing in the room. She met his eyes fearfully, but could see nothing but her own reflection in his gaze. Somehow that frightened her even more.

His lips curved in a knowing smile. "There's nowhere else," he rasped.

No one had ever spoken truer words, she thought glumly, even if his meaning was far different from her thoughts. She had traveled so far, so arduously, on a mission for help that had proved to be yet another failure. There *was* nowhere else to go. No one to help her, to help Chris.

But climbing into this man's bed was the ultimate line of demarkation. She would rather sleep outside in the rain. At least, she tried believing that she would. She opened her mouth to tell him so, but closed it again as he chuckled. Evilly, she thought.

The room dimmed abruptly and Melanie saw that two of the kerosene lamps now carried no cheery flame. Only one remained burning, and as she stared at it, it, too, lowered, but without going out. The sensation of static electricity loosed in the room intensified. Melanie could smell the clean, fresh scent of ozone, as if an electrical storm was going on inside the room instead of outside in the dark night.

"I m-mean it," she said. "No way."

Teo Sandoval chuckled again and the sound made chills work across her shoulders.

Without another word or so much as a glance in her direction, Teo turned on his heel and strode away from her. A door on the far left side of the room wrenched open with a burst of violence and whammed against the wall.

He didn't reach for the knob, Melanie realized with a distinct shock.

Teo crossed through the doorway, the king regal in his exit. Though, again, she didn't see his hand on the door, it slammed shut behind him. The thunderous report reverberated in the large, dimly lit chamber.

Elvis has left the building, Melanie thought, and nearly giggled. She immediately sobered, knowing she was on the verge of succumbing to a fit of raw hysteria. She could feel the tears and the laughter warring inside, fighting for release.

"I've been through too much for this," she murmured aloud. Discounting her whole life of battling the unusual, as well as the last nightmarish three years, she felt that she'd been through too much in just one day. She'd been lost, was tired, had watched a miracle unfold in an icy mist and had climbed what seemed a hundred miles, struggling in the rain. She'd demanded to be taken in, only to be kissed senseless and have a man nicknamed El Rayo imply he intended to share her bed. And then she'd watched as he more than adequately displayed his remarkable telekinetic talents, dimming the lights without going near them, opening and slamming the door without having touched it.

The kiss, the implication, the display of gifts normally forbidden man, all added up to one thing: she'd made a colossal error in seeking Teo Sandoval's assistance. The files had been right; he should be left alone. *Alone.*

Feeling she was treading on the very thinnest of ice, Melanie slowly crossed the huge, stone-lined chamber filled with beautifully hand-carved furniture, to reach the small open door on the opposite side of the room. At the doorway of the room, she paused, looking back over her shoulder at the door Teo had disappeared behind. A sudden crack of lightning zigzagged down the abyss beyond the sheets of glass. It lit the menacing face of the opposing mountain wall. A tremendous clap of thunder followed almost immediately, making her jump.

Was it possible that Teo Sandoval was directly responsible for the thunder and lightning? Melanie knew it was all too possible even as she wondered how she'd come to this impasse. Had he been playing some joke on her? Had he implied she would be sharing his bed only to see her blushing reaction, to hear her stammered denial?

Or was it far greater than that, was all of it some tremendous power play, some need to punish her for what had been done to him all those years ago? But couldn't he see that it wasn't her fault the PRI scientists had hurt him, had pushed him too far? He had to be made to understand that she needed his help to prevent them from trying the same thing with her son. Because her son was just like Teo had been; young, vulnerable, a victim.

She had to make Teo understand that Chris needed someone to rescue him as no one had rescued Teo. And she had to do this despite the fact that he literally frightened her very wits away.

At another crash of thunder and lightning, Melanie bolted through the doorway of the small antechamber where he said he'd placed Chris. But again she stopped abruptly. El Rayo had been true to his abbreviated words; Chris was nestled comfortably in a short, cradlelike bed. His coat and shoes had been removed and a soft, downy blanket had been draped over him and tucked into the edges of the hand-carved cradle.

Melanie felt the contrasts rather than thought about them. They were almost too large to truly understand. A man who shunned the world, hid from it, even lived perched high on a mountain top, in the mountain itself, was the same man who had saved a local villager at obvious pain to himself. A man who would have left them to the dark, the storm, a man who might be the source of the electrical display outside, had carefully stripped a tired little boy of his wet things and gently tucked him in a cradle.

Again Melanie remembered the words of the psychiatrist: *I don't know whether Teo Sandoval should be condemned or praised. But at all costs, he should be left alone.*

She hadn't followed that advice. And now she didn't know what to make of it, or the man it was penned after.

Why would Teo Sandoval have a hand-hewn cradle in a

room of his home, ready and waiting for a small child? Had he known they were coming?

Melanie shook her head. She'd seen nothing of clairvoyance indicated in Teo's files. A man of miracles, certainly, but not possessing every form of psychic ability. No, he had the cradle for other reasons. Reasons that had nothing to do with Melanie, Chris, or their need of him.

She crossed the room and lightly stroked her son's silky blond head. His baby lips were parted and his long, blond lashes fanned his rounded cheeks. Such a beautiful child, she thought, and knew it wasn't simply motherly prejudice. Chris had been remarkably beautiful even minutes after birth. The trouble was, most people failed to remember his sweetness, his innocent beauty, once they saw his toys begin to dance around him. His own father had once referred to him as the "Devil's spawn."

Biting her lip, Melanie knew she had to think of some way of convincing Teo Sandoval to help Chris learn how to control his magic. There had to be something Teo wanted, something she could give him that would tip the scales in her favor. She blushed furiously as her mind replayed every nuance of his kiss, of the way she'd returned it. But most of all because the memory of that kiss had triggered an answer to her own question.

Chris stirred slightly and Melanie drew her hand back before she woke him. They had eaten in some small, roadside café around five, so there was a very good chance he'd sleep through the night. She stood beside the cradle, wrapping her arms around her wet and cold clothing.

Chris's problems were solved for the night, but hers were just beginning. The cradlelike bed was certainly too small for her to share it with her son, and there wasn't a single other piece of furniture in the room, aside from an old-fashioned wooden highboy.

However, nothing on earth shy of a fire was going to pry

her from this room, especially not to enter Teo Sandoval's bedchamber, strip and crawl into his bed. Nothing.

She crossed to the highboy, opened one of the shutters and found a stack of blankets and pillows. For a moment she simply studied them, adding the tidy pile of comforters, quilts and down-filled pillows to the mounting puzzling details making up a disjointed picture of the man called El Rayo. She finally pulled two of the thicker blankets from the cabinet and after a moment's hesitation, spread one upon the hand-braided rag rug occupying the floor. She removed her shoes and parka before going back for one of the pillows. Wishing she could also remove her damp blouse and wet, muddy trousers, she decided she would rather clean the blankets later than strip naked in Teo Sandoval's mountain aerie.

Pulling the gaily patterned quilt over her shoulders, she sought some relief from the hard stone floor. She sighed, fully expecting to lay awake all night. She strained her ears to discern some indication of Teo's whereabouts, but aside from an occasional distant rumble of thunder, she couldn't hear anything but her son's soft breathing. Carefully, she shifted, trying not to rub the mud from her pants onto the blankets, and trying not to think about Teo's glittery, pale eyes, his dark face, his magical hands and the way they had felt against her cheeks, her neck, her breasts.

Teo pulled at the moist, cold air as if he were drowning and desperate for oxygen. He'd been unable to control the anger that had fumed in him at the shocked look in her eyes when he'd suggested she take his bed. He hadn't been able to resist strengthening her misconception when he saw that she was afraid of him.

And he still trembled from his reaction to her in the tunnel. He'd come so close to simply damning all conse-

quences and slowly bending her to the smooth rock floor
to lose himself in her kisses, in her arching body.

A crack of lightning whipped across the canyon and Teo
drew a harsh, steadying breath. *Control.* Control, he told
himself fiercely, desperately. But, God, how was he supposed to regain control when she drove him insane with
her beauty, wild with her touch, with her very presence in
his home? She had voluntarily *touched* him, hadn't seemed
to feel that apparently repelling electricity that poured from
his skin. That alone set her apart from every woman he
knew, every human he had ever met.

He'd been out into the world a few times, had masked
himself, had hidden his powers, had found a moment or
two of forgetfulness. But always his touch gave him away,
his control would slip and he'd see fear replace passion,
terror fill in the gap. And he'd cursed those who'd felt it,
who'd gazed at him so. But each time, he'd felt he was
really damning himself, his fate, his misfortune.

He knew what she wanted from him, or almost. It was
something to do with the PRI, and with their wanting her
son. He couldn't read her mind, her thoughts, like he could
do with so many others, too many others, but he knew her
need just the same, had gleaned it from her implications,
from the anger he'd heard in her voice, from her determination. And from her exhaustion. He'd once felt that tired,
that scared.

But that had been fifteen years ago. He was a different
man now.

He took hold of the wooden railing surrounding his deck
and looked down into the black chasm stretching below
him. He held on as if for life itself, willing the riot of
emotions in him to subside lest he bring the entire mountainside down with his confusion. He'd done it once, years
ago, when his mother had died. When no one had wanted

to come to her meager funeral. No one, except Pablo, and Pablo was one of the damned.

This Melanie Daniels had come with his express refusal ringing in her ears. He wanted to revile her for the desperation in her eyes, and for having a child so like he had been, who weighed nothing in his arms, who had, in sleep, pressed a chubby hand against Teo's lips, unaware that a stranger carried him, undressed him.

A knife-like pain had shot through him at the sight of the boy in that room, peacefully sleeping in that cradle. The image mocked him nearly as much as the memory of Melanie Daniels's kiss in the tunnel, her confusion in his living room. The child's room, the bed, even the blankets in the wardrobe had been created, lovingly hand-crafted, at a time when he had still believed normality was possible, at a time when he'd been foolish and so very young. In the days before the PRI had taken him. In the days when he had still believed some girl from the village would eventually share his life, his bed and, with him, create children whose laughter might drive the superstitious ghost clouds from the mountain.

Or had they been placed there afterward, when he'd believed—as he did now—that the future was only something to be lived through, that the blankets and trinkets were only the groveling offerings of the fearful people in the village? Had they been placed there as a reminder?

Somehow seeing the boy sleeping in that bed that had never held a child, that Teo had finally come to understand wouldn't ever do so, he'd been angrier than ever at Melanie for invading his home. Her presence, the presence of her son, conspired to challenge his precious hold on hard reality. Just by lying in that tiny bed, the boy made him remember wishes cast into the night long ago. And the boy's mother made him ache with a desire to talk, to share something other than solitary meals and lonelier beds.

He'd wanted to frighten her in the tunnel, had wanted to scare her half as much as she troubled him. And had been furious with her when she allowed him to succeed. She had *touched* him. She hadn't shied away in disgust, in fear. And yet words drove her eyes wide and made her hands tremble.

He slammed his open palm against the wooden railing. Another bolt of lightning whipped down the ravine. Hadn't the world done enough to him? Must he now be forced to endure a want so intense, so painful, that he'd nearly caused a riot in his own home from his own inability to subdue the fires she sparked in him?

He'd fled to his rough kitchen, and outside to the deck, all but flinging the kinetic energy from him. He'd felt it building, had seen the mock electricity playing upon her, knew it had reached her from her widening eyes, her suddenly tense shoulders. He'd let a bit loose as he'd deliberately doused two of the lamps, frightening her. The slamming door he'd been unable to control. And finally, he'd thrown the energy to the skies, augmenting the storm she'd already provoked from him. Huge droplets of rain pelted him, as if admonishing him. Thunder crashed and lightning flickered as he sent the storm outward, drove it over the mountain range. He thought of Pablo, who had sent her here, who had once again meddled in his life, causing him pain. He let the force of the storm focus at the gas station, then, irritated with his own pettiness, let it ebb.

Couldn't she understand that he'd retreated, had worked hard to stay clear of the world and its needs? He only helped the people in Loco Suerte when the restless anger and guilt in him grew too much to contain. And like some lord of ancient times, or some god they wanted to appease, the local people crept to his heavy doors, leaving offerings of food and clothing, never staying to talk with him, fearing the shadow of El Rayo, craving his blessing but never his company.

He didn't need them. Thanks to the efforts of his drunken father and, in some measure, of perverse justice, he had money enough for whatever he wanted, but he found it easier to accept the villagers gifts of clothing, food, even artwork than to refuse them. By accepting them, his reputation remained intact and his privacy was ensured.

But this woman was different. She had *touched* him. And as such, she could wreck his peace, destroy his hard-earned solitude. Already she was making him lose his control over the energy inside him. But, dear God, how he wanted her.

She needed him, he thought, and he wanted her. Somehow that should make right what seemed vaguely wrong.

"But what the hell is wrong about it?" he asked the cold, electrically kinetic night. Didn't he deserve her? Hadn't he been used enough? Hadn't he been through enough to satisfy whatever gods ruined his life?

Everyone else on the planet seemed to be able to take and take...why not him?

"It's my turn now," he said, and heard in his own harsh voice the unmistakable ring of a vow.

He let loose of the railing and with hard determination left the deck to enter the kitchen. Leaving that room, he crossed the huge living room to his bedroom. He found no appreciation of his home tonight. That he'd augmented huge caverns with stone walls and wooden beams, that he'd formed a dramatic house from sheer mountain, was unimportant now. It was simply a place, a place that now held two unexpected guests.

He wasn't surprised to find his bed empty—the dry floor mute testament that she'd never even entered the room—but he was angered.

Deliberately he crossed to the child's room and frowned when he saw the boy's mother curled up on the floor, one of Angelina Martinez's quilts warding off the cold. He stood staring at her for several moments, trying to probe her dreams, willing her to wake, and though she frowned, he couldn't break through whatever barrier she held in her mind, and she didn't stir.

He bent, his shadow covering her, and lightly touched her shoulder. She only mumbled something he couldn't make out. She then shifted away from his prodding fingers and tried burrowing deeper into the pillow.

Without consciously deciding, Teo reached beneath her and, in a fluid motion, lifted her into his arms. She still didn't wake; he found himself wondering if she would be roused by a kiss, and sneered at his own quixotic impulse.

He carried her from the child's room to his own. As he laid her down upon the bed, the blankets slipped from her and he realized for the first time that she hadn't removed her wet clothes. He frowned, considering. He knew he couldn't allow her to sleep in the damp things, she would wake with a cold or worse. But at the same time, she didn't wake when he called her name softly or lightly nudged her shoulder.

He frowned even deeper, irritated with her. She had barged into his home, cut up his peace, invaded his privacy and now she slept like the dead, leaving him to deal with the problem of her clothes.

It would serve her right if he just stripped her out of them. She would have to wonder how she'd got that way. She would wake as disoriented as he felt now, and she'd know then that he'd seen her as vulnerable as he'd been before her. It would serve her right.

But his fingers trembled at the buttons of her blouse, and his breath came raggedly at the sight of her full breasts. He couldn't resist pressing his lips first to one, then the other. But though her nipples grew hard as pebbles, she still didn't wake.

Once having removed her clothing, her deep sleep rendering her wholly vulnerable to him, more than merely trusting, even reliant upon him, he felt a deep remorse come over him even as he felt a fierce tightening in his loins. He wanted to wake her and demand she give herself to him in exchange for disturbing his peace.

Finally, almost roughly, he jerked back the covers and lifted her beneath them. He stared at her glorious body for a moment longer, then tossed the blankets over her. She sighed and stretched her body sinuously. In shock, Teo heard his own name upon her lips.

Standing above her, shaking, angry with her, more furious with himself, and wanting her so badly he could taste it, he could scarcely think. But he knew one thing: whatever wrongs he had done in his life, he wouldn't add this one to them.

He left her room with extreme reluctance. He was still angry, still throbbing with the need to take her into his arms, draw from her that cool, blessed communication of touch. The moment he closed the door, he felt an almost inordinant relief to be out of her proximity.

He again pulled at the air like a man drowning. But the roiling forces inside him didn't fight him for release. He was once again in control, if only checked by the veriest thread of willpower.

The small room on the other side of the fireplace drew him and he slowly moved to the doorway of that never-before-tenented room. Though prepared for it this time, he was nonetheless startled as again something inside him shifted at the sight of the small, exceedingly vulnerable child asleep in the bed hand-carved all those years ago.

He wondered again, almost dully this time, why he had kept the cradle. But he knew the answer: as a grim reminder that for Teo Sandoval, designated barbarian and wild animal by the PRI scientists, there was no woman in his life, no child in his cradle.

A man who could destroy with his thoughts, who possessed thunderbolts in his fingertips and frightened all he came near, could have no family. He'd kept the artifacts of the long-dead dreams as a constant reminder that for him there could be no future, no son or daughter, no wife. This empty chamber, these hand-hewn pieces of furniture served as a signal that he was destined to live alone, apart from the rest of the world, a pariah, an angry and lonely man of power.

Whatever hurt so deep inside him, wrenched even more as he studied the child. The tiny frame in the intricate cradle was no match for the PRI. He was scarcely more than a baby. Teo had been nineteen when they had gotten their hands on him, and they had nearly succeeded in driving him insane. How could this tiny child fend for himself? How could he fight their desperation, their greed? How could a few floating toys protect him from their abusive need for more and more and more?

Teo's lips twisted bitterly. The boy would have to learn to run alone. That was what the world had in store for him. He'd had to learn the hard way. So would this boy. And maybe, since he was younger than Teo had been, he might accept the tortures easier.

Teo's jaw tightened in sudden hatred for the PRI and unexpected empathy with the child sleeping so innocently in the cradle. What was happening to him? Why had he allowed a pair of luminous eyes, a pair of gentle arms, and a small, chubby, waggling hand to get to him? He couldn't afford to let this needy pair get under his skin. And the child... He knew he didn't dare even allow himself to think about the little boy more than he already had. He knew that if he did, he would be doomed, for the child brought back too many memories, too much pain.

He unnecessarily adjusted the covers and gently touched the sleeping mind. He smiled almost wistfully; no barriers here. Some cat-dog dream creature with large floppy ears and nearly sablelike fur romped on a hillside with the boy. Silently, Teo withdrew from the boy's dream and from the room.

She froze, trying not to breathe, though she knew they weren't close enough to hear her. But she knew they could find her because her guard was slipping. Why was it slipping? She could hear Chris singing a silly song about a fox, and wanted to hush him. His red ball lay on the ground in a bed of pine needles and she remembered having seen it just so in a different dream, a dream from which she woke screaming.

I have to wake up, she thought desperately. I have to wake up now, before something bad happens.

She heard her name called and could hear footsteps thudding up the hillside. She turned to see Teo running up the hill, his face a study of fury, her name on his lips.

Run, Chris, she tried to call, but no sound emitted from her lips.

Run! Run!

"Run!" she cried out loud, sitting up in bed. The dream lingered, despite the sudden shift in imagery. She'd been on a hillside, trying to get Chris to run from Teo Sandoval, from the fury on his face. And now she was in a dimly lit bedroom, light filtering in from some kind of skylight over the foot of the bed.

Where was she?

Even as the question took form in her mind, she knew the answer. She was in Teo Sandoval's mountain-king home. And with that realization came another: she was in his bed, as well. She leapt from it, as though it had burst into flames. She gasped, horrified, as she discovered herself totally nude and her clothing nowhere in sight.

"How *dare* you?" she muttered as though he was there to receive her scathing comments. "You might be some kind of a super hermit, but you have absolutely no right to undress me! You have no right to take advantage of me being so tired I couldn't have lifted a finger to stop you from doing whatever it was your perverted mind dictated!''

She jerked the white coverlet from the bed and wrapped it around her sari-style. "Damn you," she said, flinging open a set of narrow doors flanking the room. As she'd hoped, it was a closet. She pushed several woolen shirts aside, not caring if she knocked them askew. Finally, just about the time she had prepared herself for the necessity of wearing one of those shirts, she found a thick, quilted robe. She yanked it from the closet, scarcely noticing the rich velvet squares, the fine stitching. She shoved her arms into the massive robe and let the coverlet drop to the floor.

She marched from the room, ignoring how the length of the robe impeded her progress, simply hitching it higher. She swiftly crossed to the room where he'd placed Chris. She would get her son, her clothes, and leave. And if she couldn't find her clothes, she'd leave, anyway; she didn't care if she had to march down the mountain in his housecoat, didn't care if she had to fly to Timbuktu wearing it. She was leaving. *Now.*

"Chris...?" she called as she rounded the doorway. She stopped dead at the entrance to the small chamber. Chris wasn't there.

A tidal wave of adrenaline coursed through her. Where was he? She whirled and frantically surveyed the cavern stretching into seeming infinity.

Teo's unusual home looked vastly different by day, but certainly no less frightening. The huge slabs of glass, mirrors by night, now seemed to capture every stray beam from the sun and send them splashing carelessly all around the room. And the windows went nearly to the floor, revealing what she'd only guessed the night before—Teo's home truly did spill down the back side of the mountain. One step beyond those windows and a person would plummet to certain death.

Where was Chris?

She raced across the room, ignoring the dancing sunbeams, intent on only one thing: finding Chris. She hesitated between two doors. One led into the staired, dark tunnel they'd passed through last night, the other was the door Teo had mentally slammed when he'd left her.

She ran to the second one and wrenched it open. In other circumstances she might have stopped to appreciate the unusual blend of nature and manmade structure that comprised the most remarkable kitchen she'd ever seen. But she didn't care a tinker's damn about the ledges carved from the rock wall to create a storage area that held ceramic plates, cups, even pots. And she didn't care about the Spanish-tiled island bar, or the wooden deck that stretched beyond the sun-bright room. She could only focus on the small figure standing outside the kitchen, small feet inches from certain death. Her son was out on that deck, on the very edge of the world.

She stepped forward, his name forming on her lips even as she realized that if she yelled, she might possibly frighten him into jumping backward. To die.

She stepped around the bar and stopped, her hand instinctively clutching the lapels of the borrowed robe. Chris was not alone. Nor, apparently, in any great danger. One chubby hand rested on Teo Sandoval's broad shoulder, while another was stretched out, holding a slender strip of meat to a fox. A real, live fox.

Melanie held her breath as the fox delicately accepted the meat and stepped back to enjoy it. She saw now that the wood-planked deck stretched from the kitchen to the right some twenty feet out over the abyss and about that many feet wide. On the right side, it was attached to a sheer cliff face that comprised the exterior wall of the cavern making up Teo Sandoval's unusual living room. To the left, the deck disappeared up a flight of broad wooden steps. Did they lead around to the front of the mountain? To the very top of it?

The fox, having polished off the strip of food, gingerly approached Chris for more. Its tiny, red-brown eyes darted between Teo and her son. Delicate paws touched lightly on the wood deck as though ready for flight.

The double-paned glass doors leading to this wooden perch were slightly ajar and through that narrow aperture Melanie could hear Teo's soft baritone. "That's right, very slow. Don't worry, she won't bite you. She owes too much to get nasty now."

"What's her name?" Chris asked.

"I don't know," Teo said. "Why don't you make one up?" He paused, looked momentarily shocked, then nodded, and continued. "You're right. Gina's a good name for a fox."

Melanie felt the blood draining from her face. Her son and this unusual man were casually conversing *by means of telepathy*. She'd known he had the gift. She'd read about his use of it. But having lived for so many years without ever finding anyone else who used it, who could feel it, she had to cover her mouth with her hand to keep from crying out.

The only person she'd ever been able to do it with, to actually pass along information, love, was Chris. Not for the first time since she'd met Teo Sandoval, she was relieved and grateful she had closed her mind to his.

But usually Chris's communications were less than verbally conceptual, primarily comprised of images, impressions. Yet, somehow, he'd told Teo the fox's name was Gina.

Judging by the lack of Chris's ever-present collection of toys, Teo had managed to penetrate her son's usual ab-

sorption with making them dance and keep him occupied
with other interests. Was this a result of the telepathy? Or
was it simply something in Teo's personality?

Chris giggled and said something to Teo. His brown eyes
met the blue ones of the large man kneeling so casually
beside him. Even from where she was standing, Melanie
could see that trust shone from her son's gaze. Simple, easy
trust. She felt a stinging in her eyes, a swelling in her chest
at hearing his laughter, at seeing him relaxed and confident
in the company of a man the PRI files had strongly urged
leaving completely alone, a man deemed dangerous.

She was struck by the contrasts between her son and Teo
Sandoval. And the similarities. Chris was so small, so vulnerable, while Teo was large, forbidding. Chris was fair,
with honey-brown eyes. Teo was dark, with a silver-blue,
cold gaze. Both of them, baby and man, possessed enough
power in their fingers to animate an inanimate world.

Watching them, Melanie was all too aware that both of
them drew her, her son in protective need, and Teo...in
dark fascination. For a moment she wanted to reach out to
both of them, let them glimpse her understanding of their
unusual gifts, even though Teo's still frightened her. Most
of all, she wanted to be included in their amazing bond,
wanted to stretch her mind to talk to them, to let them know
she was there, wanted to be a part of this magical moment.

Teo turned then, as if sensing a slip in her guarded mind.
His blue eyes linked with hers and his heavy black eyebrows drew together in a slight frown. She slammed the
barriers into place, blocking him, needing to keep him from
knowing she felt any kind of interest in him.

Teo felt his heart jolt as though electrified. But whatever
touched him now wasn't any part of the force that had
pulsed in his veins for as long as he could remember. This
feeling was something entirely new, completely foreign.

He had thought her lovely the day before, dampened by rain, angry, snared by lantern light. But after a sleep-filled night, the smudges erased from beneath her green eyes, her hair catching every ray of the morning sun, he was sure she was beauty personified.

He slowly rose to his feet, feeling his loins tighten and knowing his heart was beating too hard, too rapidly. He *wanted* her. And now, after having seen her both by night, and in the sun's rays, he knew she had to go. And go *now*. Or he would never let her go. It was that simple.

He turned and pulled a retractable gate from the stone wall separating the deck from his living room, and swiftly attached it to the railing by means of clamp hooks, small hinges that tiny fingers couldn't pry free. At the rattle of the wooden protective gate, the fox turned and, with a flick of its bushy tail, disappeared up the stairs.

Chris cried out in sharp dismay for Gina to come back.

"She'll come back tomorrow," Teo said. "She comes every morning. Maybe tomorrow she'll bring her kits. She has three."

Chris looked up at him with solemn eyes, sending him a question. *Gina be back?*

Teo felt the question touch his mind, the mental voice tentative, uncertain, the question filled with a variety of imagery he would never have drawn upon. The wet, cold nose of the fox, the wary dark eyes, the soft tongue. Flight, return.

Again he felt that shock of knowing another person was reaching inside his mind, touching his thoughts, impressing an image upon them. It nearly stole his breath, made him yearn for more, made him wary of wanting it to continue. The boy would be leaving today. Had to leave. But how could he let the one mind he'd ever truly understand simply disappear back into the unknown world?

Tomorrow?

Yes, son. Tomorrow.

Teo felt that twist inside him at the word "son." How easily it had leapt into his head, nearly sprang to his lips. Was it because the boy was so like he'd been as a child? Or did it go deeper than that, wrapped up somehow in the confusion he felt about the mother, the touch of another telepathic mind, the explosion of memories, the recollection of dreams cast aside years before?

He pulled another gate across the steps and secured it. He'd fashioned them so long ago, he'd half expected them not to work, but they had slipped into place as though oiled, used yesterday and not designed in another lifetime. Finally he turned and opened the glass doors separating him from the woman, from Melanie Daniels, the source of a night's sleepless pacing.

Dance? he heard the boy query, sending pictures of nature's leavings floating on air.

Yes, he allowed absently.

Leaves that had landed sometime on the deck sprang into the air, swirled around Teo's head, then swept down to bob around Chris's small fingers. A pinecone drifted up from the abyss and joined the dancing leaves. From somewhere a twig spun lazily in and circled the pinecone.

Unable to take his gaze from Melanie, Teo scarcely noticed the boy's activity, though he probed at the boy for a second and received no answer. Chris was lost in concentration, blocked to any stimuli other than that of his own creation. And his mother seemed lost in some introspection, as well, her eyes on the mountain artifacts floating around her son's body.

Finally she lifted her gaze to his. She lightly touched her lips with her tongue, as if needing the moisture. He felt his loins tighten even more. She had no idea how provocative she looked, enveloped in one of the townspeople's velvet gifts, her hair tousled and golden, her lips moist and slightly parted.

He knew he had to say the words to drive her away. She, and her infant son, made him want too much, remember too much. *Need* too much.

"It's daylight," he said, and even to himself his voice sounded rough, harsh. He felt that way and the feeling annoyed him. She stood there so calmly, her entire person an invitation, her eyes wide with vulnerability while she made him crazy with want, with uncertainty. He stepped inside the kitchen. Just tell her to go, he urged himself, knowing it was the best thing to do, the only thing that would save her...the only thing that would save *him*.

"You've had your night. *Now, get out of here.*"

CHAPTER FIVE

Melanie held her ground in the broad kitchen, though she did so by sheer will alone. The sunlight at Teo's back was strong enough to throw his form into relief and he stood before her a powerfully built dark silhouette. Except for his silvery eyes. His voice might have been rough, even angered, but she thought she read something else in his eyes. Anger, certainly, but more. Something almost pleading.

Now, get out of here, he'd commanded. But his eyes told a different story, nearly begged her to leave. Why would he need for her to go? And why did the harsh voice and the pleading gaze make her feel so very sad?

She dragged her gaze from his and again watched her son at his obsessive play. Like so many other puzzling things about Teo Sandoval, the protective fence he'd snapped into place was another anomaly. A man who shunned others had a cradle in one room and protective fences around his decking. A man who claimed to want to help no one had a stack of blankets and quilts in his closets. And a man who now commanded them to leave had only moments before promised her son the fox would be back on the morrow.

Chris's concentration on the leaves, the pinecone, even the twig, were such that he'd taken on the slack expression of an autistic child. He was no such thing, of course, though she knew perfectly well that her love for him wouldn't have altered one iota if that had been the case. But Chris wasn't remotely autistic. Preliminary testing by the PRI had revealed his intelligence quotient at far beyond the normal range, while his emotional development fell somewhat short of acceptable norms.

Nothing shy of a total miracle would ever make her son "normal," but he should be free to discover a way to relate to the world, to find a guarded happiness in his own unusual gifts. And no matter what promises the PRI made, they shouldn't be allowed to get their hands on him. For everything in her warned that they would hurt him irreparably.

As they had done Teo Sandoval?

She thought then of the trust that had shone from Chris's honey eyes when he'd met Teo Sandoval's gaze. Thought of the way his little hand had rested on Teo's broad shoulder. Thought of the two heads, one so dark, the other so fair, leaning close together in contemplation of Gina, a wild fox.

There was no denying the magic in Teo's touch. Her own fear or anger couldn't be allowed to matter, nor could a psychiatrist's warning in a file put together long ago. Teo might have done extreme damage to the PRI more than a decade in the past, but she'd also witnessed him saving a mechanic, healing the man's broken body with the raw power in his hands. And she knew that he could help Chris.

She couldn't leave. Not now. Not after seeing them together, seeing how strongly Teo Sandoval affected her son, how easily he reached into her son's psyche and soothed him, encouraged him. Not after seeing how easily he accepted the kinetic energy flowing in her son, how readily her son trusted him.

No matter how he might have angered her by stripping her clothes while she slept, no matter how harshly he had spoken to her, was glaring at her even now, she couldn't leave. And however much he might frighten her or make her insides quiver like so much jelly, both for having kissed her and for her having returned that phantom kiss, her surety that he could help her son returned in full force. As did her resolve.

She had to ask him, beg him on bended knees if necessary, to let her stay. She had to get him to work with Chris, to teach him, to save him from the hands and minds of the scientists from the PRI.

"Let us stay," she said urgently, unconsciously taking a step toward the man she feared and needed so. "Chris needs your help. You can see that. You must have been like him once. You can't let them do to him what they tried to do to you. You can't!"

"You have no idea what I can or can't do," Teo said harshly.

"I do," she countered swiftly. "I saw you with him. You were kind. Tender. He needs you. I know you can help him."

Before he could voice the denial she saw on his face, she stepped another pace closer, her words tumbling out to forestall his. "I'll do anything. Pay *anything!*"

He stared at her obliquely for several long, long moments. As she had done the night before, she felt the same shiver of static electricity raising the hair on her arms, teasing at the nape of her neck. Something on the stone shelves behind her rattled. A small indication of the turmoil inside Teo? She willed herself not to turn, not to look. And she forced herself not to step back from the sudden blaze of dark, unreadable emotion in Teo's gaze.

"The price is too high for anyone to pay," he said finally, all but spitting the words at her.

Wild hope swept through her, a flash fire of possibility. "Anything," she said. "I have money. Not much. I have a house. I mean, I'm not rich, but—"

"I told you yesterday, I don't want your money!" He ground the words out through gritted teeth, a clenched jaw.

His eyebrows winged sharply upward, giving him an evil cast.

"Anything you want..." Her words trailed off. She literally clasped her hands together before him. Pleading. Or was she simply trying to subdue her nearly violent trembling?

He stared at her so long, she held her breath, hoping against hope. Finally, as though the word was dragged from him, he said, *"You."*

"What?" she asked blankly, his single word having razor-strafed the synapse in her brain.

"You said anything I want. Have it your way. You. I want *you.*"

"I don't understand...." Melanie said feebly, all too afraid that she did.

"You. *You* are the price."

Melanie felt the edges of the universe slipping away, a misty haze obscuring her view of the man so close to her she could smell his clean, mountain scent, could feel the heat emanating from his body, the electricity slipping from him, drawing her, repelling.

As if he could sense her total disorientation, her shock, he grabbed hold of her shoulders and kept her from giving in to the sudden faintness threatening to take her down. He raised a hand to her face, cupped her chin in his broad palm. His fingers pressed into her cheeks, hurting her not with his touch but with the harsh control she felt through his shaking fingers.

His blue-gray eyes burned into hers and she had the odd notion they were scoring her very soul. "You are the price, *señora.*"

With his hands upon her, holding her in place, his eyes boring into hers, there was no mistaking his message. She knew, in some wholly instinctual response, *exactly* what he meant, and yet her rational side refused to accept that anyone in this day and age could possibly be suggesting such an outrageous bargain. He was right; the price was too high.

His hand remained on her face for a moment, then his lips twisted bitterly and he pushed her away from him. Not roughly, not gently. Just dismissively. "I thought so," he growled.

Melanie could still feel every nuance and imprint of his fingers. Her entire face felt on fire, her whole body burned from that brief contact.

She dragged in a shaky breath of relief when he turned his back on her. Ripples of fear snaked down her back as she saw, in peripheral vision, several of the food items on the shelves begin to shift and slide into each other. She felt a tingling sensation along her shoulders.

"Th-that's unfair. S-society doesn't w-work that way," she stammered, attempting to temporize his bargain with some semblance of normality.

Teo whirled around and slammed his hand, palm flat, on the rough-hewn, butcher-block island in the center of his kitchen. Melanie jumped. She wouldn't have been surprised to see the Spanish tile fling off the top and slice at her. The anger in Teo's face was abject. Absolute.

"Damn society," he snarled at her. "Damn the rules of the rest of the world. Like so many, you come here, begging my help. Unlike the others, I'm not willing to accept a chunk of meat, a blanket or two. *You* came to *me*. You asked me to name my price. I named it. Accept it or don't, but don't cavil!"

Melanie shrank back against the stone wall as he advanced toward her, fury all but dancing from his eyes.

His voice carried a note of ominous menace, dark fury. "This is *my* mountain. *My* rules. You came to me against my wishes. You came willingly. Now accept the terms or get out! It's all the same to me."

* * *

Teo felt almost sick with the rage that boiled through him, but more so from the look of wretched terror on Melanie's face. Her fine features were drawn in fear, her eyes almost flat with shock. For half a moment he wanted to take back the words he'd flung at her.

And, worst of all, he'd lied to her. It wasn't the same to him at all. He'd never wanted anything—anyone—like he wanted this honey-haired woman whose mind was blocked to him, whose thoughts were occluded. He'd never craved anyone like this trembling woman whose tentative touch, accepting mouth, made him crazy and utterly weak with longing.

If only he could reach into her mind and feel a hint of want from her. He'd felt it when she'd pressed against him in the dark corridor, her body arching against his. But he could read no more of her thoughts than he could the sky or the mountains themselves. Why?

Why should it matter? She wanted something from him; he wanted her. It was that simple. She could take his offer or not. Yes or no.

She was right; he was being unfair. But there had never been a moment of fairness in his life. Born with the curse of demons and the gift of gods in his hands, he'd been raised by a father who so greatly feared his own flesh and blood that he had buried himself in bottle after bottle until finally, in drunken victory, he'd sold his own son to the PRI for a future of cash and a promise of no more flying objects. And then there was his mother, a *curandera*, a local witch, a dispenser of herbs. She had been a mountain wisewoman with a bagful of stories about possession, the powers of the devil and a sick fear of the child she'd born on a wild night years and years ago. Both were dead now, without Teo's ever having had an opportunity to correct old wrongs. Unfair.

And Pablo…what had been fair about what his beloved Pablo had done? Nothing. Nothing at all.

And the PRI, literally chaining him, injecting him with drugs, waking him at all hours, confining him and others, driving them beyond pain, beyond endurance. What had been fair about what they had done to him? Or what he'd been forced to do in retaliation?

And what was fair about a society that shunned a child such as he had been, that pointed long, accusing fingers at him even as a few coveted his gifts? Nothing.

But most of all, what was fair about having had to accept that for him there would be no normal life, that dreams and wishes were for everyone else, but not for him? And after finally accepting that terrible fate, was it fair for this wide-eyed woman to bring her infant son to him and taunt him with possibility, with desire, with her ability to touch him and not jerk back in dismay? What was fair about her teasing him with all the impossibilities in his miserable life?

"What's fair about anything?" He rasped in a velvet soft tone that clarified his anger all the more. "You're the one who came to me. You're the one disturbing my home, driving me crazy. You're the one with the need so great you can't even move away from me even though the fear is making you almost sick!"

He saw the truth of his words, the bitterness of them, work through her, parting her lips, moistening her eyes. But instead of turning away from him, or even slapping him, she shocked him by nodding.

The world seemed to hold perfectly still for a heartbeat. He could hear the very blood rushing in his veins and sought to quell the sudden flare of triumph that burst in him. But a nod wasn't enough. If he couldn't slip into her mind, glean her thoughts, her reactions, he wanted to hear the words spill from her lips. He had to read her understanding, her acceptance, in her eyes.

"What are you assenting to? My truth or my bargain?" he demanded to know. He reached for her arms, gripped her fiercely, and shook her slightly. He held her at arm's length, fighting an almost overwhelming compulsion to drag her against his chest, crush her to him, kiss away the fear he could see in her eyes, the indecision etched so clearly on her nearly colorless face.

"Define your terms," she said, freezing him.

He felt the flare of triumph transform to a swift exultation that flooded through him, hot and wild. His fingers tightened on her arms.

"Define...your...terms," she repeated. Her full lips trembled, and he longed to capture them beneath his, to spell out his terms in a means too clear to misunderstand.

"I'm waiting," she said, her voice cool if slightly breathy.

He felt a keen sense of respect for her then. And a disgust of himself, followed almost immediately by a bitterness directed at her. No one should even consider agreeing to such a bargain. No one. And he knew a moment's stinging regret; he was man enough to desire her to want him for himself, not because he was forcing her to bend to his will.

But he was also a man who had been forced to be alone too long and she was a beautiful woman, enured to magic, and needing his help.

He drew a deep breath and said slowly, clearly, coldly, "I will help you with your son. I will even protect him from the PRI. All this. In exchange for your...company."

He felt a shudder work through her, suspected her knees were buckling and that she would have fallen had he not held her erect with his fierce grip.

"D-define...company."

"Day," he said, and then concluded, "and *night*." He felt as though the words were dragged from him and were used as a whip to flay her. But he repeated them nonetheless. "You will be mine, day and night."

Melanie tried remaining perfectly still. His hands upon her arms were hurting her, but not nearly as much as his bargain was. How could she even be considering such a notion, such a mockery of everything she held dear? What he suggested was sickening, twisted. What did it say about her for even asking him to define the terms of his proposal? She couldn't possibly agree. It was insane. It was demonic.

She stared into his eyes, trying to understand what had prompted him to even suggest it. All she could read was a glittering anger, and something else, that undefinable something she'd glimpsed earlier. Not pleading, necessarily, but something inexpressibly wary and disdainful of a longing too intense to even be named aloud.

She wanted to shake her head in negation, wanted to slap him for even suggesting such a demeaning bargain. And yet, judging by the tortured expression on his face, the fierceness of his grip upon her, she knew there was nothing casual about his proposal, nothing slightly offhanded. She remembered his kiss, the feel of his hands on her breasts, the taste of him on her lips.

There was no second-guessing a man like Teo Sandoval, for there were no other men like him. He was unique, an outcast, a man whose very powers kept him separated from the society she'd bleated at him about.

At all costs, he should be left alone.

She'd asked him to save her son from people who were after him, who had hurt Teo once, and then had been shocked when he'd responded unfairly. He was right; nothing was fair. It wasn't fair that a baby should be feared because he had unusual gifts; it wasn't fair for a group of scientists to act like common thugs; and it wasn't fair of her to expect Teo Sandoval to help her with nothing in return.

But he was asking too much. He was dead right; the price was way, way too high.

She drew a deep breath, trying to understand the conflicting feelings churning inside her. The words that slipped from her mouth surprised her as much as they seemed to anger him. Why would her question make him mad? Surely the question was a natural one? Why would her question make his eyes narrow and his jaw tighten as if she had disappointed him somehow?

"How long?" she asked softly, then added in swift counter to the anger on his face, "How long would you have me stay?"

"Six months," he snapped.

Six months? Half a year? She felt that dizzying sensation again, as if the world were shifting on its axis, sucking her into a maelstrom of gravity.

"Feed Gina now?" a voice trebled from the doorway.

Dazedly, Melanie saw her son exaggeratedly step over the strip of threshold. He tugged on one of Teo's pant legs. God, he was so tiny, so defenseless.

"We feed Gina now?"

"Tomorrow," Teo said softly. Gently. Tenderly?

"Want toys," Chris said loudly.

If Melanie hadn't had such a fierce block raised in her mind, she knew she would have received a mental picture of Chris's ball, his action figure, a few other assorted items.

She didn't need the mental picture. Suddenly, materializing out of thin air was a little red ball, the action figure, a comb, even her tube of lipstick.

She couldn't help her startled, questioning look at Teo. He said nothing as Chris laughed delightedly and clapped his hands. The objects floated for a moment, then drifted toward the still open kitchen door and through it into the cavernous living room with its exquisitely carved furnishings. Chris padded after the objects, hands reaching for them, eyes alight with wonder, giggling at the novelty of toys moving under someone else's direction.

Melanie only realized Teo still had hold of her when she tried turning to follow her son.

"He'll be all right. He has them now," he said. His hands gentled on her arms, slid up her shoulders and cupped her face between the broad palms, the long fingers slipping beneath her hair, drawing her closer.

She couldn't seem to breathe. Certainly couldn't have begun to think. Her heart pounded so furiously, she felt dizzy.

"Are you agreeing to the terms?" he asked.

Even as she felt her head nodding, she wondered how she could be agreeing to anything so outrageous. She knew what he wanted of her, what he expected, and as if mocking her, her mind conjured up the softness of his bed, the fullness of his lips, the cold, hard glitter of his gaze. What had she done by coming to him for help?

"Say it," he commanded.

Say what? That she was every kind of a fool? That he terrified her? That she wanted him, for God's sake? That she needed him almost as much?

"A verbal bargain is legal and binding in New Mexico," he said menacingly. *"Say it."*

"Six months…day and night," she said tremulously.

"Or until I tire of you," he said softly, his upper lip curling slightly.

She tried pulling away at this, fury fueling her numb limbs as fear could never have done. How dare he!

His fingers pressed against the back of her skull and his face lowered slowly. She resisted his approach, but his hands held her still, not granting her freedom. She clamped her lips closed as his covered hers, held herself as rigid as possible, letting him clearly understand how little she appreciated his final words.

His lips were soft against her tight resistance. His tongue teased her sealed mouth, his fingers massaged her head, her nape. When his hands lowered, when he released her, she couldn't have said, she only knew that one moment his hands held her prisoner, the next they held her upright. One moment she'd been shutting him out, closed to him, and the next her lips were parting, her eyes closing as she drank him in.

Feeling her resistance melting away, his kiss intensified, deepened, and his hands slowly, almost lazily, memorized her curves. Unconsciously, or perhaps in a languor long ignored, Melanie found herself leaning into his embrace, clinging to his broad shoulders, pressing her fingers into his muscled flesh.

So slowly that it scarcely seemed a movement, he pulled away. She opened her eyes to find him studying her with a mocking smile playing on his lips.

"A part of my attention is elsewhere," he said, and the bitter curl of his lips accentuated. "I want all of me focused on you. And yours on me."

Melanie felt as if he'd dashed springwater on her face.

He released her so abruptly, she sagged a little. A flicker of something danced in his eyes. Triumph? Genuine amusement? She didn't know, and wasn't about to guess.

"Tonight," he promised, though to Melanie the tone made the single word a threat.

He moved away from her, out the kitchen door.

It closed softly behind him. Mocking her.

CHAPTER SIX

Teo was grateful that the boy occupied so much of his attention as they walked along the hillside flanking his home. Otherwise he would have been forced to remember the hurt—and fear—in Melanie's eyes when he'd pulled away from her and uttered his intentionally cruel remark. He would have been forced to analyze why he was so angry with her for agreeing to his bargain, even while a part of him felt like shouting the news to the skies.

He would have dwelt on the sweetness of her lips, the richness of her curves.

He would have worried at some method of undoing what he'd done to her already. In this undoing, he would simply have used the knob on the door instead of deliberately flinging his kinetic talent in her face. He would have assured her that he didn't mean to follow up on his promised threat.

But if he'd done that, he would have been lying. For nothing shy of death was going to stop him from joining her that night. The world owed him. She owed him. He owed himself.

He had to stop thinking of her. He had to stop, period.

Stop here, he commanded Chris gently.

The boy stopped and looked up at Teo. He was bent nearly backward with the effort and Teo couldn't help but smile at the upside-down, upturned face. The boy smiled back. Too easily, Teo thought. No one should trust him that much, not even this untrained, untested child.

Whatever good lay hidden inside him had been locked up years ago and had been secured with the strongest chains in the universe—the chains of distrust. And no one, not even this innocent child or his desperate mother, could pry open those forged links. He didn't even want them to try.

But without trying, the steady honey brown gaze, the baby lips curved into an upside-down smile, the rosy flush of trust snapped a single link on that ponderous chain. Much as he wanted to, he couldn't tell the boy to stop getting under his skin, partially because he didn't understand how the boy could do it so seemingly effortlessly.

But it hurt to lose even one guard, one notch of that protection against the ills of the outside world.

Six months, he thought fiercely. *I have you for six months,* he told the boy unconsciously. And was pierced through when Chris's eyes lit with pleasure. His thoughts had touched the boy, reached inside and had been received.

What was he doing? How could he have agreed to help the boy when he himself was ostracized by the world, even the small community that hid him so effectively and used him like a bane against the physical woes in their lives? How could Melanie have wanted him to train her son when she saw the teacher for what he was, a frightening, hard man? Did she want her son to be like him? God forbid.

And yet some hitherto unused part of him stretched to accommodate the needs of the boy, the wants of the mother. If only someone had tried helping him when he'd been this young. If only someone had gently guided him through what the PRI had so roughly slammed into his mind, ruthlessly carved into his soul.

If they hadn't been so desperate, so furious in their need for immediate results, it might have seemed fun to exercise his abilities before those that so craved seeing them. And hadn't a part of him reveled in the stretching of his power, hadn't he truly leapt to their challenge? The answer was a harsh yes. For a while, a part of him had warmed to the power *in* him, the invincibility.

It was only later, when he began resisting, when he had

talked with a few of the others the PRI had held inside their comfortable prison, that he had fully understood what the PRI really wanted of him, how far they were willing to go to get it and how little they cared what happened to him in the process.

"Dance?" Chris asked aloud, almost fretfully. A mental image of his entourage appeared in Teo's mind. How much of Teo's thoughts had he been privy to just then? Was this his way of shutting them out?

Teo held his breath as the images strengthened in his head. As before, Chris was communicating directly from mind to mind. It wasn't adept yet, not strong, but the boy's meaning was clear, direct. And so very, very familiar. Not the pattern, but the ability. Once again he felt rocked to his soul. He wasn't the only human being on earth who could speak with thoughts.

Dance? Chris imaged again, stronger now. Sharper in meaning and definition.

Teo shook his head. "No, son. We're going to try a new game."

He sat down on a large slab of limestone, patting the sun-warmed rock, then lifting Chris to sit beside him. The boy's weight should have seemed insignificant, minuscule, but it didn't. The feel of the child's small chest, vulnerable and so very fragile, shook him to the core. The boy felt comfortable, easy in his hands, and it made him feel that way, too.

And these newfound emotions made him feel he teetered on the edge of certain doom.

To take his mind away from the unfamiliar tingle of closeness he felt reaching out for the boy, stretching simply for him, he directed Chris's attention to a single wildflower some four feet away from them. The bright red plume of color, an Indian paintbrush by colloquial name, bobbed on the light October breeze.

"Can you make the flower dance?" Teo asked.

"No!" Chris said swiftly, distinctly.

"Why?"

Chris didn't answer. In answer, Teo's mind was suddenly filled with several conflicting images: the ground, a rope holding the flower, a vacuum cleaner sucking ferociously at the plant, Melanie crying, and finally, a dead plant in a white room, the feral, pleased face of a man in a white coat.

Teo wasn't surprised at the clarity and sharpness of the boy's imagery. Chris might be only three, but he had the focal acuity of an adult. Images had always been Teo's life, and would forever be an integral part of his talent, as they would undoubtably be the same for Chris. But he didn't understand these.

He transferred the imagery back to Chris with a mental question, *What are these, what do they mean?*

He received the same set of images, but with greater agitation. No matter how he tried, Teo couldn't grasp the correlation between Melanie's tears and Chris's reluctance to make the flower dance. Unless Melanie fell apart when Chris displayed his gifts.

But she wasn't shocked by the talent. Lord knew, he'd flung his own abilities at her and she scarcely gave any outward sign of even noticing it. And since her mind was closed to him, he couldn't probe her inner thoughts. She had stiffened, but that could be explainable by the very tension that seemed to crackle between them. He would give her a few more demonstrations, see how she reacted. And then he would ask her why Chris would see her in tears in relation to a dancing plant.

The plant rooted to the ground, he understood. It was a simple statement of fact. The plant's being grounded made the raising of it more difficult. Questions as to logistics had obviously cropped into Chris's mind. Did he break the blossom free? Did he raise the entire plant? The decisions automatically became more involved, more complex. The vacuum-cleaner-hose symbol probably related to the difficulty of uprooting the plant.

But the image that disturbed Teo the most was the dead plant in the white room, the feral-faced man in the white coat. It bothered him because he recognized those mental pictures. Not that specific room, perhaps, but enough similarity about it to know the feel and flavor of a scientific laboratory. It was more up-to-date than the labs the PRI had hustled him through, but Chris's imagery was strong and rich enough to convey the unease, the discomfort, the avid eyes of the men watching behind clouded mirrors. Psionic Research Institute scientists, trying their tricks on a three-year-old infant. And he knew from the overlying confusion and tinges of sorrow in Chris's projections that those men had already made the boy kill. Just a plant, just a small flowering plant, but their inhuman lessons had already begun. Did this image explain Melanie's tears? Her desperation?

"Okay. Let's start with the pinecone lying over there." He pointed to a large ponderosa seed casing and said, "Can you make it dance?"

Immediately the pinecone shot into the air, bobbed for a moment, then drifted toward Chris. The animation slid from the little boy's features. The baby lips parted and the eyes dulled.

"Can you hear me, Chris?" Teo asked. He received no answer. He projected the question directly at Chris's mind. He felt the wordless query deflect from the boy's thoughts, almost as though absently batted away.

He redoubled his efforts. This was the first step, clearing the blockade Chris established when making things dance. Teo knew full well what a peaceful prospect it was to shut out the world, to focus all one's attention on a single spinning thing. But, as was obvious from Melanie's rigid barrier to anyone piercing her thoughts, there were other means to guard a mind against the full onslaught of humanity's demanding thoughts. And to lose one's self so thoroughly was to invite danger.

Fire could break out and Chris would never notice it. A truck could career into a sidewalk and Chris never hear it thundering toward him. The PRI scientists could set him to whatever task they chose, then abandon him to the consequences as they had tried abandoning a younger Teo.

He didn't want to jar Chris from the intense concentration. He could remember all too well his father's sudden slap or his mother's darting swipe at the objects his younger self sent floating around a room. He remembered the disorientation, the embarrassment, the clatter of objects crashing to the floor, lying broken in a welter of confusion.

There had been no one to help him.

But Chris didn't have to face the same nightmares. *He* was there to help Chris. This notion made him feel more powerful than anything his talents had ever done for him.

He sent a minute strand of energy outward and seized the dancing pinecone. He held it perfectly still in midair. He felt Chris tugging at it, was even slightly surprised at how he had to strengthen his own effort to hold it. Then he saw a furrow cross the little brow, watched as the little lips puckered. He smiled a bit, and the curvature felt bittersweet even to himself.

Give it to me, Chris demanded suddenly. Angrily. Clear, concrete thought, unconscious command. Petulance and precociousness combined in a mind that could rock nations and slammed into his head in a mental shout. *Mine!*

Teo's smile broadened, enjoying the mental battle, the breakthrough.

You have to take it, he told the boy. He felt a poignant

elation; he had gotten through that tight web of concentration. His part of the bargain had begun.

The pinecone slipped a little when Teo thought of the part of the bargain he fully intended to institute that night.

As the shadows lengthened, Melanie found herself growing more and more tense. Not, oddly enough, out of worry for Chris. Earlier, she'd been in the kitchen wondering if she should fix lunch when a loaf of bread she'd set out on the tiled island bar suddenly disappeared. She had found the bread and a waxed paper-wrapped sheaf of thinly sliced, highly seasoned brisket in a gaily decorated basket outside the heavy wooden doors of Teo's mountain retreat.

She'd had no doubts some erstwhile townsperson had placed it there. She'd looked around, but saw no one. The basket contained no note, no explanation. Was this how Teo survived the harsh seclusion? People he helped brought him gifts of food or clothing? It made perfect sense, even if it vaguely disturbed her. It smacked of the Greeks offering libations to the gods on Mount Olympus, seeking not to help them, but to placate their wrath.

Shortly after the bread had whisked from view, the brisket had followed suit, literally having been snatched from her suddenly empty hands. Teo had obviously purloined it for a picnic lunch for he and Chris.

When it had happened, Melanie had felt an odd queasiness, a primal dislike of the unknown. She'd felt the same way when she'd reentered Teo's bedroom after they'd gone. She'd planned on finding something of his to wear, at least until she got to her car and retrieved their clothes. She'd discovered she needn't look far. Her suitcases were already resting against the doors of the closet. She hadn't had to wonder how they'd got there, nor how Teo had managed to retrieve them from a locked trunk.

She'd stood beside them for a full minute before reaching

out to open them. Her heart had beat unaccountably faster and her fingers had felt numb as she picked through the items inside. She had known Teo was a telekinetic before ever coming there. She'd *known* about him.

But knowing and continually stumbling over proofs were two different things.

She had tried telling herself that Teo's remarkable abilities were only graduated versions of Chris's talents. But they were far more than that. Chris could make his toys dance while exerting extreme concentration. Teo could manipulate the world while doing other things.

Was that what she wanted him to teach Chris? She didn't know. Maybe. But would it have to include the sense of isolation that Teo steeped himself in?

She'd hurriedly made herself a bowl of soup and almost wolfed it down, half expecting it to vanish, also. It hadn't, leaving her feeling vaguely foolish.

Not for the first time, she pondered the ramifications of having such tremendous gifts. When she was a child, she had loved watching a television program about a witch married to a mere mortal. The witch could wiggle her pretty nose and do anything she wanted. The whole thrust of the story was that doing such magical things was humorous, but wrong. Every time the witch did something with her natural talent, the husband would take her to task and, properly chastised, the witch would promise to be good, be better, never use her gifts again.

Teo was a dark, mysterious version of that witch. But he lived alone. He didn't try to do "better," didn't make any promises to the world. Or excuses. He simply withdrew from it. But unlike the witch in the story, there was no colony of like-minded twitchers who could erase the dreadful loneliness that must surround him. And if there was one, would society, in its fear and prejudice of the unknown, allow it to survive? She didn't think so.

Was there anything Teo Sandoval couldn't do? He could save a life, take one away. He could build a home directly into the wall of a mountain, he could destroy a two-story building with a flick of his finger. He could get her son to feed a fox and her to forget her fear of the dark side of him. At least for a moment.

Thinking about his gifts, she was struck suddenly with a stray hint of her own. She had dreamed of Chris singing a song about foxes and awoke to find him feeding one. But the dream, like so many she'd had in the past few months, had carried an ominous feeling, a notion that things were amiss, out of kilter. Danger stalked her in the dream. But in this morning's dream danger had worn Teo Sandoval's face, and her name had been on his lips.

What did the dreams really portend? That they were in greater danger with Teo than with the PRI? Please, she begged the darkening sky, don't let that be the case.

Eyeing the elongating shadows, wondering how to light the kerosene lanterns, she wished her mind didn't keep continually skidding into Teo's bedroom, onto that soft, down-filled bed, and devoutly wished her heart didn't accelerate at the thought.

She'd spent most of the restless day exploring her new quarters. Her home for six months. She had tried anything to make the situation seem even remotely normal, the bargain the veriest bit acceptable. But her mind kept returning to that semidarkened bedroom, to that dark tunnel that led to his home. To the kiss they'd exchanged inside its pitch-black corridors. And the kiss that morning in his sun-dappled kitchen.

She walked the length of the house, looking for matches, something to give her a clue as how to light the lanterns hanging in every room. She was struck again by the fact that except for the distinctly unusual element of having been built directly from the natural cave formations on the rock cliff, Teo's home was arranged much as a typical house might be. The largest cavern served as a living-drawing room, with hand-carved, Taos-style furniture loosely placed around a large Navajo rug near the huge glass windows. The room itself was roughly forty-by-sixty feet in width and breadth, large enough to hold an army.

She'd been pleasantly surprised to discover that the living room's kitchen-side wall was lined with hundreds upon hundreds of books. Most of the volumes in the open cases were well worn and carried Teo's name inside.

That Teo would be well read didn't surprise her so much as it added to the puzzle that comprised him. It wasn't that he didn't know the rules of society, didn't understand how the melting pot of American culture worked, it was that he rejected those rules. Many of the books she pulled from the shelves were in-depth sociological studies, others anthropological in nature. Teo had to know the rules very well.

He had simply chosen to ignore them. Or worse, to abandon them.

And what about her? She was the one who had agreed to his heinous bargain. A bargain that seemed to weigh on her with each passing second.

She went back to the kitchen to see if she could find something to make for dinner. She stood inside the darkening room and wondered how to brighten it. All that electricity that leaked from Teo's hands, she thought a little snipishly, why couldn't he arrange an electric light or two?

At least he had running water. Behind the kitchen, down a narrow rock passage, she'd discovered another large cavern. It almost shocked her at its sheer hedonism. A large skylight hung high in the rounded rock ceiling, spilling light throughout the cavelike room. A series of shower heads dotted one corner, and as she'd discovered upon using it, the water jetted from nearly every angle possible, as piping hot as she ever could have wanted. Two drains drilled directly into the rock floor apparently carried the water away. Probably, she thought wryly, straight out the side of the mountain in a sporadic waterfall.

But that couldn't be right, for the room was also equipped with a modern toilet, a sink, and a nearly mega-lithic-size bathtub that was also formed of rock but lined with some smooth agent. It was large enough to serve as a hot tub or a whirlpool, but without electricity it wouldn't have any frothy, massaging jets. Not that Teo Sandoval would have any need to rely on anything man-made to make the water churn.

The thought had sobered her. When she'd begun her search for him, she'd had only one thought in mind: Teo Sandoval hated the PRI, he was a telekinetic, he would surely help her keep her son from their clutches. Had she deliberately ignored consideration of the man behind the powers? Was that why she was in such an incredible mess?

But, aside from his unusual terms, was it really such a mess? She and her son were safe from the PRI for the first time in months. Safe from the world.

And alone with Teo in his mountain fortress. She shivered and wished the fortress wasn't quite so dark now.

As if he could read her thoughts—which she knew he couldn't for she'd kept her mind firmly clamped all day, even to the extent of being closed to Chris—the kerosene lanterns flickered, then the wicks caught and brightened, chasing shadows to the corners. And making her all too aware that he was thinking of her.

"How did it go today?" she asked the empty kitchen, needing to practice what she might say to him upon his return. "That won't work," she answered herself. The question sounded too casual, too familiar. It had the ring of the long-married couple who ask such questions more out of ritual than any real desire to know.

"Did you have any success?" she tried. But that, too,

seemed inappropriate. She wasn't even sure what "success" would mean in relation to his working with Chris. This was something she *would* have to ask him. Tonight.

She shivered anew, hating the way her thoughts always came back to that worrisome time.

From a large, wooden, insulated cupboard, she pulled another waxed paper-wrapped packet, and opened it carefully. It was thick chunks of beef. A cautious sniff proved the meat fresh and she set about trying to put together a meal. Largely by means of scent and wary tasting, she made her way through the unmarked herb containers and marinated the thick strips of beef with sweet basil, a hint of mountain thyme and a pinch or two of what might pass for oregano. She dunked the beef in a pungent red wine she found among a collection of wines in a rack on the far side of the kitchen, then dredged the strips in the crushed herbs. The kitchen was redolent with spicy odors.

Luckily the ancient stove was simply a wood-burning affair and she found wood generously stacked outside the glass doors, as well as matches for it—and the lanterns, she thought grimly—in a small wall-mounted container beside it. She took a book of the matches and marched into the living room and set them beside one of the lanterns on an end table there. She wasn't going to have him light the lanterns for her tomorrow evening. She shivered at the implication of yet another day spent in his company, the concept of thinking beyond the night looming ahead.

Slowly she returned to the kitchen, determined to find anything to take her mind from the thought of his large, down-filled bed.

It didn't take long before the iron surface of the stove was hot enough to work with.

She had the meat sautéing in the largest frying pan she'd ever seen when a commotion at the door made her whirl in exaggerated fright. She'd been listening for their approach, straining to hear any sign of their return. And now that she'd finally heard it, her heart had leapt to her throat, and her breath came in shallow, dry gasps.

He was back. And this was *tonight*.

For a moment all she could see through the glass doors leading to the deck was her own reflection, then through it, she met the pale blue eyes of the man she'd thought of every moment of the long, long day.

She felt rooted to the stone floor and didn't so much as shift an inch as he pushed the doors open and stepped through. His eyes were so piercing, so challenging, that she almost didn't notice her son riding easily against his broad shoulder.

"Mommy!" Chris cried with glee, and Melanie smiled in relief, in automatic joy.

"You're cooking," Teo said. His tone implied this was the last thing he'd ever expected her to do.

"We have to eat," she replied coolly. She'd rehearsed about thirty different things to say to him, but none fit this particular twist in conversation.

"Why?"

"Why do we have to eat?" she asked blankly.

"Why are you cooking? You don't need to. You don't have to cook or clean for me. That wasn't in the agreement," he said, frowning.

His words underscored what *was* in the bargain, even though he didn't spell it out.

"I thought Chris would be hungry," she said. "You've been gone all day." It was as close to an accusation as possible.

But Teo only looked from the pan of fragrant meat to the one containing the steaming rice. The frown on his forehead deepened. He looked genuinely perplexed. Finally he shifted Chris from one arm to the other and gave her an oblique look as he crossed the kitchen in two strides and exited down the narrow corridor to the unusual bathroom. As usual, the door opened then closed without his touching it.

She turned back to her ministrations, feeling something between pique and confusion. Her heart still beat too rapidly, her hand shook slightly. When she reached, a few minutes later, for a hand-woven pot holder she'd found earlier, she found it wasn't alone on the island bar. Her heart seemed to stop beating for a full twenty seconds.

Somehow, without her having heard a sound, without seeing anything, the table had been set. Three plates, sets of silverware, even glasses, rested on the now covered bar. Two wineglasses had been placed beside two of the settings and were already filled with a deep burgundy-colored wine.

She heard her own sharp intake of air, and slow exhalation. She tried telling herself that she should regard it as amusing, even helpful. But it wasn't intended that way, she thought. It was another of his demonstrations, another reminder that he was different, that he was frightening.

Turning away from the table, she squared her shoulders, vowing she wouldn't give him the satisfaction of knowing he'd startled her yet again, made her feel that brush with the preternatural universe.

The heat from the kitchen made her feel slightly dizzy, flushed. But when Teo stepped through the thick door, followed by his tiny and beaming shadow, Melanie knew the warmth in her cheeks had nothing to do with the fire in the wood stove, only with the man standing a few feet away from her, eyeing her with wary challenge.

He glanced at the neatly arranged place settings and back to her. A measure of mockery rested on his chiseled features. But she didn't necessarily have the feeling that mockery was turned on her.

Could she have wronged him? Could the demonstration of setting the table not have been an attempt to frighten her once again, but some need for her to accept his unusual gifts? With some chagrin, she suspected she'd come to the correct conclusion this time. *This is me,* he seemed to be saying defiantly. *This is what I am. Take it or leave it.*

She wished she dared lower her guarded mind to him to see if she was right. But she couldn't, he would see too much, would understand her extreme vulnerability, her unwary attraction to him. No, she thought, especially given the terms of their bargain, she couldn't open herself to his searing thoughts.

She turned back to the meal and carefully dished it onto a platter she'd found behind one of the cupboards. She tried quelling the riot of feelings he inspired in her, tried clinging to the realization that Teo might not want to frighten her but might be merely telling her in no uncertain terms that he wasn't ashamed of his talents. Wasn't that what she wanted for Chris?

As she set the platter on the table and lifted Chris to a bar stool, telling him to be very careful, she tried thinking of Teo in terms of the boy the PRI had—for all intents and purposes—purchased from his father. She tried seeing the damage they had inflicted on his vulnerable psyche. She tried pitying him.

But when she looked up at his hard face, his challenging eyes, she found that pity was the last emotion she could summon. Pity seemed as out of place for Teo as an ice cube in a fire storm. He would disdain anything so pathetic.

She knew the meal was delicious. She had tasted it during the preparation. The meat was tender, delicately spiced and the wine brought out a flavor both unique and rich. But now, sitting catercorner to Teo, her sleepy son separating them by only inches, the beef tasted like cardboard and the rice like so much sawdust.

They ate the meal in tense silence and the lack of conversation seemed to hammer at her ears. Every time her fork scraped against the ceramic plate, she found herself willing it to be quiet. Each time Teo's hand reached for his water or his wineglass, she would tense, as if expecting him to reach for her instead.

When the tortuous meal was finally finished, Melanie was inordinatly relieved that Chris was nearly dropping from the stool in exhaustion. At least she would have something to do, a job that would take her away from Teo's burning gaze. For the first time, dressing the limp, drooping body in his pajamas and kissing him before settling him in the soft cradle, Melanie actually wished Chris were an obstreperous baby. If he were fighting bedtime, challenging sleep, she might have an excuse to linger in this secure room. Linger and linger until the night faded into morning.

"He's asleep," Teo said from the doorway.

Instead of making her jump, this time his voice only served to drive home the wrongness of his terms, the wrong she'd done in accepting them.

"Come," he said, and when she didn't move toward him, he held out his hand.

"The dishes," she said softly.

"There's no need," he said. And while she knew that was the perfect truth, she felt such a desire to perform such a mundane task that her guard must have slipped a notch. An odd expression crossed his face, even as his gaze sharpened. He said finally, "But I haven't cleaned them yet."

She felt relief infuse her veins, allowing her to walk toward him, brush past him to leave Chris's small niche. He didn't try to touch her as she stepped by him. He didn't need to. She was already all too conscious of his scent, of the heat radiating from him.

He followed her to the kitchen and stood beside her as she ran warm water into his sink. He handed her a container of powdered soap granules that he must have acquired in a previous decade. Of course, she thought dully, he wouldn't need anything so simple as soap. He could just wish his dishes clean.

She used it sparingly and the suds rose swiftly. She stared at them almost mesmerized, needing to look at anything other than the man beside her. But she was too aware of the fact that he leaned against the wooden countertop, his arms crossed, his expression inscrutable.

He said nothing as she slid the plates into the soapy water. And still not speaking, but making her tense when he moved, he gave a single wave at the dishes in the rinse water. One by one they rose from the water, hung in the air, rotated once and slowly floated to land, soundlessly, *dry,* atop the short stack of plates.

Melanie found herself holding her breath, trying not to goggle at the display of his abilities. He was doing that on purpose, she thought. Just as he'd done the other things, setting the table, raising or dimming lights, opening and closing doors without needing to touch them.

Except for his theatrics, Melanie was struck by the sheer banality of their working together. It was too casual, too normal. Eating together, cleaning up afterward, putting a baby to sleep. It seemed to address an intimacy that didn't—couldn't—exist between them.

"Why does Chris project an image of you crying when he sends the picture of a dead plant?" Teo asked abruptly, cutting the silence that roared between them.

Melanie was inordinantly relieved that when he spoke, it was about Chris, not about the night looming ahead. "A dead plant?" she asked.

"In a white room," he said.

"At PRI," she said, comprehending the image suddenly. She felt the horror and anger she'd felt then suffusing her now. "They made him kill the plant. They tricked him into it."

Teo didn't say anything for a moment, only studied her as if seeing something he didn't particularly like.

"What?" she asked.

"Why did you let them do that to him?" he asked. "How could you let them twist his mind?"

"I didn't," she said hotly. She turned to face him, all fear of him momentarily forgotten in her anger that he would believe her capable of allowing such a thing to happen to her son. "Tom arranged the visits, all but sold Chris to them."

"Who's Tom?"

"My ex-husband," she said coldly. "Chris's father."

"I see. He sold Chris to the PRI?"

"Yes," she said, then added, "Like your father did you." She wished she could snatch the words back at the black thunder that swept across Teo's face.

After a few incredibly charged moments, Teo said, "But you have the boy now."

"Yes," she said. She couldn't help raising her chin as if daring him to question that, also. "I couldn't let them get away with their hideous games."

"Hideous games," Teo echoed. "That's what they are."

"That's why I brought him to you," she said.

"Because I would know how to train Chris…teach him all the magic they wanted to teach him, but without the madness?" he asked bitterly.

She didn't answer. What he'd said was true, but the tone made it a lie, made it seem stupid, questionable.

"What is it that you want Chris to learn?" he asked then.

She'd had most of the day to consider this question, to try to formulate some answer in her mind. "To be strong enough not to be susceptible to those such as the scientists at the PRI," she said, though the words came anything but easily.

"Why didn't you just have him do what I did?" Teo asked.

"Tear the place apart?" she countered swiftly.

Teo shrugged.

Melanie answered truthfully, "Because he didn't know how, and because I couldn't show him."

"And that's what you want me to teach him?"

"No!" she snapped, then at the flare in his silver eyes, retreated into a quieter tone. "No. But once they'd taught him that total concentration technique…I couldn't get through to him any longer. He wasn't safe from them. They could do anything to him then."

She could tell that something along those lines had already occurred to him, that she wasn't telling him anything he didn't already know.

"What did you mean when you said you couldn't get through to him any longer? Are you telepathic?" he asked.

Melanie hesitated. And finally, lied. "Just a bit," she said. "Like any mother is for her child."

She tried not to flinch away from him as he raised a hand to her temple. But she didn't succeed and his hand stopped just shy of touching her. He lowered it slowly to his side, staring at her all the while.

"How do you close your mind?" he asked her finally.

She had to look away from him. She only shook her head in answer.

After what seemed hours, he said slowly, consideringly, "In the forest today, Chris 'danced' a pinecone. I broke through his block." Incredibly, Teo chuckled. This time his laughter held no trace of the mockery that had suffused it the night before, no undercurrent other than simple amusement. "He shouted at me in that mental voice."

Melanie couldn't help but turn back to face him, couldn't help but smile. One day in Teo Sandoval's company, and Chris had already done more for him than he had for the scientists at the PRI in two months, and for her in a lifetime of coping. She'd done right in bringing her son here. She longed to tell him so, to just openly acknowledge her gratitude.

But even as her lips curved into a smile, as her eyes met his, his face seemed to change, to close, as if he'd said too much, confessed too much. He took a step closer to her. Menacingly. "I've fulfilled my part of the bargain today," he said, his meaning painfully clear.

Melanie realized that if she had hoped that the process of washing dishes, no matter how unusually they were put away, or their few minutes of conversation would have eased her anxiety, would have soothed her chaotic thoughts, she found she'd been destined for failure. The proximity to him, the warm water, the floating service, the sudden tense silence all only conspired to exacerbate the jagged-edge uncertainty that raged inside her.

No matter how much she might delay, three place settings and a couple of pans had only taken so long to clean. And no matter how much she might wish the night over, the morning dawning, her heart was beating in staccato rhythm, her lips were dry and her breath shallow and reedy. Because the raw truth was, she *did* want to fulfill her part of the bargain. She did want the night spent in Teo Sandoval's arms. No matter how wanton that might make her seem, no matter how foolish, she wanted to feel his lips upon hers, wanted him to make love to her.

Even though he frightened her senseless.

When it was perfectly obvious that nothing was left to be washed, and nothing was left to be said, Teo turned and left the room. Melanie watched him go with near heart-stopping reaction, felt she could see him still despite the closed door. Her legs were trembling, her hands shaking so hard she could scarcely manage to fold the already wrung dishcloth. She set it over the faucet and still couldn't make herself leave the kitchen.

Slowly, silently, the kitchen door swung back open. But Teo wasn't there. It was an announcement, an invitation. A command.

Feeling as though her body belonged to someone else, Melanie found herself moving through the doorway into the large living room. She walked as far as Teo's bedroom doorway.

She stopped, shocked to discover he'd already removed his shirt, was standing in the center of the room, barefoot, his broad, muscled chest naked and covered in a fine dusting of black hair. His long dark hair hung loose on his shoulders, his eyes locked into hers.

A single candle was burning on the bedside table. The flame seemed to flicker along Teo's burnished skin, reflecting in his muscles, rippling along his torso, his shoulders.

She felt her mouth go even drier. And she experienced an odd longing to lightly brush the hair on his chest with her hands, discover if it was as soft as it looked.

"I can't do this," she blurted out suddenly, and didn't bother to explain what she meant. She wanted to join him—he'd never know how much—but she needed more than a cold-blooded bargain. She craved to know him as a man, but not as payment to El Rayo.

Teo never moved, never shifted his eyes from hers as the door softly snicked closed behind her. She didn't need to turn to see its blank face, its dark portend.

"I...I need to be able to listen for Chris," she said desperately. What was she saying? That she would stay with him, but to keep the door open? What was there about the door closing that seemed to make her teeter over the edge of decision?

"I can hear him," Teo rasped, obliterating that objection. He stepped forward. And yet again, until he stood only inches from her. She could smell the herbal mixture he must use for shampoo, the wine they'd shared for dinner, felt the sharp tingle of electricity that seemed to be emanating from him. Or was it coming from herself, joining him in some unique chemistry that the two of them seemed to share?

"I was wrong," she said. "I mean it. I can't do this."

Again he didn't answer, but lifted a large hand to her face. Lightly, slowly, he traced the curve of her cheek, her jaw, with the edge of his thumb. He outlined her lips, her eyebrows and the wildly throbbing pulse in the hollow of her collarbone.

She stood there as though hypnotized. And perhaps she was, but she couldn't delude herself that it was Teo doing the hypnotizing, except by his feather-soft touch, his deliberate reflective caress.

"You are a beautiful woman, *señora*." His lips curved in a near mocking smile. "I'm very pleased you accepted my terms."

She swallowed heavily and wanted to tell him that she no longer did accept them. She even parted her lips but hesitated when he lightly flicked one of his own fingers with his tongue then shifted the moisture to her lips, massaging them softly, meaningfully.

Melanie was never more frightened in her life. And never wanted to lean into any touch as much as she did at that moment.

CHAPTER SEVEN

Teo fought the desire raging through him, fought to rein in the storm. He had never felt more truly El Rayo than tonight, than now. *God, let me have some measure of control,* he thought. But how could any man even pretend control around a woman as beautiful and as vulnerable as Melanie Daniels, especially when she stood inches from him, her lips parted, her breath coming and going raggedly?

And most especially when she had come inside this room knowing full well what he expected from her, what she had agreed to offer.

He wanted to crush her to him, to take and take and take. To drown himself in her. And for a few precious hours, make believe he was like any man with a lovely woman, pretend that sharing himself could come naturally, that touch could be a viable part of his life.

But in such a pretense a union with her would have to be one derived from mutual desire, reciprocal agreement. And he'd forced her to accept his terms…*day* and *night.* And now she was saying she couldn't comply. Didn't she understand anything about him? He didn't need her compliance. He could strip her naked with a glance, pin her against a wall—or to his bed—with a stray thought.

She'd agreed to his damnable bargain, and he'd be more than damned if he released her from it now.

"*Señora…*" he murmured, still not taking his eyes from her wide gaze. "The minute you agreed to stay, your fate was sealed. You have no choice."

"Teo…" she said, using his name directly for the first time. Unaccountably the single word seemed to reach deep inside him, though it was neither a plea nor a demand. The feeling half scared him, made him angry at her, angrier at himself. She had used his name three times now, the magical number. Once in the rain, once while asleep in his bed, and now again, her lips brushing his finger as she did so.

She couldn't leave him now, couldn't leave the room. Didn't she know that? He lowered his hand, ignoring how it trembled in need to continue touching her, to do more than simply stroke.

"For six months, you belong to me," he said. Underscoring his meaning, he sent a thought to the bed and ripped back the covers, tossing them to floor. He saw her start in surprise, watched as her eyes flicked from the empty bed to the pile of blankets on the floor. But she didn't move backward. She turned her eyes back to his and he saw they were emerald green now in understanding, perhaps in fear.

He wanted to curse at her, to demand that she not fear him. And he wanted her to simply move into his arms, wanted her to come to him, to desire *him*. To *need* him as much as he needed and wanted her. He wished he could tell her so, wished he could reach into her mind and plant the thought, the dream. But she was closed to him. Had been almost from the first moment he'd seen her.

"You're wrong," she said slowly, and if her face was pale, her lips suddenly dry, her voice tremulous, her gaze didn't so much as waver. "I belong to no one. A woman always has a choice. It's her right."

He sent a bolt of lightning across the clear sky and felt it explode against the stars, the cold night, heard the thunder echo in his soul, saw its aftermath etched on her still face.

Slowly, carefully, hearing the menace in his own deceptively soft voice, he said, "Don't talk to me of *rights, señora.* You know nothing about them. They do not exist here. Here, you are mine."

"You do not own me," she said coldly, and he felt a measure of pride for her. And regret. She was telling the truth. She might be in his home, might have sought his aid, but she wasn't seeking anything more. He might even manage to have her body, but he didn't have her mind, her heart. In forcing her to uphold her end of the bargain—his bargain—he would be using her as he himself had been used, against his will, against his desire.

He felt the confusion, the want in him striving to break free, and again sent the unchecked energy to the universe. The sky crackled and shards of light played on the skylight, refracted from her green eyes. Her lips parted in fear, in some measure of understanding, and yet she still didn't move away from him.

Some dark, long-buried part of him shivered in reaction, in question. And in answer, he told himself firmly that she *did* feel something for him, some yearning. He'd tasted it upon her lips, felt it in her trembling response to his kisses both the day before and that morning. And he could see it now in her jutting nipples, her shallow breathing.

Seeing this, knowing this about her, he suddenly understood why he'd been angry with her over her acceptance of his terms. He'd felt her want of him, a want almost as strong as his for her, but he'd been the one to force her into a corner, pushed her into this bargain. And he was angry when she'd agreed to the bargain because he was human enough to want *her* to want him, to come to him as a lover might.

He didn't want the desire to be one-sided. He knew a man would have to be dead not to want her, but what about what she might feel for him? No one could possibly know better than he just how different he was than other men, than all other men. But that didn't stop him from wanting her running her hands over his body, her mind opened to his, a plea for him on her lips. That was why he'd been angry with her, was angry still: for not wanting him, for his having had to coerce her into it.

He slid forward and slowly, deliberately, cupped her face in his hands. She stiffened but didn't pull back. He held her so for a few seconds, trying to break through the gate in her mind, trying to read her thoughts from the depths of her emerald eyes.

Almost as if of their own accord, his fingers began gently kneading, massaging her temples, the hollow beneath her ears. *Want me,* he commanded silently. But her distant expression didn't shift. *Want me,* he told her with his hands, drove home with his unwavering gaze.

Something seemed to alter in her eyes, some hint of desire, perhaps of confusion, and he slowly drew her forward, pressing a kiss to her soft, unresponsive lips. He stayed there, leisurely teasing her lips with his tongue, with his mouth, scarcely touching her, until he felt her lips quiver and heard a soft moan issue from what seemed her very soul.

He deepened his kiss, holding her to him, dropping his hands from her face to caress her shoulders, her back. She moaned again and seemed to sag against him, almost as though in relief. When her hands lifted and tentatively touched his face, stole into his unbound hair, tangled there, he pulled away slightly and met her confused gaze.

He said nothing, though thunder crashed above his bedroom, almost as if asking the question he couldn't voice, seeking the answer she would never offer.

"You'll be damned for this," she said finally.

A shaft of pure agony ripped through him. Nothing she said would have made more sense to him than that simple phrase. And nothing could have been truer.

"*Señora,*" he said softly, "I thought you understood. I'm already damned."

* * *

Melanie wanted to run from the room, wanted to lean into his hands, ached for herself, yet found herself hurting more for the boy Teo Sandoval must have been, for the pain that had created the man standing before her.

She, who distrusted most of the world, and with good reason, couldn't begin to fathom the depths of Teo's distrust, his deep-rooted anger and sense of betrayal.

He'd coldly, fearsomely, proved his point with his theatrics, his torn-aside bedcovers, the closed door, the lightning whipping across the sky, eerily reflecting in the skylight. He could have had her at any moment after she pounded on his door demanding entrance to his cavelike home. And yet he'd chosen to have her believe he had solicited her cooperation in his terrible bargain. Why?

His lips again descended to hers and as she had done in that dark corridor, and again in his strange kitchen, when sunlight had danced upon his shoulders, she couldn't help arching to meet his hands, straining to meet his kiss. What was it about this lonely, forbidding man that drew her so?

She had managed to lie to herself throughout the day, telling herself that he'd forced her into this bargain, that her body was small payment for Chris's safety, his learning of Teo's secrets. But with Teo's hands upon her, slowly molding her waist, the hollow of her back, his lips teasing her nearly senseless, she understood the truth. She'd agreed to his bargain because *she wanted him*. Because he drew her like no one had ever done before. Because in his mystery, his frightening abdication of the world, he held a dark, lonely allure that captured her imagination, her own lonely desire.

He drew back from her, silver blue eyes darkened with desire, nearly violet in their introspection, their distance. He again raised his hand to her lips and slowly, hypnotically, traced the curve of her mouth, smoothing them, soothing and sending shivers of response coursing through her.

Unconsciously, her lips pressed a kiss against his forefinger. She thought, watching him, that his eyes widened, that something flickered behind the heavy lids.

"Teo..." she breathed. "Please..."

Teo knew he was lost. He longed for words to give her, beautiful phrases that would carve out some alternate future, but with her unframed plea ringing in his ears, the kiss on his hand echoing through his entire frame, the words would wait, and sadly, he understood that they would have to wait forever.

Because there were no pretty words. For him there was no ordinary future, happy mommy, daddy, family, happy home. For him there was only extreme solitude. There was only the lonely present and the dark, infinite future of empty nights.

But she was granting him tonight. And perhaps tomorrow night. Perhaps six months. And for six months he would know a window of living, loving. That he would have to make it last a lifetime couldn't be allowed to matter now.

Her body arched against him, letting him know what he couldn't read in her thoughts, couldn't see in her face. Her hand rose to his cheek and she brushed her thumb along the muscle jumping in his jaw. Was it a question or was it the answer he'd been looking for?

In question himself, he slowly cupped a full breast in his hand. She moaned as he grazed a turgid nipple, imagining he could feel her satin skin through the silky material of her blouse. She closed her eyes and let her head fall a little to the back, allowing him greater freedom. It was all the answer he could have asked for.

Her buttons slid free of their catches and a stray thought pulled the blouse free, exposing her to his hungry gaze.

The swell of her breasts above the lacy bra was creamy, lightly freckled. A pulse beat wildly above her defined collarbone. Her eyes flickered open, then closed.

He trailed his finger down her throat, pausing at the throbbing pulse, then lower, to the cups of her bra. He was shaking almost as much as she. He savagely sent a burst of energy from him, from the room, to the heavens outside, and heard the sharp crackle of lightning, saw it reflected through the skylight.

She didn't open her eyes as his fingers peeled the lacy material from her breasts, freeing her to his hands, his gaze, and finally his mouth. He heard and felt her breath catch as his hands tested the weight of her, and then his mouth slowly laved, then suckled her turgid nipples.

Her accepting moan let him know how little she might be considering their bargain and his heart leapt in fierce triumph. Words might be important on some plane, somewhere, but for now, for this moment, it was enough to know that she did desire him, that she was a willing partner in this unusual agreement.

Melanie arched to meet his mouth, her breasts aching for his touch, the laving tongue, the soft graze of his teeth. Without conscious thought, her fingers tangled in his long, silky soft black hair and she pulled him even closer.

He slid his hands behind her without stopping his assiduous attention to her breasts. His palms flattened along her buttocks and he curled his fingers beneath her, and, surprising her, lifted her, draping her legs around his narrow, tapered waist.

She heard the sharp report of thunder outside somewhere and instinctively knew it came from Teo, but didn't care. Perhaps even reveled in it. It could have been issuing from her, she felt that strong, that powerful, that out of control.

She felt her blouse slide from her shoulders and knew

neither his fingers nor gravity played any part in its slippage. *He* had removed it with his mind. But this time, he hadn't done it with any intention to startle or frighten her. And this time, she'd wanted the obstacle removed.

As she clung to his shoulders, riding him, arching to meet his avid mouth, she felt the remainder of her clothing disappear, a tingling sensation rippling over her skin as the cool air in the room, the abrupt transition from clothed to naked, kissed her bare body. And equally swiftly, equally smoothly, his own clothes melted away as a tremendous clap of thunder exploded above them.

He carried her to the bed and slowly lowered the two of them to the down-filled mattress. They seemed to sink into the cloudlike bed in slow motion, and perhaps Teo had somehow worked his magic to make this a reality. She didn't know, and didn't care. All she knew was that his mouth was as firm and knowing as his hands, and that his touch was working its magic on and for her alone.

She had a feeling of deliberate abandon, a sensual wantonness she had never encountered before. And she reveled in being studied, explored by this unusual man, this stranger who struggled so furiously with his telekinetic powers and yet remained so slow and gentle with her.

As he leaned over her, his hand lightly stroking from knee to breast, tickling almost, his eyes were lit with some unexpressed emotion, and clap after clap of thunder echoed across the sky outside. Shards of lightning flared bright and sharp against the curved skylight and they seemed parts of herself, barriers she'd carried too long shattering before her eyes.

She wondered about Chris, if the noisy heavens would wake him, but remembered Teo's saying he could hear him. She had no doubts he meant it literally. And after a moment the worry disappeared, dropped away as easily as her clothing had gone.

She felt almost amazed at how swiftly she'd acquiesced to him, how easily she'd found herself lying nude in his bed, his large, tapering fingers slowly exploring her every curve. And how languorously she stretched beneath him, one hand on a muscled arm, the other against his face, all embarrassment absent, any nervousness gone.

His fingers traced a line from her breasts to her mound and below. As slowly as dusk, he parted her legs, slid down her body to look, to explore. He lifted his gaze to hers, perhaps in question, or it might have been in command. And achingly slowly, he lowered that gaze again, and slid a finger inside her, almost as though in contemplative discovery.

She could feel him, slick and slow inside, and automatically, unconsciously, opened to him, arching to take far more of him than he was allowing. She dimly realized that he seemed intent on taking things as slowly as possible, almost as if he had the same need she did to assimilate all the new sensations, the infinite variety of emotional reaction while discovering a lover. Or as if carving each nuance of this meeting in some private portion of his brain...or his heart.

Shocking her almost as much as her response to him was his tenderness. When he raised his head, his eyes filled with need, his lips parted as though to ask her something, she found she could read a vulnerability she had not thought possible issuing from Teo Sandoval. Something twisted inside her, and she unconsciously tightened around his enticing finger.

"Yes," she said, though he hadn't spoken. "Yes, Teo," she repeated, telling him all she could without lowering that precious guard held so precariously now in her mind. God, how she longed to drop even that, to let him know her fully, completely.

He lowered his mouth to her, and making her arch

sharply in surprise, in wonder, lightly flicked her with his tongue.

In sudden embarrassment, in some long-repressed fear of the unknown, she tried pulling away from him, but her hands were gently pushed away, then pressed gently to the mattress. And his hands were nowhere near hers, a reminder that for tonight she was his.

And even then she understood that he hadn't done this to overpower her, for he could have done that at any time. He was doing this because he planned on finishing what he'd begun and because she would have interfered with that pleasuring. He was simply letting her know that he was only beginning, that nothing she said or did would hurry him or make him abandon her now.

With her arms gently and invisibly bound to his bed, he shifted still more, and intensified his wet, tongue-hot ministration of her. His finger inside was joined by another and they seemed to flick back and forth in contrapuntal time to his laving tongue. His free hand lifted her higher, pulling her to him, his fingers kneading, sliding darkly and dangerously.

Faster and faster his fingers slid inside her as he lifted her ever higher, and his tongue lashed against her, exhorting her to a peak she'd never been to, never even dreamed of before.

Thunder crashed above them, and she could see both of their distorted reflections in the skylight above as her body began to thrum in unaccountable trembling, growing stronger and tighter, pulling her inexorably toward that cliff's edge of completion. Whatever magic he'd demonstrated before was as nothing compared to the power he was exhibiting now.

She wanted to call out for him to stop, to wait, strained against falling over that edge, but was helpless to fight the

incredible sensations sweeping through her, the assiduous-
ness of his assault on her body, on her senses.

And as her legs stiffened and her back arched, he stopped
abruptly and lifted his head. "Melanie…" he said roughly,
a call from some hidden place in his soul. His fingers stilled
inside her and his hand beneath her held her, nothing more.

Her entire body cried out for him, her heart ached for
something she couldn't even name, and without conscious
thought, she arched anew. He pressed his face to her again,
locking his lips around her sensitive apex and suddenly
bringing his fingers to wicked life.

And she didn't fall over that cliff's edge, she plummeted
from it, propelled outward, careening into weightlessness,
spinning in a gravity-free universe, her body jolted by a
thousand volts of pure energy.

And he held her out there, perhaps with his mind only,
slowing his assault on her, but not letting her go, not stopping his care. And then she understood she hadn't fallen,
after all; she was drifting, floating in a cocoon of his making.

She opened her eyes and met his. His were glassy, reflective. She reached for him, only now realizing that she
had use of her arms, that they hadn't been pinned to the
bed for some time, that perhaps she'd had only imagined
that they ever had been.

He slipped into her arms as if he'd been there a million
times before. She thought no man had ever felt so right
before. He held himself above her, and might have entered
her slowly, but she reached around him and pulled him to
her with swift need.

He filled her, paused, withdrew, and filled her again.
Needing more of him, all of him, she brushed his locked
elbows with her hands, craving his weight, the press of his
chest against hers. She wrapped her legs around him and
held him in her, rocking with him.

Teo knew only one thing, that this was the single best moment of his entire life. Never, in his wildest and brightest dreams, had he ever dared let himself go so thoroughly, so completely. Her arms were holding him tight to her, her legs locked around him, her heels pressed into his buttocks.

A lifetime of longing, and in this one woman, this miracle, he'd found a home. If only for this night. For these *six* months. Her sweet abandon intoxicated him, had made him never want to stop pleasuring her. And her lazy, understanding smile afterward, her reaching for him, had made him almost dizzy with foreign emotion.

He had no need to send the lightning from him now, she absorbed the tremendous energy with each thrust, sheathed him in satin protection, gentled him with her tight embrace, her matching rhythm. He heard her breath coming raggedly, felt her fingers curling into his shoulders, felt her tightening around him.

Suddenly, agonizingly, nothing could have stopped him then, no force on earth could equal his passion for this incredible woman whose body possessed him so. And as she cried out his name again upon her lips, her arms unbreakable bands around him, he, too, called out, and the universe seemed to split in two.

He felt he stayed there, with her in that bed, pressed deep inside her, spilling free all the hitherto undiscovered elements of his soul, and he felt he soared into space, danced with the stars and met her there, a thought or two intertwining, enjoining on some plane he'd never even known had existed before. And in this plane, perhaps a place of his own creation, overwhelmed by his own longing, he stretched for her, revealed his need for a future, his burying of the dream, and felt her tentative understanding, a careful acceptance.

He opened his eyes to meet hers, to see if he'd dreamed this union. She lay beneath him, her head turned slightly to face him. Her eyes were half open, glazed, and an uncertain smile tugged at the corner of her lips. He kissed that smile slowly, tasting her, tasting himself upon her.

He felt her heartbeat slowing, steadying, and knew his own was doing the same thing. He hated coming back to earth, losing that thread of connection with her. As she drifted into full consciousness, he saw a guardedness steal across her face and felt the barrier once again fully raise against him, shutting him out, blocking him. A cold fist seemed to clench around his heart, and a restless fear crept into his mind.

The dream had been just that, nothing more. And now that they were both awake, reality was only a breath away. He wanted to kiss her to passion again, to drive her from her body anew, to take her with him to that strange and beautiful plane where she understood him, where he could share with her the secrets of the universe, but he was spent and had no power left to use. She had taken it all.

No magic remained. Now it was simply night, and he a man of raw force who had been stripped of his power. She was the Delilah who had stolen his locks no matter how tangled her fingers might yet be in his hair.

He had never felt so vulnerable before, so drained of comprehension, of strength. She had melted beneath his touch, and in doing so, had melted some essential part of him. But in her wary gaze, he felt all was lost because her closed mind underscored the differences between them, the missing elements.

"Teo...?" she breathed, his name and a hundred questions rolled into a single word.

He didn't answer, couldn't have begun to explain that while this may have been the single most glorious union of his life, he wanted more. And more still. He wanted inside that mind she somehow closed to him. He wanted into her heart. Even if he was incapable of allowing her into his.

She had given her body freely, but except for that moment of union on an alternate plane, a plane most likely derived from his own need, his own imagination, her mind remained closed to him. And her heart was as much a mystery as ever.

She had parted for him, taken him to her, but while her body had yearned for him, she had only given him a measure of her trust. He wanted it all.

She feared him. He knew that, had even encouraged that fear, fanned it. But it wasn't like the fear the townspeople held of him. Certainly unlike the emotion the scientists had exhibited at the PRI. But he knew she feared him nonetheless, and in a way he couldn't fathom, couldn't begin to comprehend.

If only he could get inside her thoughts, he could will her to trust him. Like the forest animals did, like the wary townspeople did, like Chris did.

But somehow that wouldn't be enough with Melanie. The thought came to him suddenly that her name fit so easily in his mind, against the roof of his mouth, unspoken, untried. He'd called her *señora* as much to distance her as to frighten her. He longed to say her name aloud, and remembered that he had. During the height of his passion for her. During his loving her.

"Melanie," he mouthed, as if breathing her name would make it come all that much easier. It hurt to even whisper it. *Give me your trust,* he urged her silently.

Years ago, he thought grimly, men—outsiders—had tried to take from him that essential component uniquely his, had tried taking it without permission, without asking. They had tried bending him to their will. Who could possibly know how differently things might have turned out had they thought to earn his trust, his respect?

Wasn't he even now desiring the same thing from Melanie? He wanted her trust, but without having earned it. He'd demanded she stay, give herself to him fully, but had offered her only the training of her remarkably talented son in return, not letting her have even the barest hint of what he truly thought of her, truly desired of her.

Confused, frustrated by his own tail-chasing thoughts, he pushed off her and rolled over. He lay, staring at the dull, unlit skylight, staring out at the dimly visible stars. He could feel her warm, dewy skin next to his, felt the completion they'd reached emanating from her.

But he couldn't pierce her thoughts.

Melanie felt she could still feel him against her, could still hear his heart scudding against her breasts. She felt shattered, whole, empty and filled all at the same time. And she tried understanding the whisper of her name, the sudden darkening of his eyes.

In the time they had shared, in the shadowed half light, he had transcended mere humanity and become the embodiment of the stuff dreams are made of. And he'd made her feel as if she had done the same.

And yet she'd read a disappointment, a deeper need in his gaze. She wanted to turn to him, to ask him why, to ask him to explain what he was thinking.

But while she'd been delightfully abandoned in his lovemaking, she felt curiously reticent in his silence. Their union had been as dark as midnight and as filled with shadows as the deepest cavern, but it had also been lit with the light of a thousand stars, had seemed to spin around the universe itself.

She longed to open her mind to him, to glimpse what he truly was, to share an element of herself with him. But he had retreated from her, both bodily and emotionally. She didn't know this stranger, this now quiet man whose magical touch had sent her spinning through space.

After several silent moments Teo pushed from the bed and stood at the side of it staring at the wall as if it were a crystal ball that could spill forth answers. Finally he turned his gaze down on her and smiled bitterly. She felt herself growing afraid again.

"Gracias, señora," he said in a tone more cold than the sudden iciness creeping through her veins. "Until tomorrow, then." Without another word, he turned and left the bedroom.

He slowly pulled the door closed behind him. The covers remained puddled on the floor. The candle flame sputtered in the wake of the brief draft left by his departure.

And in the final release of the night, Melanie felt tears spilling down her cheeks. She couldn't have been so mistaken, she thought. What had passed between them had been as magical for him as it had been for her...hadn't it?

A few seconds later a distant rumble of thunder reached her ears.

And she fell asleep with the taste of Teo and tears intermingled on her bruised lips.

CHAPTER EIGHT

Wake up, Man.

Teo froze. For a moment he felt totally disoriented, as if he were still asleep, dreaming. His head seemed filled with this alien presence, a small but potent touch. And then he remembered. Chris. *Chris.*

Chris was talking to him, again…in his head.

Wake up, Man.

My name is Teo, he corrected automatically, for what seemed the thousandth time. He sent an image of himself, a sound pattern, an identifier with his mental acknowledgment.

He didn't open his eyes, though he smiled. The small voice in his head was still as much a novelty as it had been the first morning the boy had stretched mental fingers across his mind.

No matter how many times in the past two weeks the boy's thoughts touched his, he still found himself intrigued, his heart pounding just a little faster, his mental patterns quickly shifting to accommodate this delicate, baby-soft brush of thoughts, the multilayered, half-conceived questions, curious, only dimly projected answers.

And no matter how much he might have expected the mental bond, considering the child was like himself in so many ways, it still came as a surprise and an added boon.

But the mental communication with the son had a negative side, as well. It served to strengthen the barriers he felt with the child's mother. No matter how he'd hammered at her mind, tried probing at all hours of the day and night, Melanie remained as firmly closed to him as he kept his heavy doors barricaded when not using them. Was the analogy apt? Was she somehow able to throw a bar across doors in her mind?

She was able to do *something,* create some kind of wall that shut him out as effectively as any guard tower had done against an advancing army. Except at night, when her mind seemed to wander while her body lay in deepest sleep. And then, upon rare occasions, he could glimpse a snippet of her dreams, her nightmares.

Unfortunately, all those night excursions told him, aside from the fact that she was obviously frightened of—and attracted to—him, was that her conscious mind couldn't fully control the wants, needs and fears of her unconscious thoughts. Not while she was sleeping, at any rate.

He felt Chris's soft, patting touch, a quest for reassurance, a request for play. He smiled, still not opening his eyes, knowing exactly where the boy stood, what cartoon-figure pajamas he was wearing, what he wanted to do next.

Not for the first time in the past two weeks of pure heaven and hell combined, he wished he could do the same with the boy's mother. *Melanie,* he sent silently. The stray thought stole to his bedroom, and he found her there, partially blocked to him as always, able to keep him from fully understanding her thoughts, even in sleep.

He wondered anew at the strange and uneasy rhythm they had fallen into. After that first incredible, shattering night with her, he'd had difficulty even meeting her eyes the next day, had kept Chris out on the mountain until evening shadows had stretched the trees to the hills.

And when they'd returned home, she'd again had dinner prepared, an incredibly delicious concoction of pork, piñon nuts and some subtle herb that had apparently been soaked in his brandy. But she hadn't met his gaze, no matter how much he'd willed her to. She'd been stiff, quiet and, like him, seemingly uncomfortable about the complete abandonment they'd shared the night before. And perhaps, also like him, too conscious of his parting words.

If only she didn't keep that damnable blockade in her mind. He'd know what she wanted, know how deeply he'd cut her with his demonstrations of power. But he'd also know how deeply he might have touched her...and perhaps discover if it had been anywhere near as intensely as she had affected him.

He had no way of knowing, no way of understanding...except as normal men might know, as normal men might blunder in the dark, searching for explanation, praying for some glimmer of comprehension. They were living together, focused on a mission that should have drawn them closer, but didn't. Couldn't. They were together in all ways that seemed to count, and yet Teo keenly felt the gulf that separated them.

Perhaps it was the all-too-intense perplexity that kept him from entering his own bedroom that second night. Or perhaps it was some sense of his own unfairness. Whatever the case had been, she hadn't said a thing when he didn't join her. And she didn't comment on his absence the following night, though he thought he'd caught a glimpse of her studying him in puzzlement the next morning.

He didn't join her the night after that, either. If she'd shown him so much as a single signal that she would have welcomed him there, nothing shy of an earthquake or tornado could have kept him from it. But she gave no indication that she would have appreciated his attention, that she had even noticed his absence.

She hadn't asked where he and Chris went during the day, seeming to prefer the solitude of his home to the unease she obviously felt in his company. By the fourth night of this, he was nearly insane with wanting her and yet staying away from his own bed.

Each night, either before or shortly after dinner, she had

watched what her son had learned that day, always expressing encouragement and reassurance to her son. But never, by look or deed, had she acknowledged that the teacher might deserve reward, might need recognition for his efforts. But, staying away from her was undiluted torture.

Except the fifth night, unable to sleep, unable to stop thinking about her lying so close yet as distant in thought as any citadel, he had paced the living room, sending bolt after bolt of lightning to the sky, reveling in its shattering release.

Finally, fueled by his own fury, angered by her neglect, her refusal to open her mind, her rejection of his gaze, he hadn't been able to stay away. If not able to break through the barriers in her mind, he could at least open the bedroom doors. And he'd done that with the flourish of a man pushed beyond his endurance.

As if it had happened only seconds before, he could still visualize every nanosecond of his approach to his own room. She had sat up with a small gasp of fear, gazed at him with wide, emerald eyes, her face warm with sleep. Her lips parted, and her chest rose and fell. She had looked languorous and he had felt like molten steel.

He hadn't said a word as he'd crossed the room to her side, and he didn't remember her speaking, either. Without reaching for them, he'd torn the covers from the bed, not in question but in command.

She had given a strange, soft sigh and shifted slightly, not to deny him, but to accommodate his bulk on the feather-light mattress. And if their loving had been fueled by frustration, even a tinge of angry need, and if she had kept him from understanding her mind, he had nonetheless lost himself in her touch, in her loving. And, hopefully, she had done the same. She had cried out, his name upon her lips, her fingers bands of iron on his shoulders. But she hadn't said a word beyond his name.

And he'd left her, as he had that first night with her, wondering what on earth he was to think about her...what he was supposed to *feel*. Especially when he was left totally replete yet completely in the dark as to knowing what she was thinking.

There were times in this past week, this second week of her company, he'd positively hated her for not letting him know. And never more so than when she opened to him so thoroughly during the night, but kept her mind tauntingly, teasingly remote. He couldn't breach her, couldn't knock down the walls of her mind. No matter how hard he might try, no matter what tactics he sought to use.

But the sheer physical unity alone held him, never failing to draw him like a magnet. He could no more resist returning to her, night after night, than he could have cut off his own limbs. In her arms, he found whatever solace he had spent a lifetime aching for, and if it didn't quench all thirsts, it made him try to believe that thirst was only relative, always subjective.

But as always, he would leave her to sleep alone, a part of him hoping she felt his loss as keenly as he did hers. He felt afraid of her somehow, afraid of sleeping next to her, fearful of curling her to him, watching her drift from him in sleep as she would eventually do in reality. And he left because he felt flayed raw by the time spent in intimacy so deep—and so piercing—that he felt stripped to his very core.

But always, overriding everything, blanketing the realization that he couldn't—try as he might—reach into her mind, couldn't bring her to her knees, couldn't force her to beg for his love...to beg him to give her his, was the notion that he wasn't alone anymore.

Whenever the notion popped into his head, as it all too often did, he tried squelching it as quickly as it entered. The understanding that he wasn't alone came too close to dreams he couldn't achieve, futures that could never be. And it drove home the knowledge that six months didn't make a future, they only carved a moment in the present. And even those six months were already slipping away. He couldn't stop time any more than he could hold Chris back from stretching his gifts, or keep Melanie from leaving eventually.

But with this boy's touch in his mind, Melanie's scent still upon his skin, it was hard not to dream, not to wish for a future. Here in his home, a woman nightly accepted his touch, and openly, if silently, enchanted him by sharing in the delights of human contact. And with Melanie, with Chris—another in the whole universe who could speak as he could, could tap minds, could stretch mental fingers across odd synaptic connections and join in thought—he'd found a family. A hope for the future. A reason for living.

His heart pounded with the promise even as the dream crumbled when he mentally reviewed the short time left to him. God, he'd been insane to even dare dream, however briefly.

Teo. Man. Big Man. Big House Man. Chris's imagery made Teo smile. He opened his eyes and met the honey-brown eyes of the boy who looked nothing like him, but could have been his child he was so much like him in all other respects.

Play with me, Teo? The thought entered his head. All other people he'd heard, had listened in on their thoughts, had only carried thoughts and vague pictures in their minds, loosely strung together images. Chris's touch in his head, however, was filled with flavor, with nuance. Like a voice, it carried timbre, pitch, vibration.

Teo felt he'd spent his entire lifetime hearing only humming, and now, in a few special days, had been introduced to a symphony.

He studied the boy, sending a variety of reassuring images himself. He loved the sensation of the moment when their thoughts snagged, wove together as though knitted by unseen hands. And that weave, those patterns unique to him, to the boy, seemed to exchange emotions, thoughts that felt totally alien in their comfort, their ease. Overriding all his own imagery was one emotion that, until this mentally woven pattern with Chris, had remained utterly foreign to Teo. The feeling was something akin to protection, safety, concern, enjoyment. Teo almost dared believe its name was love, though never having felt it before, couldn't make the full connection to faith in it.

He hardened his heart and sharpened his thoughts. He couldn't afford to allow himself to drift into that kind of wishful thinking. The boy—and his beautiful, perplexing mother—would be gone in less than six months.

Play now? Chris asked him again silently, musically. Now the inner voice was more wistful.

Teo reached out his hand as he sent a soft mental encouragement to the child. The boy's face lightened and his hands clasped together in anticipation.

Play. Chris said, "No dance." His own self-admonition was result of the many times Teo had said the same thing, had offered a new trick in exchange for the enticement of slipping into that solitary world of total concentration.

What he couldn't tell the boy—much less, Melanie—was that he'd begun to wonder how much of his own world wasn't exactly like the boy's innocent dancing of toys. How much of his own solitary, fiercely guarded universe wasn't just an extension of the need to withdraw from the world, to shut it out? And in this realization came the obvious rejoinder—Melanie and Chris had broken through, were daily challenging his ability to live alone just as he was daily challenging Chris.

"No dance now," Teo concurred, smiling. But he wanted to tell the boy to go ahead, to dance his toys all he could ever want to, that he'd keep him safe, that he'd never let anyone harm him ever again.

However, he didn't want this unusual channel of communication closed to him as it would be if the child concentrated on making things levitate. This morning, today, and damning the impossible future, he wanted this new pattern to remain open, fluid.

Chris's little face was all but obscured by his own large hand, but the baby skin felt so soft, so morning warm. Almost as soft as his mother's. Teo's smile faltered as Chris's grin widened. Just three, an engaging smile on full lips so like his mother's that the sight of them made Teo's heart skip a notch, Chris had no awareness—besides a dead plant and some bad men in white coats—of the dangers and betrayals that lurked in the world.

They won't have you, he vowed. And for the first time in these two weeks of miracles, he knew this pledge came from a good part of him, a true part. A part he'd too long ignored, feared.

Who?

Teo shook his head and ruffled the boy's hair. While not at all the same color, it felt as soft and silky as his mother's.

Man. Teo, the boy's thoughts came through contentedly.

He didn't have to ask how the boy had come to be at his side instead of in his cradle. Only half a month had passed, but the boy had shown remarkable strides.

He hadn't teleported from the cradle to Teo's sofa, but had spilled himself from the raised bed, gently tipping the cradle until he was free. It was just another indication of how strong the boy's talents really were. Teo felt a wave of pride suffusing his stiff muscles, his tired body.

When had *he* first exhibited signs of controlling his universe? So early he couldn't remember, but surely it couldn't have been accomplished as easily nor as early as Chris was doing. He tried telling himself he was only feeling the natural pride of a mentor watch his pupil grasping difficult tasks. But he had the distinct sensation of being the proud daddy watching his child take his first toddling steps.

He remembered the first morning Chris had freed himself, had pattered into the living room, standing beside the sofa, prodding Teo's mind until he woke. And he remembered the look of shock on Melanie's face when she came out of the bedroom the morning after that and found Chris dancing his toys while Teo slept, oblivious to the miracle.

Each day had brought Chris's different talents to the surface. And for the first time in his life, Teo had to wonder what it had been like for his superstitious parents, watching their only offspring making things float around the room, fly from the dressers, pitching toys at them if he was angered or thwarted.

Had Chris been like that? If so, it was no small wonder that Melanie had appeared so weary that first night. What she must have been through in Chris's young life. He knew from vague images in Chris's mind that his father—Melanie's *ex*-husband, Teo reminded himself—had been afraid of his own son and had left Melanie to cope with Chris on her own.

Teo remembered the shadows he'd seen beneath her eyes that first evening, the total exhaustion that had kept her from even waking while he removed her wet clothing the night she'd appeared at his home. A visceral pain shot through him as he recalled she had appeared anything but sleepy last night. As always, she had been liquid fire in his hands.

But he wanted more of her. Needed more. He needed to get beyond that barrier in her mind, the barrier around her heart. He couldn't give her anything in return, except his protection, his need for her. But, by God, wasn't that enough? Why didn't it feel like it was?

He rolled to a sitting position on the short Taos sofa in

his living room. He grimaced at the sudden crick in his neck. Why did he always leave her bedroom? He knew about the fears, but did it have a more subtle message, such as *you'll have no more of me?* Pride, he told himself. Foolishness, he answered back.

But the truth was what he already knew; he always left her because he was truly afraid, fearful of how she made him feel, terrified that he would begin to need her, not simply want her.

Are you hungry? he asked the boy, as he did now every morning.

"Yes!" Chris all but shouted, his usual exuberant response.

What a kid!

"Gina hungry, too!"

Teo stretched both body and mind. He felt every nuance of the too many nights spent on the too short sofa. And every tight, protesting muscle remembered the time spent with Melanie. His mind, meanwhile, told him that the fox, Gina, was indeed hungry and waiting for her feeders on the deck. He again pushed into his own bedroom, and could sense Melanie sleeping there, but couldn't probe her mind.

Does your mother keep her mind closed all the time? Teo asked Chris suddenly. He was careful to limit his mental imagery to concepts a small child would recognize, a gate, a wall, Melanie's smile, his own thoughts, Chris's ability to hear them, a question.

The little boy stared at him for a moment, then cocked his head to the side. "Don't know," he said simply. But his mind snapped various conflicting pictures at Teo. Melanie loving Chris; Melanie playing patty-cake, heart talking; Melanie frightened; a huge, brick wall from Rapunzel's castle; Chris battering at the wall in frustration; Melanie holding Chris and running from bad men in white coats; a dead plant; a living rose; a red ball lying on the ground.

With each picture, Chris's agitation increased. If the voice in his mind had volume measurable to outside terms, the boy would have been shouting at him. Was shouting.

Even as he probed for understanding, Teo felt a ripple in the air between himself and Chris, was certain he saw a shimmer of refracted light, then before he could stop the boy, a dozen small objects—a vase, a candle holder, a pen, a book of matches that should have been in the kitchen but wasn't and a button that had fallen off one of Teo's shirts weeks before—rose from the tables and floor and began to spin slowly, lazily around the boy's suddenly slack face.

"Chris?" Teo asked, then repeated it in his mind, stronger, *Chris?*

But he received no answer, no indication that he was being heard. What was it about his question that bothered Chris so? Was it Melanie's "heart talking" that triggered the need for reclusion? Or was it the lack of it? Whatever bothered him, it was obviously associated with the dead plant in the PRI laboratory and with Melanie's fear. And yet, hadn't he also sent the picture of her playing with her son?

And what on earth was that bit about the fairy-tale castle tower? And the rose?

As it was so very early, and because Gina could wait for her morning meal, Teo lifted Chris into his arms and made his way to the subcave he'd converted into a washroom. The makeshift toys danced in their wake.

He set Chris upon one of the rock benches, almost effortlessly deflecting the swirling toys, and turned on a few of the shower jets. As he stood beneath the nearly scalding water, trying not to think of Melanie standing there during the days while he was absent, he sent several questions to young Chris, but the boy remained oblivious to his prodding thoughts. The objects he'd made to dance still rotated around him, and his concentration blocked Teo thoroughly.

There would be time enough to shift the boy's concentration. He had succeeded a bit more each day, knew it would require even less effort today. The boy was penny bright and eager for learning. Today, Teo would begin the slow, careful task of introducing dual strengths, stretching possibilities, and setting limitations.

If only he'd had someone do that with him, he thought again. Perhaps his confusion during the past two weeks would never have happened. He wouldn't have lost himself so thoroughly in Melanie's embrace, wouldn't have felt so confused, so deserted when it was over, despite the fact she'd never once tried to leave his side.

When he was clean, and after he'd dried and dressed with rather more care than he usually expended on his clothing, he hefted Chris to his side and carted him to the kitchen. There he still didn't break Chris's concentration as he gathered the basket filled with wrapped meat left on his doorstop the night before. He fried the meat, tipped it into an earthenware bowl, and prepared to step outside.

Before sliding the door open, he mentally reached out and grabbed the dozen or so floating items Chris had lifted from the living room. Chris resisted the seizure of his toys. *They will scare Gina,* Teo projected firmly. He sent a few pictures of Gina happy, Gina scared, Gina running away after seeing the knickknacks floating around her.

Chris opposed him, tugging at the toys-that-weren't-toys just as Teo suspected any small child would do if handling them manually. Teo strengthened his Gina-scared images. He felt the indecision in Chris's hold on the objects. Finally the boy released his mental grip on the toys and the slack expression on his face disappeared. Only the day before, while resisting Teo's intrusive interruption, Chris had slammed a pinecone directly at Teo's nose. His laughter and firm mental reprimand had snapped Chris from his reverie. Today, only mild reinforcement was necessary.

"Gina not go away?"

"She's still here," Teo said. He sent the objects back to the living room. He pointed through the glass doors. "See? She's waiting for us."

He felt a shiver run down his back. How simply he said those words, used pronouns he'd never used before two weeks ago. She's waiting for *us*. Just a word, but one that linked them together, that bound them as a stronger unit somehow.

And the notion stretched beyond Chris, to his mother, as well. It seemed so natural to transfer the words related to a hungry, and frightened wild creature waiting outside the door to the sleeping woman in his bedroom. *She's* waiting.

For him? Not likely. Not after his hard, nightly dismissal of her. But they had been together those nights in total harmony, complete union. He couldn't be wrong about that.

And he had her for six months, less two weeks. The loss of half a month seemed enormous. A few days ago the notion of sharing a half year with her had seemed nearly a lifetime. This morning it felt less than the blink of an eye, the whisper of his name on her lips. Already the pain of her inevitable departure wrenched at him, hurt him. Infuriated him.

He slammed a mental door on such thoughts and took a deep breath to settle his suddenly gathering energy. How could he teach a young student control when he himself felt none?

He lifted the bowl in one hand while still holding Chris in the other. "My hands are full," he said. "Can you open the door?" He reinforced his question with a mental image of what he wanted Chris to do. In the woods, during their days alone together, he'd had Chris try several lifting and shifting techniques. But he'd never tried anything so close to home.

Chris shook his head. "No," he said aloud.

"Try opening it," Teo said.

Again, in agitation, Chris projected the image of the dead plant into Teo's mind. It was followed by a clear image of shattered glass.

"No," Teo said, smiling, understanding the imagery. "It won't hurt the door. It's just like the stick you moved in the woods yesterday." *Watch.*

He tried holding Chris's thoughts with him as he slowly placed his command on the glass. It was so much a habit with him to slide the door open without use of his hands that he had a moment's difficulty thinking about the effort.

"Can't," Chris said, but Teo knew the boy meant "won't."

He slid the door closed, then open again. And repeated the whole process. "Your turn," he said.

He could feel—hear—Chris's desire to please the large man who held him. Could hear the puzzlement in the little boy's mind, the uncertainty.

Chris looked at the door. Teo felt the strength of the boy's concentration.

"You don't have to work at it. Open it like you pick up your toys."

Chris frowned. A couple of items on Teo's cupboard shelves lifted into the air, but the door stayed shut.

"Too hard," Chris said, pouting a little. The spices he'd sent into the air dropped to the cabinets with a clatter. Chris's head whirled in surprise.

"It's okay, *niño*," Teo said, and smiled. Chris had, unknowingly, crossed a major hurdle. He'd been concentrating on the door, and managed to lift objects elsewhere. *And,* most important, he'd done both those things without totally losing himself in the attempt.

Teo slid the door open and carried Chris outside to the crisp, clean mountain air. The door slid closed behind them and Chris clapped his hands.

Teo smiled crookedly, feeling off balance. When had anyone ever genuinely applauded his unusual talents? The scientists at the PRI had certainly been eager to harness them, to use them, but at every juncture, at every stride in development, they'd become more and more fearful, more leery of him. And, eventually, more greedy. And here was a three-year-old boy who simply praised a minor task that he hadn't been able to accomplish.

He squelched a sudden, wholly childish desire to show off, to let Chris catch a glimpse of what he could really do. This urge etched his crooked smile with a tinge of bitterness.

Melanie knew. She'd known before she had brought her son to him. She'd read the files. She knew he was capable of destroying an entire wing of a building, knew he had reduced the mind of one scientist to complete mush. And she'd seen the evidence of his abilities a dozen different times and, while she hadn't applauded, she hadn't run from him.

No, she'd opened her arms and drawn him inside her, giving herself fully night after beautiful night, holding back nothing but her thoughts. And in return for that favor, for that sharing, and because he selfishly had wanted everything, he'd slapped her with words or silence, left her with tears in her eyes, his kisses still warm on her body.

God, what kind of a man was he? What kind of a monster?

He felt a tap on his shoulder and focused his attention on Chris's brown eyes, his baby face. "Mommy sleeping," he said. He held a chubby finger to his lips and exaggerated a shushing sound.

He'd spent so many years without anyone able to hear his thoughts, he'd momentarily forgotten how easily the boy could. He could see from the untroubled expression on

Chris's face that he hadn't understood the complexity of Teo's musings, only that they had been directed at Melanie.

"We'll let her sleep, shall we?" Teo said, kneeling down, letting Chris slide from his arms to stand beside him. He held out a piece of meat for the fox. She took it delicately and moved off a few inches to nibble on it.

"Chris do it," the boy said, reaching into the bowl for a piece. He held it out, imperiously demanding Gina take it.

"Yes," Teo said, his hand on the tiny shoulder. Protectively, he thought. Supportively. Or was it possessively? Somehow the distinction didn't seem to matter. The sun was bright, the air was fresh, and today was only the beginning of the third week in a six-month-long miracle.

"Don't worry," Chris said, but Teo couldn't tell whether the remark was directed at him or at the fox.

"I'll try not to, son," Teo said.

"No bad guys here," Chris offered in a complacent tone. Teo wondered.

CHAPTER NINE

*T*he sky was dark with rain clouds, or perhaps an early snow. It was late afternoon and the birds and forest animals were silent, still. She was inside, but could discern no movement through the heavy sheets of glass. Her heart pounded and her ears rang with the strain of listening to nothing. Something was out there. She could feel it. Smell it almost. Where was Chris? She'd been looking for him, running from room to room in Teo's home. A shaft of pain shot through her as she thought of Teo. And then came a stark, raw terror.

She heard a voice calling her and thought it might be Pablo from the gas station. "Lady, leave/come quickly!" She ran up through the corridor leading out of Teo's strange home and burst through the heavy wooden doors. Across the clearing she could see something lying on the ground and didn't know what it was. Rags. Please let it be rags. Near it, clearer than the rags, was Chris's red ball, lying on some pine needles.

She heard something moving behind her, and something nearby. From the corner of her eye, she saw a vague, indistinct flash of white, and something brighter, something that reflected the sharp, glittering lightning streaking across the cloud-heavy sky. A needle of some kind. A knife?

She knew she had to run. Knew something was close. But her legs wouldn't move. And from far away, from the pile of rags lying beside the ball, she heard "M-o-m-m-y!"

Oh, please, don't let those rags be Chris! she prayed, and tried to run to him.

She heard something beside her again and turned. Teo

was running toward her, sparks flying from his fingers, anger lining his face with a harsh blue light. His lips were pulled back in a grimace and his fingers were curled like claws as he reached for her. And he had blood smeared across his palms, mud covering his clothing. She screamed and screamed—

And woke, her throat aching from the harsh release, the echo of the scream taunting her. Her heart pounded in undiluted terror. Where was Chris? Where was Teo? Was the dream a prophetic vision or was it only a product of her fevered, tortured fears? She'd seen the ball before, many times now, and the pine needles. And Teo running at her. But she'd never seen the needle before, or had it been a knife? Had she seen the blood before? The blue light? Was Teo the something that lurked outside, waiting for her? Whatever, she'd always awakened screaming, or trying to. That part was the same. Always the fear of Teo Sandoval.

And she did fear him, more than she had ever feared anything or anyone. But was the fear born of his powers or her reaction to him as a man? She hadn't feared him the night before even as she was wholly and utterly terrified. The same applied to all the nights she'd spent in his arms, locked in his embrace. Which was the truth? Which feeling was to be trusted? Or were they both the truth, both real?

With Teo Sandoval, where did fear end and faith begin? Somebody had told her once that fear was the precursor of faith, the carrot that led the fearful to that place of control. Was that where Teo was leading her, down a path that led to her ultimate lack of control, to a position of powerlessness?

She pulled on her robe and went in search of Chris. As she moved through the house, remnants of her dream clung to her mind. She felt she was reenacting scenes from the nightmare, except that the sunlight filtering through the glass now was bright and dappled golden, where in the dream it had been distant and gray. This was morning, that had been late afternoon surely.

But she still couldn't find Chris. He wasn't in his room, nor in the kitchen, nor even the bathroom. Teo was also obviously gone. Remains of a breakfast were in evidence on the countertop flanking the sink. This should have relieved her, should have chased the dream back into the world of shadows, but somehow didn't.

Everything appeared the same as it had every morning in this bizarre life she'd thrown herself and her son into. Nights spent in passion as deep and intense and as achingly poignant as a great masterpiece of art. Days spent alone, roaming Teo Sandoval's unusual home, trying to glean some understanding of the man who so haunted her every thought, reading his well-worn books, studying the intricate carvings, fingering the handmade quilts he carefully folded away.

A semblance of a strange pattern had materialized between them, between all of them. By day, Teo was Chris's mentor, a teacher, a master magician with a half-pint apprentice. By night, the lover. But there was nothing in the middle, no by-play, no interaction. And he would leave her in the night, as though having had his fill of her, as if having pleasured her, pleasured himself, he had no further use of her.

She had discovered much about him by roaming freely through his home, his books, even his clothes. She picked up only small bits of information: a scrap gleaned from an underlined passage in a book—*My relatives are not all dead, but they are surely all damned. And I am the one who determines the hell they occupy;* a newspaper clipping about a strange rockslide in the steep canyon above Loco Suerte—*Geologists Baffled Over Freak Avalanche;* a framed photograph found upside down behind some of the books in the large wall unit in his living room—*two men*

*who looked alike, who resembled younger versions of the
man at the gas station, and a woman with long black hair
and hard, cold eyes holding a baby.*

There were many such items, many such tidbits that contained clues to the personality that made up Teo Sandoval.
But they were all only puzzle pieces strewn across a table
too large to be fully recognizable, a puzzle too complex to
comprehend. Like the other things that she'd found out
about him, they only posed more questions, greater contrasts.

She had often wanted to ask him about the things she
discovered, wanted to seek an explanation for the many
questions tormenting her. But his shuttered gaze and his
stiff silence daunted her, made her all too aware that she,
too, was a mystery to him and he was determined she remain one.

She would have to be satisfied with the strange alliance
they'd forged, if only for Chris's sake. She might be getting
more restless by the day, by the night, but Chris was bloom-
ing. His gifts were obviously gaining strength by the moment, expanding into areas she'd only vaguely suspected
he was capable of approaching. And with each newfound
"trick," he'd seemed more complacent, happier.

Teo had done that for him. Teo was giving him a strong
sense of self-worth even as he pushed him to greater and
greater heights. Hadn't he done the same for her? Each
night in his arms, didn't she give in to the passion that had
always lain dormant in her body, in her heart?

But each night seemed to widen the chasm that stretched
between she and Teo, because each night drove home those
puzzle pieces she couldn't make fit. What was he? What
did he really want from her? Why did she seem to need
him so?

Strange questions, stranger man. Strangest bargain in the

history of bargaining. And yet, all seemed to be well, all was working. Or had been.

But today was different. A nearly full pot of coffee waited for her on the old-fashioned stove as it always did. A loaf of fresh bread and some hand-pressed cheese waited for her on the island bar as it had every morning, little considerations that had somehow only daily served to make her feel more off balance, more insecure.

Today, in the wake of the intensity of the dream, the terror rife within it, the feelings of disorientation were even greater.

If she showered in that unusual washroom or soaked in that huge, hot pool of water, the day might seem more normal, less charged by the dream. If, afterward, she strolled outside to find some new offering on Teo's doorstep, a small token of some townsperson's gratitude—or fear—the day might seem less dominated by the leavings of the night.

But nothing felt right today. Was it only the dream? Was the dream true? If so, where did truth and supposition collide? How could she begin to interpret the differences and separate illusion from reality?

The truth was that she couldn't. Nothing in life seemed real anymore. She was living with—*sleeping with*—a man like no other on earth. She was running for her life and for her son's protection from a privately funded organization that seemed to have no qualms about circumventing any and all laws, including her permanent removal to gain control of Chris.

And for all that her talents seemed minuscule when held in comparison to Chris's and Teo's, she *was* clairvoyant. Always had been. She couldn't allow herself the luxury of forgetting that important detail. She *knew* when things were going to happen. Not always, not definitively, but enough, and often enough, to trust her sense that things *were* amiss this morning.

The dreams had to mean that the PRI was nearby, or that danger existed here on the mountain. They certainly pointed to the fact that Chris was in danger. And what about Teo's role in her chaotic dream? She wouldn't know unless she dropped her careful guard and let her mind roam at will. She wouldn't be able to ascertain the extent of the danger, the confines of the truth unless she did so.

She forced herself to pour a cup of coffee, as much to steady herself as to take in the jolt of caffeine. She drank it thoughtfully, slowly, trying to tell herself not to worry, not to panic. Teo had taken Chris out on the mountain every day, for most of the day, ever since they'd arrived. He had never lost him, hadn't harmed him.

Just as he hadn't harmed her the night before or any of the nights before that. Not physically, at any rate. But while each night was as glorious as the previous, the whole arrangement was beginning to tear at her soul. Because sometime in the space between their first night together and this morning she'd discovered she wanted more. With each union, she found herself fighting to hold on to her guard, fighting not to cling to him, keep him at her side, not to beg him to sleep beside her, abandon himself in dreams, his strong arms wrapped around her, holding her close.

She wanted, leveled at her, that tender look he transferred to Chris. She wanted the smile she sometimes glimpsed on his face turned in her direction. She wanted that gentle voice he used in loving her spoken during the course of the evening, proffered after a meal, or while cleaning up the dishes. She wanted to ask him what he thought about some of the books in his library, the drawings on his walls. She wanted to know why he looked sad sometimes and angry at others.

As long as she thought about Teo, what it felt like to be

in his arms, what her legs felt like against his, she could almost forget about the dreams, the feeling that something was dreadfully wrong. But even thinking this much, she had to raise her hand to her mouth to mask the slow moan of anxiety that threatened escape this morning.

What if henchmen from the PRI came upon Teo and Chris unaware?

She shook her head. Nothing could come upon Teo Sandoval without him being aware. It simply wasn't possible. Why else had she sought him? And yet, the PRI *had* taken Teo once. Why had she never wondered how before? She remembered that underlined passage in the book, the line about relatives being damned. She knew his father had betrayed him. Had someone else done so, as well? She thought of the look of hatred he'd sent at Pablo that first rainy afternoon, of the phrase he'd used when she'd tried deflecting his anger against Pablo for having sent her up the mountain to find Teo: *If I am…it has nothing to do with you.* What had Pablo done to him? She knew Teo's father had literally sold him, almost exactly as Chris's father had when he'd transferred his custodial rights to the PRI. But the PRI files had been clear on the point that there was no love lost between father and son in Teo's case.

So how had the PRI gotten their hands on Teo? What had they done to him that drove him to the point of total destruction of the PRI's laboratory wing?

Did any of this even matter now? Fifteen years had passed and Teo's life was still as different as a life could possibly be. But, somehow, she suspected that it all *did* matter, that it all fit together in some complex alignment of causes and effects.

This morning, however, it was the dream, the prickling of her arms, that kept snaring her thoughts, that kept insisting that something was wrong. She still carried the image of that pile of rags calling her name, that pile of clothes that could only be a person. *Please, not Chris!* Another part of her added a codicil to that half-formed prayer—*please, not Teo!*

What if the PRI people had somehow snatched Chris from Teo, were using him against Teo? It was possible. She'd seen with her own eyes the great tenderness, the affection Teo had for her son. She had no clue what he really felt or even thought about her, knew one thing from his lovemaking, an entirely different interpretation according to his prolonged silences, his gruff comments, but she knew what he felt about Chris. He displayed that gentleness, that regard, openly and easily.

She'd even caught glimpses of him studying Chris as if perplexed by the very ease of their relationship. Was Chris the clue to the cradle in the small room, the baby gate around the deck? Had Teo at one time hoped for a family? Craved one, planned to have one? There had been no clues in the files relating to any wife, girlfriend. He was a loner, the notes had said, a complete recluse.

But Melanie now knew that wasn't exactly the truth. He might be reclusive, might hold himself apart from the rest of the world, but he entered it when one of the townspeople needed him. He saved lives. She'd seen it with her own eyes. And if he was capable of that, capable of the tenderness he displayed with Chris, the sensitivity he let her glimpse in the flare of lightning during the night, then he was also capable of having dreamed of having a family.

She realized suddenly that a family was exactly what he had bargained for in his six-month definition of terms. She to play the wife, Chris the child and Teo the lord protector. But, she thought sadly, they were the farthest thing from a real family. Real families talked, laughed, found inside jokes and curled up together on shabby sofas to read books to each other, relate day's events.

She shook her head. If real families did that, then she,

like Teo, had never known what family life could be like. While hers had never been as remote as Teo's, while she had never been literally sold for her unusual gifts, her talents had always been regarded more as curse than blessing, as Teo's had been. As Chris's had been, except by her, and even she had her moments.

But in Chris, in her son who held every nuance of Teo's tremendous powers in his baby hands, Teo had found a child of his own genes, those mysterious strands of DNA that formed another telekinetic. And if Teo Sandoval was capable of love, he loved Chris.

Therefore, if PRI henchmen threatened to hurt Chris, if they already had him, they could coerce Teo into inactivity out of fear of also hurting Chris in any attempt at retaliation.

She set down her mug with a sharp thud, spilling some of the coffee onto the tiled bar. This couldn't go on. No matter how far afield her thoughts traveled, they always circled back to the awareness of something awry.

She was simply nervous, had cabin fever. She'd been too long alone in the daytime, had spent the nights in too much longing, too much passion, too much pain at not allowing her guard to slip and her mind to mingle with his.

But if she had given in to that sharp desire, that longing, he'd have known how much their time together really meant to her, how she had never known such splendor in her life. And he'd know, and perhaps so would she, how little she understood him. If she lowered that guard, he would know, from the thunder outside to the light flickering through the skylight, she'd come to want the dark man filling her in every possible way...more than she'd ever dreamed it possible to want someone.

But he still frightened her, not with his powers, but with his anger, his ability to withdraw from the world, his defiance of any and all rules of society. Was want enough to engender trust? Could it ever?

If only she had dropped the barriers blocking him from her thoughts, if only she'd let him understand some of her own abilities, she thought now, she would be able to let him know how terrified she was that something was wrong.

If she had ever let him in, then perhaps she could now call to him, have him return, bringing a safe and happy Chris with him, proving all her fears silly things, after all.

Her arms were cold and she found herself wishing, praying, that Teo was back, that she could confide some of her fears in him. But he wasn't the sort of man one went running to with confessions of nerves. He might have been tender the night before, but that tenderness didn't extend to the world outside his bed. She knew this instinctively. She'd seen the truth of this in his shuttered gaze, that distant look he gave her before leaving his bedroom each night. Even if she'd seen it through eyes glazed with tears.

What possessed her to even imagine that a man like Teo Sandoval would be capable of such emotions as gentleness, chivalry? *Chris,* she answered herself. *Remember Chris.* But she wasn't Chris. She was Melanie, a woman who seemed to anger Teo as much as she aroused him. What made her think she could simply confide her fears and he would melt them away as easily as he melted her?

Again her heart seemed to hold an answer: the night before he had been as gentle and considerate of her body as any woman could ever dream of. Certainly that she had ever longed for.

Again she ached to lower that guard just long enough to stretch for Chris, find him, make certain he was safe, that he was happy. Make certain that he was safe with Teo.

She paced the kitchen, stared out at the sunny deck. It wasn't dark and cloudy. Or had that part of the dream been metaphor? She wouldn't know unless she opened herself to the elements, opened her mind to find out.

God, if she only dared. A part of her felt starved for the contact with Chris, ached to open herself to the man who knew every facet of her already.

Was she only fighting herself? Was this a heart's trick to get her to open herself to Teo? A simple subterfuge... your child is in danger, better unveil your thoughts to the man who intrigues you so. You need to know what's going on...open up. Was it only a ploy to let Teo know her confusion, her fears, her longing for him, her hurt as a result of his nightly abandonment of her?

Because if she so much as opened a crack in her closed mind, she would also slip into Teo's. It was inevitable. And so incredibly tempting. And more dangerous than anything she had ever done before.

He would see how much he'd hurt her every night, not with his hands, not with his loving, never that, not that part of him, and certainly not with his possession of her, but by his dismissal, his callous disregard of what had passed between them. And she would be forced to see why he would leave her afterward, why he would love her as exquisitely as an artist loves the canvas dearly painted, and then proceed to abandon it. And she would catch glimpses of the Teo that used to be, along with the Teo that was now. She wasn't certain she was ready for any of that.

But she longed to know and suspected that she might just be manufacturing this entire fear of the PRI this morning just so she would have an excuse to touch Teo's mind.

She all but flung herself from the kitchen to the washroom. During her shower, the multiple jets massaging her long-untested muscles from all sides, she wrestled with the question of whether or not to lower her guard. Through dressing, even through cleaning the few breakfast dishes, the frightening notion of opening herself to him chased around in her head. And the equally frightening notion of *not* opening, only to discover that her feeling had been right and something was terribly wrong.

She was still weighing the consequences when a sudden bolt of lightning shot down the abyss beyond the deck. It was followed by a tremendous clap of thunder. Teo's mark...but Teo wasn't there.

The thunder seemed to continue long after it should. A huge, clamorous sound. The pounding seemed to echo all around her, seemingly from the rock walls themselves.

Blam...Blam...Blam!

She froze in confusion, in fear. *This*...this must have been what her dream portended. Dear God, what was happening?

Blam...Blam...Blam!

Perhaps because she'd been thinking so desperately about lowering her guard, or perhaps because she suddenly realized how vulnerable she was here alone, or maybe because the terrible pounding struck her numb with fear, she threw open the doors of her mind and sent her thoughts in a frantic quest for her son, for the man he'd adopted as father...the man she'd all but adopted as a dark fantasy of a husband.

The block was only lowered for a split second, a heartbeat's length of time, but it was long enough that she brushed the mind of the man standing outside Teo's remarkable house, the source of all that noise. She saw the long corridor leading into Teo's home and understood in that nanosecond that the tunnel acted as some kind of amplifier, an echo chamber. No wonder she'd heard it so clearly, so distortedly. And no wonder that Teo had heard her the first night she'd arrived, despite the cacophonous thunderstorm.

She tried reigning in her mind, pulling it back behind her mental gates, knowing now who stood outside Teo's home. She knew what the pounding was, but she'd held herself too long isolated and, as if galloping of its own volition, gloriously free for a brief, unfettered moment, her mind soared outward, seeking her son and the man beside him.

She stretched across the mountainside, questing, searching, aching for contact. When she found them, she nearly sagged to her knees. *They were safe.* They were sitting together, Chris leaning against Teo's broad form, smiling, saying something aloud about the squirrel above them in a tree.

Incredibly, Melanie saw them through both sets of eyes, Teo's to Chris and vice versa. And she felt a whisper of the emotions each held for the other. She caught her breath as she reached deeper and saw that Teo was thinking that Chris looked so much like her that it made him hurt. What could he mean? Why did it hurt her, also?

"Mommy!" Chris cried out at the same time Teo stiffened, a shocked expression freezing his face. *Mommy! Heart talk! I make loud noise!*

Chris! she nearly cried aloud in joy. She felt his mind embrace hers eagerly, with innocent delight, with a tinge of relief. And she almost reeled with the incredible beauty of mingling her thoughts with her son's again. It had been only two weeks since she had closed her mind, and she'd seen him each day, kissed him each night, yet the loss of this special communication had made the time seem like centuries.

It had only been two weeks, and yet, like a child will do in such a brief time, he'd grown stronger, had solidified images in his mind, as though the addition of another mind had augmented his, taught him clearer mental pictures. Their heart talk had escalated to nearly complete communication. No more the simple pictures, the string of vague, sometimes incomprehensible images.

She held her breath, missing the days she'd been closed to him, missing the small and infinite ways he'd been changing even as she'd been there so near to him. Had she been inadvertently punishing both of them to protect herself from Teo's telepathic abilities? To keep Teo from knowing too much about her, had she denied both her son and herself the most simple of life's joys?

At the same time she wondered this, she could feel Teo, and unconsciously stretched against his thoughts like a cat against a warm hearthstone. She basked in his tenderness for Chris, his want of her...his confusion. She wanted to know more, but didn't want to probe too deeply. She might not like the answers she found. People seldom did when they were eavesdropping, and there was no greater form of eavesdropping than telepathy.

Teo, she whispered mentally, wanting him to accept her, needing him to understand what had driven her to opening now. Unconsciously, so lost in his mind that she didn't edit her mental imagery, she let him know why she'd dropped her careful guard, her fear that something was amiss, her joy in releasing her mind, her great happiness in touching Chris again. And perhaps, on some level, she was also letting him know what she felt when he left the bedroom at night, what she was worried about in relation to Chris. All this, perhaps far more, in the single mental breathing of his name.

She suddenly felt herself grabbed and roughly held captive. Not physically, though it might as well have been.

Melanie.

She felt Teo's knowledge of who had entered his mind, who had stolen into his thoughts and mingled there for a moment. Teo had felt her lowered guard, her questing mind. He'd seen her mental imagery, her projected thoughts, but hadn't fully processed them yet. He seized her with all his might and lunged toward her mind. She could feel a measure of unbridled shock, a hint of raw triumph, and a strong surge of a dark, unnamed need propelling him, catapulting him across the countryside and deep into her mind.

Melanie.

Rocking from his mental blast, his determined probing, the richness of his thought-induced voice, and terrified of the depths to which he would quest—and aware for the first time how deeply, shockingly intimate such a communication could be—Melanie slammed the gate closed in her mind, shaking, dying to know more, aching to renew the contact, regretting the brief contact they had shared for it only added to the barriers separating them, and, like everything else about Teo, served to underscore their basic, innate similarities.

Trembling, not from fear of whoever stood outside—her brief foray into the world again had allowed her a glimpse of the mind outside, and the identity of the man it belonged to—but shaken to the core by that nearly instantaneous brush with the inner Teo, she stumbled from the kitchen and up the long corridor to the front doors. She scarcely noticed that the tunnel had been pitch black; it was almost a relief after the flares of light emanating from Teo's thoughts.

She gulped for air, then threw open the large doors.

"Can I help you?" she asked breathlessly.

"No, *señora*," the man on the portal said. "I am hoping I can help *you*. And Teo."

Carrying Chris securely in his arms, Teo raced down the final embankment leading to the hill above his home. How long had he been running? Had he even really touched feet to the ground? He didn't know, couldn't even answer himself. All he knew was that he had to get to his house. Not for the first time, he wished that telekinetic ability conferred the talent to teleport. But it didn't. At least, not in his case.

As he ran, he desperately tried not to think of Melanie's touch in his mind. It had been shock enough two weeks ago to feel Chris deliberately sending his baby thoughts into his mind. But when Melanie had asked for his help with Chris, he had expected the boy to possess many of his own gifts.

He remembered the first time he saw her, remembered feeling the block slam into place in her mind. He even remembered thinking that her son was like her. But he'd never expected anything like he'd just encountered. Why hadn't he guessed that she could communicate with him directly, that she could send her thoughts as well as block him from penetrating hers? Was her block as easy as she'd made it seem?

He'd been angered by her block, but only because he hadn't been able to probe her thoughts, her needs. He'd never guessed she could do the same with him. Why had she kept him shut out?

He'd never guessed she could do more than block him, hadn't suspected that she had that same ability to reach inside a person's mind and literally touch the very thoughts spinning around. He'd been able to read others' minds for years and years. And never, outside of flickers of it from his family when he'd been younger, not until this unusual pair had he ever had someone do the same to him. He understood now, for the first time, how enticing the sensation could be. And how unsettling.

Her mental touch seemed to linger, as her scent had persisted on his skin, the memory of her remarkable loving yet remained in his thoughts. In both loving and in mental voice, she possessed a soft touch, lush with understanding, honeyed with depth. And somewhat skittish, wary.

Their nights together had told him that she had accepted

him on levels no human being had ever done before. But now, today, her fear and her certainty that danger awaited them clearly etched in his mind, he understood that she accepted him fully, was completely aware, and if not totally comfortable with all facets of his talents, that she at least understood them. Needed them.

And he understood that when she sought him, no matter how inadvertent the brush had felt, she had touched him more intimately than he ever could have dreamed of, could have conjured by any use of his remarkable talents. She was like him. Perhaps not in all ways, but in the most essential of all components. His heart raced at the thought, at the possibilities.

And, still running, thinking about the ramifications, his heart thundered at the sudden understanding of one of the many images that had lingered in her brief touch. Someone was at the doors of his home. And Melanie would be opening the doors. She might be in grave danger.

She'd closed to him just as quickly as she had opened, so he couldn't know just what the danger might be, what the fear in her had portended. All he knew was that nothing this side of heaven would prevent him from reaching her side, from helping her. She was his. And a man protected his own. It was that simple, no matter how complicated it might feel in his mind, in his heart.

But even as he ran, he tried probing at her, seeking more information, seeking that incredibly soft voice, those nuances in her imagery. How could she block him? Even he didn't know how to totally close his mind to the outside world.

He faltered, slowed to an unsteady jog when he wondered what all she might have understood about him when she did touch him. He had probed at her, and she had slammed her mind closed. He had not been shut to her. She could know everything about him. Everything. She'd deflected his mental probe easily, but he had no such ability. If she unveiled her mind again, she could reach in and pluck anything she might wish to know.

He stumbled, did a wild dance, used a bit of extra energy to rearrange the ground beneath him, and Chris giggled as he clung to his shoulder, blond hair flying out in baby-soft curls. For a moment Teo wished he could simply turn back time and be as carefree as this child he carried. As accepting of the vagaries of a strange and terrifying set of gifts.

They rounded the final hill leading to the clearing, and though they were too far away to see who stood upon his portal, talking urgently with Melanie, Teo was able to breach the distance with his mind. And as abruptly as Melanie's mind had brushed his and retreated, he reached for the mind of the man who stood outside his home, hat in his trembling hands. He could only read strange discomfort, half-formed apologies, betrayal. And danger.

And because of these incomplete thoughts, this half-blocked mind, Teo knew who it was who stood there, who had dared come to his home, knowing he wasn't welcome.

And, with black anger and hatred, Teo wanted to send a bolt of lightning from the sky, pull it up from the ground, and strike Pablo where he stood. He wished with all his might that he could do what he'd longed to do years ago…kill him dead.

He didn't know what stopped him, what held him back. He hadn't understood that fifteen years ago, didn't understand it now. How could he want something so badly, have it in his power to do precisely that, and then not do it?

CHAPTER TEN

During the short time she'd sent her mind questing, before she'd flung the doors of Teo's home outward, Melanie had already touched the man outside and knew him to be a mild telepath himself.

The brush with his mind also told her that something had hurt him long ago, had twisted the gifts. In that brief glimmer of time, she had sensed fear, betrayal, hurt, and yet, abject apology.

He cleared his throat, then said, "You remember me, *señora?* I am called Pablo Sandoval." He didn't meet her eyes, looked down at his shifting feet, the rotating grease-stained hat in his hands. His very diffidence, his nervousness, let her know instinctively that he'd come to the mountain only by the most dire necessity. Nothing else would have made him brave Teo's wrath.

When he looked up, she felt nearly assaulted by the man's need to tell someone all the horrible things he'd done in his life, and when his mouth worked, she thought he might free the one thing he was obviously certain would damn him for all eternity. And she wasn't sure she wanted to hear whatever it might be.

"Señora."

"Yes?" Was he never going to explain why he was there? Why had he pounded on the door so furiously?

"I am Teo's uncle," he said. And because of his tone, his pleading look, she wanted to lower her guard again, to understand what he was trying to tell her. The line from the book played through her mind, accompanied by the burning look of hatred that Teo had leveled at him that first afternoon.

Because he was here on this morning when the dreams wouldn't fade, when his pounding had mingled with the thunder outside and frightened her, she wanted to tell him to go away, to leave them alone. Even with her guard raised, she had the feeling that whatever he wanted to tell her would change her life completely.

But she kept the guard firmly in place, and the questions that would have flooded through her upon its release. This man was Teo's uncle? She remembered the photograph, the man who looked like him. Had that been Teo's father? The one who had sold his only son all those years ago?

But this man was the one who had sent her to Teo, told her how to find him. She remembered how he'd crossed himself as she'd driven out of sight and how she'd wondered if he was praying for her safety or his own. Now she wondered if he hadn't been praying for something else altogether.

"¿*Señora*? Is *he* here?" he asked in a husky, conspiratorial whisper.

"Why?"

"Because I have to talk to you. I need to tell you something very important. But I don't wish him to know I was here."

Melanie felt a frission of fear snake down her back. The presentment of danger echoed again. The voice in her dream, the one who called for her to come/leave quickly...it had been Pablo Sandoval's voice. Teo's uncle, however impossible that might seem.

"Do you want to come in?" she said, decided finally.

The look of horror on his face would have been comical had the house belonged to anyone else. "No! *Señora,* he must not know I was here! It's bad enough the way things are, but for me to go inside his house...I think he would kill me. And, for the things I did to him, I would deserve it. You understand?''

Melanie didn't understand and wanted to protest this assumption that Teo would kill anyone, but couldn't in all honesty. She didn't know Teo Sandoval well enough to know what he might or might not do. All she knew of him had been gleaned from the PRI files, files depicting him as the most terrifying man of power in all of history. A man of extreme conscience. A man to be left alone.

And yet, what she'd learned of him in watching him with Chris, in knowing him from lying in his arms, the heat radiating from his body, drawing every bit of sustenance from his lips, those things had no place in understanding the destructive side of Teo.

"We can talk out here. It won't take long," Pablo said. He looked at her expectantly, as if she was supposed to give some formulaic response. She didn't know what it might be and remained silent.

He nodded, but she still didn't know what he expected of her and so again kept quiet.

Finally he stepped a pace closer and said in a deep, rough tone, "*Señora,* you have to go away."

"What?" She slipped back a step.

"You must take your son and leave. *¡Rápidamente!*"

"But why?" Melanie asked, stalling, not wanting to know, afraid she understood the reason all too well.

His next words confirmed her worst fears.

"The institute men have been in Loco Suerte, looking for you. It won't be long until they find you here."

He had seen Chris in the car that afternoon. He was Teo's uncle. He would know what the PRI was all about, what they were after. He had directed her to Teo's door, hadn't he? Was this warning an atonement for some past misdeed? Or was he simply warning her because he knew what they had once done to Teo?

"Thank you for telling me," she said, involuntarily crossing her breasts with her hand as though the outside force could still the too rapid heartbeat, quell the tidal wave of fear that washed through her.

He was right, she thought, she had to run. And *now*. But then she remembered the simple terms of Teo's strange bargain. *I will protect him from the PRI.*

"Teo will protect Chris," she said somewhat defiantly, almost as if trying to convince herself.

Instead of running a hand through his thick, still-black hair as anyone nervously trying to convey a point might do, he only looked down at the grease-stained hat in his hand, and cranked the brim a half turn to the right. He looked back up, his dark eyes meeting hers with a glittering intensity. For the first time she recognized Teo in him. She felt her breath catch anew.

"You don't understand, *señora*. I know he will try to save you, to save your son. But, I ask you, who will protect Teo? They took him once. Don't you see? If they want your *niño* badly enough to come here looking for him, do you think they will let a man who already scares them stand in their way?"

"But they can't harm Teo," she murmured, afraid of the meaning in his words, the intensity in his gaze. "No one can get close enough to him to hurt him."

Was this, in some way, the essential element that held Teo apart from others, the one thing that made her unable or unwilling to totally give herself to him? A man who couldn't be hurt was a man capable of inflicting great pain on others.

But Teo had been hurt in his life. Deeper hurts than some people would be able to imagine, she thought. She amended her earlier comment. "No one could hurt him now, at any rate."

Pablo looked at her, sadly. His lips twisted bitterly, with

a pain she could all too easily imagine. He said slowly, emphatically, "They can *kill* him, *señora*. They can simply *kill* him."

Melanie felt a chill wash from her shoulders to her calves. "No," she said. Her single negative came out like a full-blown statement of fact. But her heart begged the question.

He seemed to sense her uncertainty for he pressed on. "I know what they are like! Don't you think I've had to live with that memory for all my days, every day for the last fifteen years?"

"But—"

"There aren't any arguments, *señora*! I lied to Teo, took him to the men who paid Ernesto for him. I stood there and watched as they poked needles in his arms and listened as he cried my name out loud. I know what they did to him. I know how they hurt him. He has never been the same, *señora*. He knows they cannot take him now...he can be of no use to them the way he is."

She said urgently, "You're right. He knows this. They know it. They can't use him. They don't dare try."

He advanced a step, all but spitting the words at her as he said, "Exactly, *señora*! Now, they have no choice. They cannot use him, he will not let them get close. But they want your boy. And Teo is in their way. So...they will kill him. If you don't leave, they will kill him."

"Why are you...telling me this?" Melanie asked. She felt as if her throat was closing around her breathing, choking her.

"Because I sent you here. Leading them right to him! Again. Don't you understand, *señora*? I have betrayed my own blood. He trusted me and I betrayed him. I once handed Teo to the men who used him, no matter for what motives, for what reasons. And now, again, I have brought him to them. Through *you*. Please, *señora*, leave now. Go away. I will tell the men you left, I'll point them in the wrong direction. Even if they try their tricks on me, they would understand nothing. But please, don't make me betray him twice!''

Melanie felt her mind was reeling. Suddenly she understood so much about Teo, so much about his past. It wasn't a matter of having to delve into his mind, it was a matter of putting one piece of the puzzle next to another and coming up with the whole.

This man, Teo's uncle, had been instrumental in betraying Teo Sandoval to the PRI, had been the one who had helped turn Teo into the dark man he was today, who had helped steal the dreams of his youth from him. And, for the first time since she'd run from the PRI, she understood what she, too, had asked of him. Not just his protection, but an end to his seclusion.

''He wouldn't believe I didn't drive them to him again, leave him to that nightmare. He was only a boy, a starry-eyed young man who believed that he could control the power in his hands by working with wood. You've seen his house, the way he builds, the beauty he creates. He does this with his hands, *señora,* not with his magic.

''When Ernesto told me that we would be rich beyond our dreams, I didn't care. You understand? I didn't care about the money. I believed the institute would teach Teo things, give him an education, take him from the mountains, let him lead a normal life,'' Pablo said.

He stepped back then, turned and stared at the rock escarpment on the far side of the abyss. ''He did that, you know. When Angelina died. When no one but me came to the funeral because everyone was afraid of the witch. But he was already changed by then. He was different. Because of me.''

When he finally turned his gaze back to hers, his eyes seemed flat, dulled by self-realization, glazed with a pain that had been too long endured. He said, "Do you see? I told myself he would have a better life, *señora,* but I lied. I knew what they would do. In my heart—" he slapped his chest with his battered hat "—here. I *knew.* And I took him to them anyway."

Melanie pulled back from him in sick distaste as she realized the role he'd played, the part he'd acted so perfectly, so perfidiously. Like Tom, Pablo and Teo's father had sold the young Teo, had disregarded the human being, had seen only the opportunity. Poor Pinocchio, she thought, trying to envision the younger version of Teo, the betrayed young man with the power of gods in his hands. What had they wrought between them, the PRI, Teo's father, this broken excuse for an uncle?

Like Tom, Teo's father might have sold the young Teo to the PRI, but it had been Pablo—and she understood Teo's underlined, obscure reference about his long-damned relatives now—who had transported the boy to the hell he was forced to occupy. This Pablo had been the one to promise good things, even as he had broken those promises, broken the boy who'd believed in them.

She had only been concerned that they not find her son, that Teo protect them, train Chris to be like him, and therefore to become invincible. But she had forgotten the most basic truth of all: the men at the PRI had taken Teo once, they could do it again. But Pablo was right; they didn't want him now, couldn't use him as they would use Chris.

So, knowing them well, it only followed that they would simply have to eradicate him, as they had planned to do to her. That way two of the PRI's most pressing problems would be solved in one fell swoop. The most dangerous man to the PRI would be eliminated and so would any remaining obstacle to their obtaining young Chris Daniels.

And it would all be her fault.

Her head swam in confusion, her heart thundered in attempts at denial. Of all things, she would never have wanted Teo Sandoval to come to any harm. And, now more than ever, she couldn't bear the thought.

"You mustn't tell him I was here," Pablo said again. "He won't believe me if I tell him I only wanted to help. He hates me now. Perhaps rightfully so. But you must save him, *señora*. You're the only one who can."

Melanie held on to her mental blockade by the merest thread of willpower. Everything in her wanted to reach out to Teo and Chris, assure herself again of their safety.

And now, when she felt—knew—it was too late, she wanted to tell Teo of her confusion about him, of how she wanted and needed him, and yes, even feared him, almost as much as she feared what he produced in her.

Oh, God. Pablo was right; she couldn't bring the PRI into Teo's home.

"I can't just leave without some kind of explanation," she said feebly, then added, thinking of the terms of their bargain, "He won't believe me, anyway."

Pablo looked away, up at the mountains for a moment, then back at her for an even longer time. He seemed to be studying her, perhaps trying to read her mind as his nephew could do.

Finally he said, "Tell him that you don't love him, *señora*. He will let you go, then."

Melanie couldn't help the instinctive cry of protest that rose to her lips, even escaped them. She swallowed heavily and started to tell Pablo that love had nothing to do with the bargain she and Teo had struck, but the words stuck in her mouth as her heart remembered the long nights spent in each other's arms, the look of tenderness on his face when he played with her son, the confusion she felt for him, about him. And, perhaps strongest of all, her reaction to the realization that the PRI might kill Teo.

Dear God, was she falling in love with Teo Sandoval?

If she hadn't been told to tell him she wasn't, would she ever have realized she might be? That it was too late, that she already did love him, perhaps had for days without even knowing it?

"Or tell him you hate the mountain and have to go back to civilization. Tell him anything. But go. By tomorrow morning. I'll do everything to keep them away until tomorrow night. But I heard one of them say more were coming then. And these are psychics, like Teo. Like your son. Maybe like you and me. But they will come here then. And they will let nothing get in their way. We both know that, *señora*. I will try and block them from seeing which way you travel. Everyone will try to help. But you must go."

He hesitated, then met her eyes directly. "Or Teo dies."

With his last, definitively harsh statement, Pablo turned and began loping across the left side of the clearing, onto the rough track, then disappeared over the edge of the mountain.

Melanie watched him go, leaden, feeling as if he'd taken her heart with him. How could the sun still shine so brightly? How could the clearing meadow be green and dotted with blue asters and Indian paintbrush? How could the sky be clear and the breezes cool when everything inside her felt dead?

She turned to go back inside the house when a movement off to her right caught her eye. *Teo,* she thought, and without intending to, jolted free a crack in her guard.

A blast of multilayered emotions, flavored with his rich, dark tone, whorled into her mind, sprinkling anger, joy, triumph, despair, confusion and longing across her own too beleaguered thoughts. With a tremendous effort, she shoved the gates closed again, and clung to the porch railing for support she sorely needed. He'd never know how difficult it was to close him out now. Now that she understood she

had brought him into danger, now that she knew she would
be leaving him.

But perhaps, most of all, because she understood that she
didn't *want* to leave now. Didn't want to leave, ever.

He set Chris down halfway across the clearing and Melanie felt a brush of the dream's presentment. *Run, Chris!*
she wanted to cry, but held her tongue. The sky was still
light and cloudless. No red ball took up most of Chris's
hands. Nothing in white shimmered at her left and no knife
blade or needle reflected the lightning that wasn't flaring in
the sky.

"Mommy! We runned! You heart talked and we runned
to you!"

His face was filled with simple joy, baby-face dirty with
his journey on the mountain, eyes bright with delight at
seeing her.

"Teo carried me and we runned. He danced the
ground!"

Tears welled in her eyes as she scooped him up and held
him tightly to her chest, burying her face against the soft
warmth of his hair, drinking in his little-boy scent. The
choices were too sharp—her son's future, Teo's safety. Neither were certain, both were nebulous. But if she stayed
with Teo, told him about the PRI, he would want a battle,
and with them having nothing to lose, they would win. And
with what he had already taught Chris, they had a slim
chance of escaping them again.

She heard Teo's approach, but didn't raise her eyes to
meet his. She couldn't. She knew too much, felt too much
now. And she was raw after her conversation with Pablo,
her realization of how she'd endangered him forefront in
her mind, along with the terrifying understanding of how
she'd come to feel for him, what she'd come to feel.

She couldn't gaze at him now, knowing what she did.
He would read her fear, her love, her decision to leave him.

A sob rose in her chest, fought for release. She hugged Chris even tighter, felt him patting her back in baby slaps.

Scalding, hot tears burned her cheeks, seared her throat. My God, she thought, they had mingled their minds, just for a moment or two, but having touched, she was certain the imprint would remain forever. A part of her would now and always be searching to find that rare and glorious connection again.

And she had to leave. Tonight. Tomorrow morning at the latest. A pain deeper than any she'd ever known before coursed through her, tearing her apart. And the worst part of the pain was caused when she understood that he would never know how much she wanted to stay.

Teo lit a fire in the huge fireplace. His hands were shaking, he thought, and not for the first time discovered he had no power to control his own body. He could mend the broken ribs, the punctured lungs in Demo Aguilar, he could make a mountain crumble and fall into the abyss, he could destroy an entire building with one glance, but he couldn't suppress his own anxiety, couldn't stem the trembling in his own hands.

What had Pablo said to Melanie?

Whatever it was, she hadn't spoken to him since they'd come back inside the caves. She was blocked to him, as always, but he felt a difference in her now, almost as though he could feel her struggle to maintain that barrier.

When he asked her point-blank, she only shook her head, not looking at him. And when he'd pressed the question, she'd finally mumbled something about his wanting to make certain she'd found the mountain all right, that she wasn't lost in the mountains somewhere.

"After two weeks?" Teo had said sarcastically.

"He came as a kindness," she'd snapped then, and left the room.

He had wanted to follow, certain she was lying to him, not understanding why, but most of all, not understanding the tears that threatened to spill across her cheeks, the tightly reined-in pain he felt was about to pour out of her. What had Pablo done? What had he said to make her shake so? To make her look at him as if all hope were gone?

Before, he would have just demanded that she tell him; he would have threatened, hectored, sent bolts of lightning zigzagging down the ravine, but this evening, on this night of revelations, having touched her thoughts, having felt her mind touch his, something in her eyes, in her pallor, had kept him from even voicing a question.

Pablo would never have dared to come to this mountain if Melanie hadn't been there, if she hadn't been alone. He knew better. Why today? And why did it make him feel nervous, uncertain? His uncle was of no more significance than a fly in a windstorm. Less, perhaps. He could swat him away easily. The man was so trapped in the guilt he so thoroughly deserved that nothing Teo could do or say would ever make him whole again.

But Pablo had said something. Teo had felt the measure of danger in the older man's twisted thoughts.

The fire caught and he stared at the flames, mesmerized by the memories of the past, the impossibilities of the future.

Everyone in Loco Suerte was aware that Pablo had helped Teo's father to persuade him to forswear the mountain's safety for a day, to take him into town, to the movies in the city, he'd said. And everyone knew that he'd handed Teo instead, to the men from the PRI.

No one but Teo and Pablo knew how he had screamed his uncle's name when the white-coated men had restrained him, chaining him for all intents and purposes, and then pumped him so full of drugs that his mind was totally stripped and his thoughts had felt on fire, his control shattered by their devices and their greed.

Strangely, the part that always seemed to bother Teo the most was that he and his uncle had never seen the movie. If only the man had taken him to the show, let him watch in innocent oblivion, and then given him away, perhaps he wouldn't feel so bitter. As it was, even the smallest of joys, the most mundane of promises, had been broken.

And who gave a damn about the tears in Pablo's eyes after the men who talked with him had walked up to his nephew and jabbed a hypodermic into his arm? Pablo had left him to them, hadn't he? Wasn't that what he had to remember now?

His beloved uncle, Pablo. No better than his father, Ernesto. No worse than his mother. Pablo, his last living relative. One of the damned.

The important thing to remember tonight was that Melanie had mentally touched him twice. He still reeled from that experience. Craved even more. If she opened to him again, he vowed, he would proceed slowly, softly, not swamp her like some crazed fool eager for something he'd hadn't understood or recognized.

The flames heated his face and his hands and he remembered how Melanie had buried her face in Chris's sunlit hair. If Chris weren't long asleep now, he would do the same. He understood that need for some kind of affirmation, some kind of proof that life was a good thing.

Melanie...? he quested, probed gently, but received no mental answer. He knew she was in the kitchen, could feel her leaning against the glass doors looking out at the star-studded night. He could sense an indecision in her, a question, but beyond that couldn't break through her tower-strong walls.

As if sensing he was trying to reach her, he felt her move from the kitchen, tensed as she pushed open the door to the living room. He slowly turned to look at her. He felt his breath catch in his chest. She was so incredibly lovely.

She crossed a good half of his living room before faltering, then stopping, almost as if something she read in his face kept her from coming any closer.

Suddenly he didn't want things to be the way they had been. He didn't want to steal into her room in the middle of the night, like some thief taking what he could, then slipping away, disappearing. He wanted all of her, wanted her to come to him. Needed her to seek his company. But, of all things, he couldn't ask this. It was not something one could ask.

She stood perfectly still, apparently waiting for him to say something. Anything.

"What did Pablo say to you?" he asked again, gently this time. "I can tell he frightened you. What did he want?"

She flushed bright with color for a second, then paled alarmingly. Her pallor was such that he pushed to his feet, ready to go to her.

She opened her mouth, perhaps to tell him what Pablo had said, then a terrible sorrow washed over her face and she shook her head.

"I can't," she said. He thought he'd seen misery before, but now suspected he'd only caught reflections of it. Her face was a study in confusion and pain.

"You can't...what?" He almost didn't want to hear her answer. His heart began pounding too painfully in his chest. He felt like he couldn't breathe. Don't say it, he wanted to command. Don't tell me you can't stay.

"Teo...?" she said, making his name a question, as many times in the night she'd made of it a benediction. Another of the chains around his heart snapped loose, making him feel off-balance, free but frightened of the freedom.

When he didn't say anything, only waited to hear what

she wanted, she raised a hand to her forehead, touched it lightly, then smiled crookedly. A tear escaped from her eye and snaked down her cheek. She didn't try to brush it away.

"I...I...could we sit in front of the fire for a while?"

"Of course," he said. He almost marveled at how cool his voice sounded, how calm. He felt anything but. *Melanie*...

She wiped the tear from her face and moved closer.

"I can draw a sofa over," he said, and half wondered at himself for offering. And, for the first time since she'd come to his home, come into his life, he realized that he'd always *done*, not asked. Was it because there was such a fine line between asking and pleading, pleading and begging?

"No," she said, almost as if answering his internal question. Would that she could open up to him, really understand his thoughts.

But all she said was "Let's sit on the floor, on the rug."

He felt his breath catch as he realized the implications of her earlier question, the simple answer. *Let's...we...*

He waited until she had settled on the thick sheepskin rug in front of the huge stone hearth before sitting down himself. He sat some three feet from her, wanting to be closer, wanting to ripple the rug and draw her to him automatically.

"I'm afraid," she said finally.

No power on heaven or earth could have kept him from reaching across that three-foot breach to draw her close to him, to wrap her in his arms, to hold her slender form against his body.

"Shh. I'm here," he said. The words were the same she'd spoken to him that day in the station plaza when Demo had been hurt and he had mended the bones.

A sob broke from her and she pressed her face against his chest.

"Querida, everything's fine. You're here. I'm here. Chris is safe." His assurance sounded off kilter even to himself. It sounded like a challenge to fate...come and get us, we're waiting.

He could understand why her hands convulsed around his arms, why her face pressed even tighter against his chest. But he couldn't understand why she fought lowering her guard. He could feel the struggle, almost a war raging inside her.

"Melanie..." he said, then trailed off, hoping she would understand from his voice, his embrace what he wanted her to see without words.

She raised her head, tears drenching her emerald eyes, her lips taut with some inner fight.

"Teo...if I..."

"If you...?

"Make love to me," she said abruptly, raising a shaking hand to his face. "Real love. All night. A forever night. Please. And when it's over, when we're drifting back from wherever it is we go...stay with me tonight. Please."

For a moment he truly believed he was asleep and was dreaming. And then he understood the most profound truth of all, that all he'd ever wanted, all he'd ever dreamed of, was hearing those words from this woman. And he understood suddenly that dreams did have a place in his life again, that the future was only what a person made of it, not what destiny dictated. And the dreams of the future could come true.

"Melanie," he murmured before lowering his lips to hers. Even as he tasted her slowly, loving the way she molded to him, he felt a flare of raw joy infusing his veins. She had come to him, had asked him for company, for loving. She wanted *him,* had begged him for a night, a forever night.

She'd seen inside him and knew what he was, knew what he wanted in his heart of hearts.

Let me in, too, he called to her, pleaded with her, but though he felt her waver in her control, the block remained in her mind. He felt almost desperate to understand that she was a different woman than he'd thought her all along, and yet was afraid of what she would find, afraid of what he would.

With her hands on his face, exploring the planes of his features, tracing his eyelids, the curve of his lips, he realized that some part of him, the biggest part, perhaps, had never expected this moment to really happen. Wanting something to come to pass and having it do so were two entirely different things. From the first moment he'd seen her, he had wanted her to come to him, not to have to beg her to do so.

And now she had. Could that reality be projected onto other dreams, as well? He'd demanded she stay for six months. Was it possible that she would ask to stay longer?

His heart began beating in heavy, almost painful thuds. He, who had long since buried the dream of home and family, had been granted a taste of what family could mean. If it were to disappear now, the pain of it would surely crush him. Was his want and need of her enough to hold her to his side? Dear God, he prayed, let it be so.

She'd seen a glimpse of his thoughts, his heart. Did he dare tell her what she'd seen, what she could see? And then he realized he had never answered her with words, never responded verbally to the question that seemed to have been torn from her very soul.

"*Querida*...I'll stay with you. Of course, I'll stay," he murmured against her arching throat.

He didn't understand her quickly swallowed sob, didn't know why her hands bunched in his hair for a moment as if weathering a severe storm...or as if afraid to let him go.

CHAPTER ELEVEN

Teo's admission that he'd stay with her through this one last-a-lifetime night almost broke Melanie's heart. She longed to open her mind to him, to let him see how much this concession meant to her, how much she wanted to stay with him for far more than one night, how much she wanted to be with him morning, noon, summer and winter, sharing all of the long dark nights, the strangely beautiful mountain days.

She felt like a fraud for not telling him what Pablo had said, for not being honest with him now that she was brave enough to ask him to stay with her tonight because tomorrow she would be gone.

But there was nothing the least fraudulent about how she wanted him tonight. This would be their last time, the union that would have to put paid to a lifetime of lonely nights, nights she knew would be spent remembering their brief time together, dreams spent longing for that mental voice, that physical touch. Nights and long, long days spent knowing that she had to leave the one man on earth whom she might have been able to truly love. Did love.

Tears welled anew at the realization, the understanding that she could no longer hide from the truth. She loved Teo Sandoval. Wanted him, needed him. *Loved* him.

If she told him she was leaving, he would demand the reason why, and if she told him, he would vehemently deny the conclusions she and Pablo had drawn. He would, in all likelihood, lash his incredible power at the skies, misunderstand that all she was truly thinking of was his safety.

Those two momentary brushes with his mind had told her far more than anything he ever could have told her verbally.

Her initial impression of him, before she'd closed her mind to him that first afternoon, had been absolutely correct. For Teo Sandoval, alone was an entirely different concept than for others. His loneliness was so acute, so ingrained, that it really was an altogether different emotion than what others might feel. And it was born of his difference from other people.

Knowing this, and understanding how he must now be feeling at having encountered two others with elements of his own differences, his own gifts, she knew how thoroughly he would fight to keep them at his side. She knew that feeling well. She had never been so happy as the moment when she realized that her genes had passed along to Chris the ability to share his thoughts. And she knew that Teo must have felt the same way. Scared, tingly, absolutely joyous at finding another.

For her it had been like waking up one morning after a lifetime of being the only sighted person in a blind colony and discovering another sighted person had drifted into her life. And she had never had the traumas, the agonies that Teo had suffered. How much greater his awe, his joy must be.

She was prepared to take that away from him? Yes, to save his life. Better he be alone again, without them, than to not be there at all.

God, how she wanted to tell him the truth. The reasons for her leaving. Wanted to tell him now, so he would believe the tears in her eyes, the trembling of her hands, and see the pain this was causing her. Without them, without the tears, the pain, would he believe that someone could care enough about him to want to keep him safe? Trust was a learned behavior, she thought, it didn't come automatically. She, of all people, knew that so well. Just as she was beginning to know him. To *love* him.

It was almost a relief to finally admit she had fallen in love with Teo Sandoval. But, with this admission, she also knew, instinctively, that she couldn't tell him, couldn't even let him begin to guess her love, because if he did, he would never let her go, would never let her save him.

With his lips upon her throat, his hands roaming her curves, molding her breasts to his broad palms, it didn't seem to matter that she'd only realized this love for him when she knew she had to leave him. It had taken understanding that she'd brought him danger, that she was in danger of losing him, to make her realize the truth. Leaving him now, knowing how she felt about him, understanding him better than anyone else ever could or would, was the hardest thing she'd ever have to do in her life.

And it was so difficult to keep her mental guards in place. Like her body melted beneath his hands, his tongue, she could feel that carefully erected mental barrier beginning to slip, starting to erode. She struggled to keep it in place, as she'd been fighting all afternoon, all evening. If only she knew how to open without totally opening. If she could only feel him, share only those thoughts that related to the moment, to *him*, to this final night together. But she couldn't do that without revealing to him that the PRI men were nearby, that she was leaving him forever, leaving…to save him.

But would she want to live without him?

She had no choice. She had Chris to think about. And Teo. Her wants couldn't be allowed to matter now. Not with the two people she loved more than anything else in jeopardy. She knew, without having to lower her guard, that the PRI would stop at nothing to get Chris, including killing Teo, killing her. And she knew their only chance of survival—all their survival—was to get as far away from this mountain as was possible in the early morning hours.

But nothing, no amount of danger, no amount of threat from the PRI, was going to steal this night, this moment, this farewell from her.

His hands parted her blouse, exposed her breasts to his careful attention. Before, he'd used his talents to strip them both, to peel away the barriers of clothing in a tingling whisper of electricity. But, as if wanting to travel this particular journey as slowly as possible, and as enticingly, tonight he slowly undressed her by purely manual efforts.

Though there hadn't been a time they had spent together that hadn't been glorious, incredibly passionate and achingly beautiful, this slow, deliberate seduction surpassed them all, exceeded every dream she might have had about him, of being with him. Or was she feeling this way because for the first time she knew she loved him, that she wanted to love him for all time?

But underlying everything, perhaps accentuating all touches, all nuances, was the knowledge that this would have to be the last time, the final chapter in their bizarre and unique relationship. Because she knew the PRI wouldn't give up on Chris. Not until he was fully grown, and perhaps not even then—they had tried to use Teo when he was nineteen, hadn't they?—would they back away from Chris. And she didn't dare try to rely on Teo's protection, when they would kill him to get to Chris.

No, she daren't try to ever contact Teo Sandoval again. If she did, his life would again be in peril, his solitude in jeopardy. This final realization seared her and made her clutch him to her almost angrily, as if needing to deny the truth of it.

This would be the last time. The words, the understanding of them, chased around in her mind, making her desperate to lose herself in his loving, to forget tomorrow in his touch tonight. But, oh, how she ached for a tomorrow with him, a future, just a hope of promise, all the while knowing it could never be.

Never before had he allowed her to undress him, and she found herself almost mesmerized by the way his buttons wove through his flannel shirt, the way the zipper hissed as she pulled it down, freeing him. And never before had he allowed her to take such time, such exquisite pains to taste him, to feel him, to let him know her teasing fingers, her lips.

When she heard him groan aloud, the sound seeming to come from somewhere deep inside him, she tore his shirt from his arms, pulled his pants free of his legs and tossed the articles away from their bed on the sheepskin. She then pushed him back onto the rug, bending over him, aching for him, aching more for herself.

She wasn't worried that Chris would interrupt them; she knew Teo's mind was linked with his, if distantly. He would know if Chris woke, would know if Chris was tipping his little bed, padding out of the bedroom. Just as she would know if she dared let her guard drop.

She didn't dare think about Chris. To think about him was to remember tomorrow, remember that all tomorrows—if she lived long enough to have them—would be spent without Teo. And if she thought about that, she wouldn't be able to love him now, give him everything in her.

If she thought about the lack of happy futures, the sad twists of destiny, she would simply curl up in his arms and cry and cry and cry. She had to go and didn't want to. How could fate have been so cruel as to pair her with this dark man only to have her fall in love with him just as she understood she had to leave him, just as fate was wrenching him from her side?

His teeth grazed her bared nipple, electrifying her, snapping her back to the present, to this glorious moment. As she arched to allow him even greater access, she understood that tonight she would give the best she had to give, the most she had to offer. Tonight, she would be his wife, his lover, and she would lock away every single gesture, each nuance of taste, touch, smell, and file them forever in her mind, in her heart.

The heat from the fire seemed to stoke the flames in each of them. His fingers ignited passion even as his tongue fueled an eruption of equal ardor in her. He rolled her over and his long hair brushed across her breasts, making her nipples pucker and ache for a stronger touch. His muscled body rippled gold and his want was evident in his throbbing manhood, hard and vibrant, which pressed against her thigh.

She rolled again, sweeping his arms out to the side, kissing the sensitive hollow of his throat, letting her own hair tease him. She felt strong and wholly woman as she straddled him, pinning him this time, not with her hands but with her desire, meeting his gaze, seeing him vulnerable for the first time, understanding now what she never had before this moment: that all he'd ever wanted from her was for her to ask him to be with her, was for her to want him back.

She had to blink back tears at this sudden understanding of him, knowing now how lost he must have felt during the past two weeks, more lost than she perhaps, needing her love, craving her acceptance of him. She wondered if this newfound understanding came from her equally newfound comprehension of her love of him or if it was a product of the moments when their minds had linked, sharing not so much surface, concrete thoughts as those that lay buried deep within souls, the commingling of heart and mind, thought and deed.

Surely, no matter what she might now comprehend or

might be feeling, those remnants of exchanged thought, the unvoiced but recognized thought patterns shared and re-shared, those were the emotions, the enhancers that lent depth to their lovemaking now. And perhaps, because of that depth, he would know that she did want him, that her self-imposed nakedness, her wrapping her body so tightly, so purposefully around his, had nothing to do with their bargain, had only to do with the two of them, with the chemistry—and far more—that sprang so seemingly effortlessly between them.

But without lowering her mental guard to him, she couldn't be certain he understood. He had a right to know. It was vital that he be left with the clear understanding that she did want him, that she always had, that she always would. Without the intermingling of thoughts, there was another way...the way used by countless other lovers, a way as old and venerated as the earth itself.

"No one has ever made me feel like this before," she said as she ran her hands through the soft, tight curls on his dark chest. "I didn't believe I could ever feel this open, this...hungry for a touch, a kiss. I have never wanted anyone like this before. Teo...I never will."

He looked stunned for a moment, as if by speaking she'd broken some great unwritten law. But his hands raised to her shoulders and in their fierce grip she understood that he was only feeling things that *he'd* never felt before. Like her.

She half raised, and in slow deliberation, sheathed him, sliding down, encasing him in her own well of want and need. His grip on her shoulders tightened for a moment, then he shifted his hands, sliding one to a breast, cupping it, snaring a taut nipple between his thumb and forefinger. He placed his other hand behind her, gripping her buttocks, rocking her, sliding her, touching her in ways only he could.

And she knew from his bowed body, his matching rhythm, what it was to ride the wind, to soar on the edge of the hurricane. How could she even contemplate leaving this, turning her back on the promise inherent in his touch, in his abandon?

But how could she not, when the alternative meant his death?

Teo gave himself to the rhythm she created for them, arching to stay with her, dying to explode, determined not to lose control. With each thrust, he seemed to hear her voice, her honey-rich tone. And, whether in reality or in his heart, he heard her say, "I have never...wanted anyone...like this before...Teo...I never will."

He felt he was drowning in her, in her words, in the concreteness of them, in the pure solidity of them. They were real, vibrant, viable. He felt he could build a mansion with them, create a stairway to heaven with the sheer weight of them. He felt they were drawing every bit of him into her...mind, body and loneliest, darkest soul.

Tonight, it didn't seem to matter that their thoughts didn't mingle, that he couldn't probe the secrets of her mind. Tonight, she'd given him words, had granted him the benefit of speech. Tonight, she had offered him the solace, the impetus of her desire. If he couldn't have the deepest parts of her, he thought in wonder, then he had to believe that she had given him something in exchange that was beyond price. She had given him the promise of a tomorrow.

As miraculous as her loving had always been, this time, this night, transcended them all. Faster and faster they rocked, intertwined, woven together, losing their separateness in a unity so absolute that it seemed to defy the laws of physics. Somehow, sometime during their joining they had truly become one.

And when he felt her suddenly freeze and heard her cry out his name, he clasped her sharply to him, holding her, letting her fly, but staying with her, keeping her with him, as he knew now that he wanted to do so for all time. He wanted this, knowing in his soul that it could never be, that for him there was no future. Yet the thought persisted...*for all time.*

Her muscles clenched around him, spasmed, and she cried out yet again—"Teo!"—and for a flicker of a second he felt her in his mind, also, her rich melody of unveiled thought searching, brushing, mingling with his. She drifted away, as softly as a midnight kiss, and he let her go, didn't attempt to probe any deeper, didn't try to hold her with him.

She would never know how much he wanted to believe there was all the time in the world to try to reach her, to slip into her thoughts, intertwine there as they were now intertwined, commingled touching.

He sensed a great difference in her tonight, felt it in her loving, in her shuddering, exquisite release, and he felt that difference echo inside himself, as well. She had granted him words, had touched his mind, however briefly.

What she had done was what he had most feared when she'd first arrived. She had caused him to doubt the burial of his dreams, the funeral of his youth. She had made him think things were possible, made him want things, want more and more, not just of her, but of Chris, of day-to-day living, of life itself. Of time.

He truly wished that all they would need was time. But six months was only a moment, just a whisper of a name during a long lonely night or the brush of a like mind during a rare moment of passion. And in six months, she would be gone. She would live up to her bargain and be gone then. Out of his life. Disappearing as thoroughly as ever he might have done.

She slumped against his chest, her breathing ragged, her hair blending with his. Her eyes opened, luminous with unshed tears, a question, a sorrow too great to express trembling on her lips. Why did she look at him so? What was she thinking? Was she reading his mind, knowing he couldn't believe in the future no matter how much she made him want to?

The entire world seemed off-balance suddenly, as though from the time of his birth until this very moment, it had been a spinning top, whirling in a frenzied, furious line, and now, abruptly, it had keeled askew. It was as if his entire life had been spent waiting for this one woman. If it had been any other time, any other circumstance, and he'd been alone, he might have dropped to his knees, planted his lips upon the ground and thanked the powers that be for understanding his need for relief, his need for delivery from the pain he'd endured his entire life.

He felt her tears upon his face and raised his hands to cup her cheeks, feathering his thumbs across her sculpted features to smooth the moisture away, to tell her, without words, how deeply he was moved. *Don't ever leave me,* he thought at her. *You must stay with me. Forever. I will not let you go, now. You woke the dreams, you have to stay to tend them.*

Did she hear him? Could she?

She opened her eyes, looking down at him, her lips parted, her breathing still rapid, shallow. She rocked slower now, but tightly, liquid and steel combined. Her eyes were glossy with unshed tears, her skin dewy, and she appeared wholly vulnerable. A single tear crept down the curvature of her cheek. As he gazed deep into her eyes, he felt the explosion gathering in him.

He wanted to say something before his hopeless struggle with control was gone. He wanted to say something miraculous, a phrase or word that would bind her to him for all time.

"Melanie..." he breathed out, feeling himself going, feeling the tightening spirals forcing him upward, arching him, bucking him. Now, he thought. Now. And faster and faster the coils tightened, pulling him with them. Now. Now.

The words broke free, even if his greatest thought couldn't. "Stay—" *I'm losing myself in you.* "—with—" *I'm dying/living/believing in a tomorrow.* "—me!" *I'm drowning in you, filling you with all I have to offer.* "Melanie!" he rasped. He bucked against her, in her, and felt as if she pulled all of him inside.

Over her shattered sob, he commanded, "Stay..." *Oh, dear God, Melanie, stay with me!* "You *must* stay!"

And then he was gone, whisked away into an explosion of thought, body and emotion, whirling in that universe she seemed to create for the two of them, and he felt her there although he didn't understand the thread of sorrow that seemed to permeate her.

When he opened his eyes, he found her crying. "Ah, señora...querida," he said. *Darling.* And then, as though dragged from him, he murmured against her cheek, holding her tight to his chest, "Don't cry, *querida*. There's time. God willing, there's time."

And though his words should have made her relax, smile at least, she didn't, she convulsed in swift release of pain. And while he didn't understand her sudden flood of tears, he held her to him, rocking her gently, murmuring her name over and over.

But for the first time in his adult life, even as he held her weeping in his arms, he felt the glimmer of hope that tomorrow could be a reality, that belief and trust might be words that could be used and relied upon.

"You will stay," he said, and then again, "You will stay

with me.'' It was only much later that he understood he hadn't asked her to stay, that he'd commanded it. And only much, much later that he remembered he'd spoken the words as a talisman against losing her.

Melanie woke and lay perfectly still, listening to Teo's soft, steady breathing. His long black hair, smelling of herbs, of pine, of her, spilled across the pillow, half masking his face, blanketing her hand, which had rested the night against his shoulder.

She remembered the tenderness with which he had carried her to the bedroom after her tears had abated. She hadn't been able to tell him why she cried, that his harsh command for her to stay with him—a demand she would have given all she owned or ever knew to accede to—had totally undone her, that she had no reserves left to hide behind. Except her carefully guarded mind, and that, now, was only focused on his safety, on Chris's.

He'd ground out the words in his height of passion, but she hadn't been deluded into believing them extravagant, words tossed away at the moment of release. No, his command, his order, had come from the depths of his heart, his soul. With those words, he hadn't needed to add others, such as longing, need, want, *love*. He had shown her, had demonstrated the emotions she'd craved every night for the longest weeks of her life. Everything he had to offer her had been steeped in each syllable, each desperate sibilant, even if he didn't know it, or wasn't willing to admit it.

And that he'd said them even as she knew that she was leaving—had to leave for his sake—had torn her apart, cut at her in a way she'd never known before, would never know again but would remember every day, every night, for the rest of her life.

Somehow, his doing so now, on the eve of her departure made a mockery of everything he'd said, every emotion he'd dredged up. Because she knew instinctively that only he could have done so had he begun to believe that she might stay, that she could stay. He hadn't asked her to stay with him that first day in his kitchen, he'd tried forcing her into a corner.

And while she might have believed that he had manipulated her all that long, long second day in his home, she had known at his first kiss, and truly knew now, that she would have stayed with him no matter what the terms of his bargain might have been.

But not Teo. He wasn't the type of man who stumbled around in a morass of self-pity, of self-questioning. He was, as the PRI files had designated him, a man of extreme conscience. That didn't mean he would always fight on the side of right or good, that he would forever wear a white hat and ride off into a sunset. On the contrary, it meant he would only fight if he saw a ferocious need to fight...and it wouldn't matter whether right or good had anything to do with it. It would only matter how Teo Sandoval perceived it.

And Teo Sandoval wanted her to stay.

And, for his sake, she had to go.

Somehow his acceptance of her lame excuses for her tears had made her feel all the worse, made her ache to tell him the truth, to let him know how much she wanted to tell him yes, she would stay. If only she could.

One of his muscled arms covered her, all the blanket she'd needed through the dark, cool night. She had seen him angry, sending thunderbolts to strafe the sky; she had seen him passionate, exhorting her body to heights of intensity she'd not believed truly possible before; she'd seen him confused, perplexed by her, amused and tender with her son.

But until now, asleep, lips parted, brow smooth and untroubled, long, dark lashes fanning golden cheeks, watching him with love in her heart, departure in her mind, she realized she hadn't known him at all. Spent, passion laid to rest, he looked as impervious to the world's chaos as ever and yet there was a vital difference. He was so very young.

In his power, with his multilayered talents, his forbidding stare, his glittering silver-blue gaze, she'd forgotten that he was only thirty-four or thirty-five years old. The anger gone, the keep-the-world-at-bay attitude absent, Teo appeared what he was: a man on the threshold of life, decades before him, a long stream of time stretching into the future. Time to find love, family, creativity.

He could find all of that now, she told herself. She tried believing he would seek out the world now, because now he would want it more than he would need to shut it out. She tried to convince herself that he could find all that once she left him.

But she shivered as a stray truth, an understanding of him, chilled her. He wouldn't see her departure as helping him, as a noble gesture. He would see it as betrayal. As another betrayal. She knew how thoroughly he'd poured his heart free tonight, and he would see her leaving him as ultimate repudiation of his request. Of him. And he would damn her for it.

As she was damning herself. Because now, knowing she loved him, she couldn't understand how she was supposed to imagine living without him. Was this why she'd traveled all those miles, run that fast and furious, only to find him and then have to leave?

With tears threatening her anew, she slid from beneath him, pulled the covers over his bare, half-turned shoulder, and quickly dressed. She kept her mind firmly sealed as she snuck from his bedroom, across the cavernous living room and through to the kitchen. Once there, she found pen and paper in a small drawer and after two or three false starts, managed to leave Teo a note.

This horrible task complete, she quickly roused Chris, dressed him, and with only one or two reinforced mental messages—done so quickly that Teo couldn't have heard them in his deep sleep—managed to collect her son, his few things and, hopefully, her own thoughts.

She carried Chris out to the living room, holding a finger across her lips, again adding the notion of Teo sleeping.

The first light of morning crept down the abyss, sending shards of shadows across the huge windows, letting in the grayest of dawn's rays. Melanie held Chris for a moment, standing before the mammoth windows, looking out for the last time, wondering how she'd ever been frightened of the glorious view, the expanse of quiet and peace, wondering how she'd ever found it strange, bizarre. This view, this room, these windows, all were simply an extension of Teo. All—the cavern, the monolithic mirrorlike windows, the view of the abyss and the mountain wall facing it—were breathtaking, spectacular, a little frightening. Unique. Like the man who had created them.

Chris stirred in her arms. "Feed Gina?" he whispered.

"Not now," she murmured, and felt a pang of guilt. The first time in his young life that he'd ever had a semblance of normality, a creature to feed, to love, a man who wasn't frightened of him, who had worked with him to strengthen his gifts, and she had to take him away.

They'd run to get here, to be safe in the home of the mountain king, and now were running for safety, both for the safety of her son and the very man they'd sought for protection. How many times would they be running in Chris's lifetime? Would the running turn Chris into another Teo, a man who hated society, who shut it out, who demanded rather than asked, who repudiated rather than sought in even the most simple of contacts?

But if Pablo was right, if she didn't leave now, there wouldn't be any running at all. At least not for her. Not for

Teo. And Chris wouldn't be allowed the opportunity to escape a second time.

She didn't really have a concrete plan of action in mind, only escape and sparing Teo's life. Like so many had in the late sixties and early seventies, she figured she would try the route to Canada and hope for anonymity, hope that the short time with Teo's brand of psychic training had been enough to allow Chris some protection, and if not that completely, had at least gained some obscurity. Strength enough, perhaps, to continue to elude the determined PRI scientists. Certainly, Chris was changed.

So was she. Irrevocably. Inalterably.

As it had from the moment she'd first read it, the line from the PRI file raced through her mind. *I don't know whether Teo Sandoval should be condemned or praised. But at all costs, he should be left alone.* She hadn't left him alone, and she had fallen in love. And he had changed her entire life, her love, her heart.

Yes, she was changed. Even one week ago she might have hesitated leaving this mountain, might have blurted out Pablo's discovery to Teo, begged him to do something, anything to save Chris, save her, and hopefully do so without hurting himself. But she was different now, and if the difference came from loving him, she was the better for it.

She would survive the trek to Canada, she would make a home for herself and Chris, and try not to think about Teo, try to believe that she could find a life without him. And if the PRI traced them there, they would go elsewhere. There was an entire world lying out there; surely somewhere in it was a place for a mother and child to hide.

And if they were lonely, at least running now would spare Teo. She tried telling herself that it would be enough to know he would still be in the world, still be alive. But she wasn't sure that anything other than being locked in his arms, his lips pressed to hers, would ever be enough.

"Make loud noise now, Mommy?" Chris asked.

"No," she said absently, not sure what he was talking about. "Now we have to be very quiet."

"Wake Teo up," he commanded.

"No." More firmly this time.

She looked around the huge living room, memorizing it, taking in the spaciousness, the incredible attention to detail, folding it into her heart. What had once frightened her, what had repelled her, now soothed, even drew her. Amazing home...amazing man. Man of her heart, mystery of her soul.

She crept across the living room, edging toward the door leading out of the main quarters. She gave one last glance at the semidark room. In this light the room appeared much as it had in her dream. Was this an integral part of her nightmare? Gray eyes, gray room...broken heart?

Tears welled in her eyes when they reached the closed door to the kitchen. In there, he had kissed her for the second time, had scared her with his place-setting theatrics, and had fed a small mountain fox with her son. And there, on the island bar, lay the note she had felt compelled to leave him. The note explaining why she had to go.

She felt she owed him an explanation, owed him a reason. But most of all, she owed him the knowledge that the PRI henchmen would be looking for her here. And that he was in danger from them. And that she was leaving... because she couldn't bring them down on him a second time, because she believed the men that served the PRI didn't believe in second chances. And, alone in the kitchen, tears running down her face, she'd added a final line to this final note. *I love you.*

There was no explanation of that line, no elaboration. Just the three words, the most important three words in life. Or in separation. The most terrible three words in all the earth when one was leaving.

She traversed the black corridor by instinct alone, her mind on the first time she'd entered it, her heart on the phantom that had kissed her there in the dark. *I knew even then,* she thought, but the realization had stayed within the confines of her own barricaded mind.

"Toys, Mommy?" Chris asked.

"Shh. Wait till we get to the car," she whispered, remembering how the tunnel served as an echo chamber. She remembered everything. Too well.

Tears threatened again and she fought them back with nothing other than sheer determination. She had to get Chris away from here, for both his sake and for Teo's.

"Ride in the car?" Chris asked.

"Yes."

"Go to town?"

"No," she said, then added, "Sort of, honey. But definitely going, anyway."

"Mommy kiss Teo," Chris said about the time they reached the heavy front doors.

"Yes," she said again, wondering how much he might have glimpsed through her short drop of guard, how much he might have seen through Teo.

"Make loud noise now?" Chris asked, apparently not interested in pursuing Mommy-kissing-Teo.

"Not now," she said. "Later." She wrestled with the huge doors while trying to maintain her grip on her son and her handbag. She hadn't bothered with her suitcases; clothes, a few personal items, things like that didn't matter now. She was leaving behind the only thing in the world that mattered to her besides Chris—Teo.

When she finally wrenched the heavy doors open, she paused. Although the reasons for her departure were of the noblest, were the purest of reasons, she suddenly felt again that she was betraying Teo, leaving him, letting the PRI swarm around him once more. She had led them to him, and she was sneaking away from him when he needed her most. Suddenly she felt she was abandoning him just as she'd broken through that fiercely held reticence. Was she doing the right thing?

Pablo had betrayed Teo once, years before. Could he be doing the same thing to her? Getting her to run out into the night, straight into the arms of the PRI?

No. His pain had been genuine, his fears wise. She had to get Chris out of there and hope that Teo would be safe. *Please, God, keep him safe. Keep us all safe.* But somehow, as if reading her lines of destiny from a far and totally emotionless plane of existence, she felt her prayers were too late. Far, far too late.

As she pushed the large doors closed, she opened her mind and stretched to Teo's sleeping form. She lightly rested her mental touch against his dreaming mind, stiffening against the incredibly enticing feel of his thoughts, his rich, broad thinking.

Farewell...I love you, Teo.

She pulled back before he could wake and find her in the very act of doing the opposite of what he'd so tenderly, so passionately asked the night before. She was leaving, for all their sakes. But why did it feel as if she were being incredibly foolish, utterly selfish? And why couldn't she stop crying?

Without the rain, by the early morning light, the trek down the mountain was much easier than it had been by stormy night. Despite the tears that blurred her vision.

That night her heart had been filled with desperation, with the need to persuade Teo to take them in. Now her heart was filled with despair at the idea of leaving him, and fueling her steps was worry—hard, stark worry. Would they survive the next few hours? Would Teo understand her departure? Would he see it as a betrayal of his honest admission, his heartfelt request the night before, his demand that she stay with him?

Just let them get far enough away from him so that they would all be safe, she repeated over and over, a litany against whatever was to come.

"Car, Mommy," Chris said, pointing to her car. The rented Buick was no longer wedged to the bumpers in mud. It was sitting alongside the narrow track, nose pointed down the mountain to freedom. She hadn't left it that way. She'd left it mired in mud, stalled. And in the weeks she'd been with Teo she hadn't once considered the time ticking on the rental clock. The world had ceased to matter while she'd been with him.

The world scarcely mattered now. The only things that mattered were Chris and Teo, the two strongest telekinetics in the known world...and the two most vulnerable.

She stared at the car, motionless as she hadn't been since Pablo had left Teo's home the day before. The righted car pointed to—what?—Teo's having straightened it, fixing it the night she'd arrived, hoping it would make it easier for her to leave? Couldn't it have been Pablo, doing so to expidite her departure? Or was it the PRI arranging her neat exit—straight into their clutches?

She had the feeling that if Teo knew she was leaving, the car not only wouldn't start, but it might actually fly away and crash into a pile of rocks somewhere. And if Pablo had done it, he surely wouldn't have stripped the car of mud, of muck. Nor would the PRI.

The car was ready for them because of Teo. He had done it. He had prepared it. But when? How long ago? The night she'd come? The night in the rain, the night he was so angry at their intrusion into his life? The morning his eyes had begged her to leave and she had wondered why he'd needed her to go away?

She knew the reason now. She felt she understood almost

everything. He had wanted her to leave because she threatened his very existence. She could have placed his entire life in jeopardy just by coming here. She could challenge his solitude, make him wake up, make him want things he'd thought himself inured to. That was what the please-leave look in his eyes had meant.

But she had ignored him. The memory brought fresh tears to her eyes. She had insisted that she stay, had even agreed to his less-than-ridiculous bargain.

Oh, he had tried to get her to leave. He had done everything but demand she get out of his life, and had sent thunderbolts to punctuate his need for her to go. But she had insisted, accepted his terms, his demands, his qualms and, in doing so, had placed him...and her son...in grave danger.

What have I done? she wondered. And on the heels of that thought, *What should I do now?*

She knew, instinctively, that Teo would never accept her reasons for fleeing this mountain. He would never understand her need to know he was safe, immune from the PRI.

As if that were an answer, Melanie started forward, spurred on.

She slid behind the wheel after depositing Chris in the front seat and fastening his safety belt. She fished the keys from her handbag, didn't care that her hands were shaking so badly that she had difficulty holding the single car key. But she did think about Teo taking her hands in his, holding them, kissing away the trembling, kissing away her tears. Oh, dear God, she thought.

The car sputtered to life and after only letting it warm up a moment, Melanie released the emergency brake and shifted the car into gear. With each revolution of the wheels, Melanie's heart grew heavier and heavier. By the time they reached the turn-off, tears were again streaming down her face. She turned left, instead of right—the way she'd come a scant two weeks before.

It felt like a lifetime ago.

CHAPTER TWELVE

Teo stretched and opened his eyes abruptly, realizing immediately where he was, who should be beside him but wasn't.

"Melanie?" he called softly. When she didn't answer, he told himself not to worry, that she was only in another part of the house and couldn't hear him. He would have to get her to trust him enough to lower that damnable guard in her mind. He ached to feel her thoughts touch his again.

He'd dreamed of her doing just that, a touch like a kiss, a melding of thoughts, connections that spelled great tenderness, *love* and something else. Something that had made him long to reach for her, hold her close to him, comfort her...console himself. He frowned, sitting up. The something else had been a goodbye.

He remembered it clearly now. *Farewell...I love you.*

He sent his mind questing for young Chris. And didn't find him. Was he dancing his toys? Was that why he was blocking Teo's touch? He stepped up the call, making it a summons. Still no response.

He stretched his thoughts outward, questing them, searching them out in his home. But couldn't conjure an image of them anywhere. A shaft of pure panic needled his heart, and he felt a jab of undiluted rage that he immediately tried to squelch.

She couldn't have lied to me. She couldn't have.

But what he meant was, of course she had lied to him; didn't everyone lie eventually? Wasn't betrayal a natural step in the evolution of a relationship? It certainly had been in his case. So, while he might fight the notion of lying, he'd been expecting it all along. And what he really felt was sick to his very heart.

He swung his legs from the bed and jerked on a pair of pants. Not bothering to dress any more than that, he strode from his bedroom, searching for the pair he had dared to allow to go to sleep, believing they could be the family he'd finally given up hoping for.

"Melanie?" he called from the cloud-gray living room. At the lack of an answer, he checked Chris's room. Not there, either. He narrowed his eyes at the rumpled quilt, the silent room, the lack of a miniature hooded parka and little shoes. He touched the cradle and felt the blankets not cold, but not warm, either.

She wouldn't have gone. Not after last night. Not now.

But his heart knew otherwise. Of course she had gone. Instead of six months, she had given him two weeks. Instead of a dream, a future, she'd given him another taste of bitterness to add to his lifetime supply of betrayals.

In the deepest part of himself, he'd known she wouldn't stay. He had known it wouldn't happen. Even as he had cried her name and called for her to stay with him, even at the moment of truly wanting the dream to blossom into reality, he had known, truly known it wouldn't ever happen.

Energy rippled across his shoulders, down his arms, and he flicked the residue to the skies. Several small jagged-edged bolts of lightning cut through the sky, separating his home from the mountains across it.

But why had she left now? Now, when he so wanted her to stay? Could he be wrong?

Were they out on the mountain somewhere? Didn't Melanie know it could be dangerous? What if the PRI's hit men had managed to trace them and found them out there all alone? Mentally blocked or not, Melanie was essentially defenseless and Chris's new capabilities were as unstable as any new form of learning would be to a three-year-old child.

He waved open the door to the kitchen, walked through to the washroom. Not there, nor in the kitchen. He was on his way to the deck, to check the fencing, the steps leading around to the side of the mountain, when he saw the note lying on the island bar. It was scarcely larger than one of the Spanish tiles.

He stared at it for several seconds as if he might ignore it, go on with the search for his newfound family, for some semblance of the peace he'd felt in his dreams, in the moments before drifting to sleep with Melanie curled to his body, locked in his arms the night before.

He knew with absolute certainty, with heart-stopping clarity, that the note, the words inked on white paper, meant the end of the dream. And if he picked it up, read it, the words would make the ending all the more real, the more desperately final.

He began to shake and threw off the excess energy, scarcely clearing it from the deck before the thunder cracked with a ricochet effect.

Finally, quelling the waves of denial that coursed through him, he snatched the small piece of paper from the bar. He had to read it twice before he understood even a small portion of what Melanie had tried to tell him. And a third time before the psychic impressions she'd left behind coalesced and took shape.

She had left him; he understood that. Hell, he'd expected it all along...until last night. But she'd said her leaving was for his sake. What kind of a fool did she think he was?

But as he held the note, another image crept into his mind. His uncle. Pablo had told her something. Done something. Her leaving was Pablo's doing. After fifteen long years, he had finally found himself on the edge of happiness...and once again his uncle had betrayed him.

And Melanie, too. Whatever motives she might have had, whatever she might have believed from Pablo's twisted mind, she had stolen the best part of Teo in her departure. She had taken Chris and she had taken the dream. Like a thief, she had plundered his heart, his hope of a future, the night spent in her arms. She had left while he'd slept. She had asked him to stay with her and left him when he did.

I love you. She'd said it in his dream, penned it on this damnable note. How could she leave him, then? How could she say she loved him and then go? How could she tell him so…and then go? If she hadn't…if she hadn't told him, he might never have known, might never have had to face the fact that he might love her, as well.

A primal, animal-like groan escaped him. "N0!" he yelled as he held the note out from him and sent some of his rage at it. It burst into flame and dropped to the ground in a pirouetting spiral of fire.

If Pablo didn't tell him where she went, that would be his fate, as well.

He didn't dare think what he would do to Melanie. All he knew was that he would find her because he'd be damned if he would be cheated of a single day of his promised six months. And he'd be double damned if he ever begged her for anything again.

He smiled as the lightning snapped down the abyss, and if the smile on his lips felt evil, angry, that was all right. He felt that way, too.

Melanie had driven some twenty miles up the narrow road leading away from Loco Suerte. She'd been lost when she stumbled across it; she was even more lost now. When she had come to New Mexico, driven into these dark, prime examples of why early settlers had designated the entire range the Rocky Mountains, she had been tired, nearly despairing of finding Teo Sandoval, the only man who could possibly help her.

Now she was lost in them once again, tired, dried tracks of tears staining her cheeks, and in despair over leaving him, the only man who had brought her to life. She glanced over at Chris. He was sullenly staring up through the window at the sky. She had snapped at him only moments earlier when he'd asked for what seemed the hundredth time if he could make the loud noise.

That she had immediately regretted her brief flare of temper, and had apologized as swiftly, didn't seem to matter to Chris. He'd told her in no uncertain terms that he wanted Teo.

"Go home to Teo," he'd said. *Now!* he'd commanded her mentally.

When they had achieved some five miles from the turn-off, she'd cautiously lowered her barriers. She couldn't feel Teo, and resisted the impulse to send her mind questing for him. Nor could she detect any sign of the PRI, although every pore seemed to absorb a sense of danger all around her, all around Chris.

At first Chris had been intrigued at the full sharing of thoughts, but he'd soon become readjusted to having his mother with him again. That was when he'd begun asking for Teo, and asking to make the loud noise. He projected a few perplexing images at her, pinecones bursting into flame, Teo's lightning, rocks rolling down a cloud bank, but she'd ignored the images, concentrating on getting them as far away from Teo as was possible.

Car stop, Chris offered.

"No," she said aloud, but he only shot her a "no" look himself and projected the concept again. *Car stop.*

"I can't stop the car, honey. The bad men are nearby. They're looking for us. We have to go."

He projected an image of Teo making men in white coats

dance on the air as Chris did his toys. And then that perplexing image of rocks rolling down a cloud bank came again. Melanie shook her head. "They would hurt Teo," she said aloud.

Dead plant...Teo?

The imagery was grizzly and chillingly apt. *Yes,* she answered sadly.

Chris hadn't spoken after that, only stared at the gathering clouds outside the windshield of the Buick. They rounded yet another curve in this seemingly endless strip of hairpin turns.

And what she saw ahead of them made her heart leap in horror.

Teo had taken the shortcut to the back of his uncle's gas station. He was at the back door in less than fifteen minutes and through it and into the small apartment Pablo used in less than one.

Pablo was in the act of pouring a cup of coffee when Teo burst into the room. If Teo hadn't been so angry, so furious, he might have smiled at the picture of terror Pablo presented when he caught sight of his nephew in the narrow doorway.

"Where is she?" Teo asked coldly, quietly.

Pablo hadn't lowered the coffeepot; he continued to stare at Teo as if he were the devil and not his own blood that had walked in that door. All the while he stared, he was pouring coffee onto the cabinet, the floor.

"Where is she?" Teo demanded again, faster, harder. He took a step into the room.

"I d-don't know wh-where she is, Teo," Pablo said.

"Don't dare call me by my name, *Uncle.* You have no right to use it. What did you tell her yesterday?" *What did you say to her that made her lie to me last night, steal away like a thief this morning?*

He thought he saw a measure of relief cross Pablo's face at his question, though nothing relieved the pallor brought on by his sneer at his relative's title, the shock fanned by his sudden appearance after fifteen long years.

"What did you tell her?" Teo asked again. Upon not receiving a reply, without mercy, he hammered his way through the imperfect block and straight into his uncle's confused mind. With no care whatsoever, he trampled across feelings, guilts and fears. Without speed, without deliberate softening of the patterns, he pummeled Pablo's mind like an overzealous baker might punch bread.

He searched through the muck that made up Pablo Sandoval's mind, uncaring that this was the man who had taught him how to fish, who had taken him for long walks in the woods, who had given him his first bow and arrow set, only remembering that this was the man who had wronged him once long ago, and again only the day before. Now.

He caught a line or two...*He'll protect us—* Melanie's voice. Spoken yesterday, or two weeks ago? When? Pablo's voice, *Tell him you don't love him... He will let you go, then.*

He paused, his heart beating erratically now, because she hadn't told him that. Pablo was right; had she told him she *didn't* love him, couldn't do so, no power on earth, and certainly none he possessed, would have kept her there. Instead she had written a note of goodbye...and said she *did* love him.

Slower, with a little more care, he continued his search. He felt staggered by the contradictions, the conflicting thoughts. *Love...betrayal...forgive me, Teo... Run, señora, and take your boy with you... They will kill him if you stay...you stay and Teo dies...Angelina never should have married Ernesto, that drunken coward...Teo was like my own son…Teo burned my mind that day long ago.… Help me, God… Stop, you're hurting me, Teo…Teo!*

Teo pulled back, lessening his furious mental hold, his mental trampling of Pablo's already damaged psyche. He found he was shaking, as much from the rage that had propelled him down the mountainside as from confusion over what he'd discovered in his foray into the wilds of Pablo's mind.

To his shock, perhaps his horror, he'd discovered that while his uncle certainly felt tremendous guilt in the role he'd played in betraying Teo, the deepest emotion he had felt toward Teo all these years was more akin to sympathy. *Pity.*

He half lifted his hand as though he would strike his uncle. He felt the energy coursing through him. He tossed a bolt of lightning to the sky in swift reprisal, rough demonstration.

"Don't pity me, old man," he snapped.

Pablo stared at him a moment, then straightened slowly. His eyes were as dark as the coffee spilled upon the cabinet beside him, and as liquid. "I don't pity you now, *niño.* You have made yourself this way, not me. All I feel for you is sadness."

Teo knew this wasn't the whole truth; Pablo also felt a tremendous amount of fear…deservedly so. "You dared to interfere in my life again, *Uncle,*" Teo growled at him.

Pablo shook his head but didn't lower his gaze, didn't look away in the fear that shook his body. "What life, Teo? Answer me that, if you can."

"My life!"

"Again, I ask you…what life? The great El Rayo, who grants the villagers a glimpse of his wonderful power? Accepting food and clothing from the poor because they fear you too much to just knock on your door to say thank you?"

"Stop this!" Teo yelled, and sent another burst of energy to the skies directly above Pablo's home. A tremendous clap of thunder followed, making Pablo flinch backward and nearly slip in the coffee. But his eyes never left Teo's.

"That woman, she cares for you enough that she would rather leave you than see you hurt. She wants to save you. As I do. But you, all you think of is revenge. All you care about is finding her for your sake. All you care about is beating down the old man who betrayed you all those years ago. Poor Teo, poor El Rayo."

Teo threw a bolt of pure energy directly at Pablo. As his uncle yelled and leapt sideways, Teo angrily deflected it, sending it crashing into the wall above Pablo's Formica-topped cabinet. The wall shook and burst into flame, then seemed to melt, the old adobe mud and stucco dripping molten lavalike mud from a hole roughly the size of a basketball.

He told himself he hadn't stopped the energy from striking Pablo out of any misguided sense of familial recognition, out of any long-buried loyalty. He'd stopped it only because he still didn't know what he needed to know... where Melanie was, where she'd taken Chris.

But as he watched his uncle's face go from pallid to ashen, he found it bothered him more than he might have guessed to actually talk with his uncle, face-to-face, alone again after all these years. And he found he couldn't ignore what he'd plundered during that foray into the man's mind.

He had loved this man once. Had almost worshiped him. Pablo had been the uncle who had not only taught him how to fish, but how to carve the intricate carvings on his pieces of wood. He had listened to his nephew's thoughts, and though unable to do much more than send a disjointed image or two, he had never made Teo feel self-conscious about his gifts whenever he was with him. Which had been almost daily.

He'd given Teo his interest in the wild creatures of the forest, and in the unique world of books. All Teo knew of loving came from this man. As did a great body of his knowledge of betrayal.

"Just tell me where she is."

"I don't know. Why don't you find out?"

Ruthlessly shoving such memories away, Teo again plundered his uncle's thoughts. His lack of care, his deliberate heavy-handedness drove Pablo to his knees, crying out in pain, grabbing his head on either side of his eyes.

"Where is she?" he demanded.

"Stop, Teo! I don't know where she is! She's gone!" *She had to go, to save her son…to save* you. *The PRI won't care about you now. Just the boy. Let her go. Let me go.*

"How did you get her to leave?" Teo demanded aloud as he thought the question at Pablo, hard enough to make the older man moan before answering.

"I told her— Ah-h-h, stop this, Teo, I beg you.… I told her—"

Teo leapt past the web of lies Pablo had already constructed in his mind to account for the whereabouts of Melanie Daniels and her son Chris. Then he seized one and dragged it to the surface of Pablo's terrified mind. He studied it from all angles, listened to it with all senses. This one was the truth. This was how he'd persuaded her to flee Teo's home. *If you don't leave, they will kill him. Teo. They will kill Teo.*

It was what he had told her, this was the fulcrum Pablo had used to pry Melanie from his home.

"How could you have told her such a thing?" Teo asked. He didn't ask it in anger. If he'd thought about it, he would have said he asked in a dull puzzlement. But it went deeper than that, it pierced the very core of his confusion about Pablo, about Melanie, about society as a whole.

Perhaps what he really wanted to know was why Pablo

had told her that the PRI would kill him to get to Chris. And why, believing it, Melanie would take Chris out into almost certain danger rather than let it happen. A possible answer to this last question formed in his mind, but he didn't dare consider it, couldn't believe it could possibly be true.

Pablo didn't answer, only moaned, rocking forward, still holding his head.

"Uncle," he said, and this time the word wasn't a denigration, wasn't used as a sword. "Why would you tell her such a thing? You know it isn't true."

"But she...didn't," Pablo gasped.

"You wanted her to leave me...." Teo said. He felt stunned, saddened, betrayed anew.

"No. No, I wanted you to fight for her," Pablo said. "I wanted you to be a man again, not a god."

For a full second Teo couldn't even think. He couldn't begin to comprehend the magnitude of what Pablo had done. Fifteen years ago he had felt the same way, watching his uncle stare at him through tear-filled eyes as the men holding Teo had jabbed him yet again with a drug-filled needle.

"You didn't," he said, stunned into neutrality. "You couldn't have."

"I had to," Pablo said.

"Why?" He was so stunned that he didn't think to reach into his uncle's mind for the answer this time. He lifted him from the ground and shook him. "Damn it! Tell me why!"

"To save you," Pablo said, his feet dangling some five inches above the ground, his eyes wild with fear, his hands twitching uselessly at his sides.

Teo only stared at him as the realization of what his uncle had done sank in. As the realization of what Melanie had done began to seep through. "You fool. You incredible fool. My God, do you know what you've done?"

"You're here!" Pablo said, as though that were all in the world that could matter on this morning of disaster.

"*¡Tío!*" Teo screamed at him as he released and flung him away, letting him drop to the floor. How long had it been since he used the Spanish diminutive for uncle? He knew, but didn't care. "Don't you understand? You sent her into danger. *Danger,* Pablo. The PRI intends to *kill* her, *Tío.* She knows this. They will do *anything* to get their hands on Chris. If they find her, they will kill her."

"Oh, *Dios,*" Pablo moaned. "I didn't know this, I swear. I only thought that if she left, you would follow her. I saw the way you looked at her that day with Demo...I saw, you understand. It was the first time I have ever seen you look that way. And you let her stay. She never came back down the mountain. I thought, if she left...for you...you would see that you could have a life. That she loved you enough, you see? That you could finally trust somebody again."

And strangely, though his heart thundered in fear for Melanie and Chris, and for all that his blood seemed to be boiling with the energy that seared through him, Teo found he couldn't hate the pathetic man groveling on the floor before him.

Pablo had been wrong, very wrong, but he'd brought Teo one truth: Melanie did indeed love him.

On the heels of that truth, he found another. He loved her, too. Really loved her. He didn't just want her, and he didn't just need her. Nor did he love her as a mere extension of his long lost dreams of having a wife and a family. No, he loved her for herself, *as* herself. As a beautiful, vibrant woman who had graced the world with a remarkable child, a woman who wasn't afraid of the talents and gifts hidden in either the child or himself.

It was then he knew a shame so deep that it nearly made

his knees buckle as he thought of how he'd treated her all along, testing her at every juncture, frightening her, ignoring her, teasing her. Commanding her. Aching for her, but using her nonetheless. Doing this all though he'd known, instinctively, that she was the one woman in all the world for him.

And he'd done this all because he couldn't believe that for Teo Sandoval, man of power, lonely man of the mountain, things could possibly go right. Because he'd been unable to accept the notion that Melanie might really want him for himself, want him not just as a protector but as a lover, as a surrogate father for her child, as someone she might want to talk with, to be with throughout her life. And, perhaps most damning of all, he'd convinced himself that he didn't dare trust her.

And she had left the mountain, facing certain terror, certain danger, all because *she loved him*, wanted to spare him.

Making him moan out loud was the realization of the torture she must have endured the night before. When she'd cried, asked him to stay the night with her, had sobbed against his shoulder, she had known she would be leaving him…for *his* sake.

Oh, God, he could hardly bear the pain of knowing what she'd done for him.

Please, God, let me find her in time. The prayer rang through his mind and his soul, because he knew with absolute certainty that he couldn't live without her. Couldn't live without her love, without her son. She wasn't a part of the dream, she *was* the dream.

He stared down at the weak man on the floor before him, the man he had once loved, who even now had thought to help him in his own twisted way.

I love you came a momentary clear projection from Pablo's chaotic thoughts. The same words Melanie had used in both the note and the dream. *I love you.*

Teo had long since loosed the mental hold on his uncle, and now he reached out and took Pablo by the arm, drawing him to his feet. He wouldn't have been surprised to find blood on his uncle's face, broken vessels upon his cheeks, but aside from his extreme pallor, there was no sign of physical distress.

"I need your help, Uncle," Teo said.

Pablo's eyes raised to his, sudden liquid blurring them, making them huge in surprise, in hope. "Anything, *niño*."

"You have to drive your truck. I don't have a license anymore, and I will have to be looking for them."

Pablo immediately dove a hand into his coffee-stained pants and drew out a key ring. "Let's go."

They climbed into Pablo's old Chevy pickup and Teo didn't even notice the heavy clang of the metal doors slamming closed. His mind was already questing, searching the highways, skimming the mountainsides.

He felt impaled on the seat as a single blast of thought burst into his mind. *Teo!*

Melanie. He reached for the strand of psychic energy, slipped, missed. She was too far away. He couldn't grasp her, couldn't hold her. *Melanie?* He tried sending out to her in response, but still couldn't find her, couldn't feel her thoughts.

But what he'd felt had sent a knife through his heart, slicing him to ribbons. Don't let it be too late, he begged.

"Teo...?" his uncle asked nervously, concern edging his voice.

He frowned heavily, concentrating, trying to reconnect with that single, cold, terrified strand of thought. He turned his head left, then right...and caught a fragrance of her, a nuance of her rich tone.

"Toward Tierra Amarillo," Teo said, then repeated it louder, more surely. He hadn't found them, but he could feel a trace of Chris's mind, and the smell of Melanie's rental Buick, which he'd cleaned so perfectly the first night she'd arrived so that she could leave the next morning. He wished now that he'd simply demolished the thing.

"She'll be all right," Pablo muttered, throwing the pickup into gear. Revving the motor, he jerked it onto the narrow two-lane highway.

Teo looked at the dark thunderhead gathering in the sky, the thick ghost clouds creeping down the mountains. An owl flew overhead and Teo's neck rippled with superstitous reaction. The hairs on his neck raised in an almost superstitious premonition.

A part of him wanted to tell his uncle that if she wasn't all right, if anything had happened to her, he would tear Pablo limb from limb and throw him to the mountain lions. But, in truth, he couldn't have done that, nor would he want to. Because if anything had happened to Melanie and Chris...nothing in this life would matter. Nothing at all.

At Melanie's gasp of horror, Chris struggled to sit up higher, see over the dashboard, but the seatbelt held him restrained. She automatically applied the brakes, stretching a hand out to protect her son. *Safe,* she tried to project. But all she could think was *trapped,* doomed, *lost.*

Off, off, off! Chris projected, but to her shock, not at her. She felt the imagery, felt his touch, but also felt something whoosh by her, saw the air inside the car begin to shimmer. Suddenly Chris's child-proof safety harness snapped free, belt ends dangling in the air. Chris paid no attention to this remarkable feat. He stretched up to sit on his knees, using the dashboard as a support.

"Car stop," Chris said, pointing.

"Yes," she affirmed dully, understanding what he'd been trying to tell her now. She had assumed she'd known all there was to know about Chris's gifts, about his multi-layered talents. But he'd stretched those talents with Teo.

He had *known* what lay ahead, at least a mile back, he had *known* what lay in wait. And had tried to warn her.

Blocking the road, rigged to face each other nose-to-nose, were two black station wagons, unmarked, obviously intending serious business. Why hadn't she seen this, heard the thoughts of the men inside? And where was the white the dream had warned her about?

Where was Teo? Immediately, the memory from the dream—Teo with blood spilling down his front, calling her name, his hands outstretched, blood upon them—sprang her mind into galvanized action, and her block dropped open and her thoughts spilled free, like floodwater escaping a broken dam.

Teo, she cried out frantically. And then, stronger, *TEO.*

Was it too late? They were blocking her, were they already at Teo's mountain home? Was he safe? Had she left too late?

Too late…too late…the words seemed to reverberate in her head, echo in her heart.

Teo! Hear me, Teo! Desperation, need and love all combined to spike her thoughts with adrenaline, sending them careening wildly, questingly. Needfully.

The two black cars were totally blocking both lanes of traffic on this narrow road. From some dim recess of her still rational mind, Melanie knew she had a slim margin for escape and she used every bit of lore she'd ever read or seen on car escapes to pull off a miracle.

She forced herself to let up on the brakes, then, in what seemed sheer lunacy, jammed her foot down on the gas pedal with all her might. With the smooth action known to Buicks, the car leapt forward, and without so much as a whine, whizzed toward the parked cars. Hoping she'd gathered enough speed, she urgently pulled up on the emergency brake and cranked the wheel sharply to the left.

Please…please…please, she thought as she heard the

scream of the tires on the road, felt the sickening conflicting message shudder through the car. For a single blessed moment she actually felt the rear end of the car slowly sliding on its squealing tires, almost as though in slow motion, and knew that stunt seen so often in movies—the mythic J-turn—was a reality, that it was truly working for her now.

All the while—a matter of some five seconds or less—she mentally yelled at Chris to depress the lock button. They wouldn't be able to get in for a few minutes at any rate. Just let her have enough time to turn the car around and head back toward Loco Suerte. Toward Teo.

Teo!

Car stop! Chris suddenly screamed in her mind.

The force of his mental command, his warning, made her wince, lose control of the wheel for a moment. "Chris..." she started to protest, then trailed off as the car, in midswing, abruptly died. It didn't stop its wide swing immediately, however, it continued to glide as though on ice, until it gently rocked to a halt.

And now she and Chris were also straddled across the road. From her side window she had a direct view of the station wagons blocking the way, the two men inside each of them.

She gave a rough sob, a choked sound that was somewhere between a scream and a whimper, and urgently tried cranking the key downward. Nothing happened. There was no engine-about-to-turn-over sound, no *click-click-click* of a starter on the fritz. Nothing. No sound at all except her ragged, sobbing breathing and, oddly, Chris's clapping.

And then she understood. This was no malfunction of the rental Buick. This was nothing she had done, either. The clapping hands said it all.

Chris had stopped the car. With his mental command. Dear Lord, Chris had stopped their only means of escape!

"Oh, honey!" she cried. "Don't stop the car now! Those

are the bad men—" *Bad men! Bad men!* "—We need the car to get away."

"Make loud noise now, Mommy?"

The men stepped out of their cars. There was something incredibly strange and ominous about them. And not just because they were after her son. As if seeing them through a camera lens, Melanie watched them round the cars, standing a little to the sides of each one, hands extended, palms exposed, as though trying to tell her that there was absolutely nothing up their sleeves.

Fear, paralyzing, crippling fear, glued her to the seat, made her heart nearly stop, her breath catch in her lungs.

TEO! TEO! she projected, unconsciously. She had no sense of him nearby, no sense of him at all, but she sent the thought lurching outward, racing back to Loco Suerte, back to the mountain aerie, back to where she should never have left mostly, back to the man she should never have abandoned.

Even as her mind sought him, desperately, achingly, she watched as all four men began walking toward their Chris-stalled car. She frowned as she realized why they looked so ominous, so odd. All four of the men wore strange-looking, slightly ridiculous helmets, as if they were three-piece-suit bikers.

Even knowing she was in the gravest of dangers, she felt a bubble of hysterical laughter trying to break free. She covered her mouth to hold it in, but a small sound—a ragged, tattered thread of noise—escaped anyway.

But it didn't sound like a laugh. It sounded suspiciously like a sob.

As if still seeing them lens-small, Melanie felt she wasn't watching real men at all, but movie characters, actors, people pretending to be thugs, hit men. Perhaps even men trying to behave like creatures from outer space. She wished it were true, but knew it wasn't.

These men were walking toward her car to take her son from her with force.

And as she frozenly stared out the side window at them, watching their slow, very cautious approach to her car, she suddenly understood why they were wearing helmets, what the helmets portended.

The helmets were lead-lined, might, in fact, be lead clear through. And she couldn't read a thought from a single one of them. They were like the gloves the scientists had used when handling Chris, and the same had probably been used when touching Teo all those years ago.

They were wearing the helmets to block their thoughts from the very people they sought to capture. They had escaped detection this way. They knew she was telepathic, didn't perhaps know the extent of her abilities, but they knew enough, nonetheless. She had spilled it all during the early days of the wining-and-dining that the PRI had done for her, in the days when filling out forms and taking tests had seemed perfectly normal, even adventurous.

And they knew Chris was one of the strongest telepaths ever recorded.

But though her mind had been blocked all this time, Chris's had been open. They could have taken them at any time. Why this elaborate dodge? Had they conned Pablo into helping them again?

Then she felt a wave of nausea sweep over her as she understood the full import of what she was seeing. Her own block from Teo had helped them, while the helmets had protected them from Chris or Teo's discovering their presence.

And even after she'd lowered her precious guard, she hadn't felt their thoughts, only the danger. She hadn't known they hid around the curve in the road.

But Chris had. He had known. Despite the helmets, despite their caution, he had known. *Car stop*. He'd most definitely known.

"Can you still read their thoughts, Chris?" she asked suddenly, hopefully.

He didn't so much as glance her way. His eyes were fixed on the men slowly narrowing the some hundred yards separating them.

"Make loud noise now, Mommy?" Chris asked again, louder.

He was only three. Just a baby. He didn't understand what they wanted from him, what they would do to him. And they were breaching the distance. They would have what they wanted within moments.

"Fine. Yes," she said, defeat pulsing through her veins. "Make any noise you like, Chris." Make the loud noise, make your toys dance, bend a rainbow upside down and fill it full of green ice cream. It's all the same to me. Do whatever your little heart desires...because it's very likely, it'll be the last thing you ever do on your own.

"Make a very, very loud noise, honey. A huge, humongous noise."

The air in the car seemed to shimmer again, as if they were sitting in the center of some kind of force field. She had the sensation of air being drawn out of the car as if transforming it into a vacuum. And she could see the four men looking around in some confusion, as if Mother Nature was suddenly changing the rules on them.

My God, she thought, what had Teo taught him? She'd seen the little tricks, the careful lifting of the coffeepot, the pouring of the coffee without spilling a drop, the opening of a cabinet, the slow, deliberate closure. But she'd witnessed nothing like this. Nothing.

The shimmer she'd seen in the car stretched outside now, enveloping the space between their stalled car and the two cars blocking the road. It gathered strength, form, size, twisting, writhing, a wall of translucent, rippling sparkle.

"Chris...?" she started to ask, then trailed off as the four men some twenty yards from their barricaded cars began backing away from the imposing, impossible shimmer.

"Rocks," Chris said distinctly, and Melanie had the briefest of mental images of his rocks on the cloud bank in the space between her car and those of the PRI henchmen. Suddenly, that space was filled with a blinding ball of fire, accompanied by the loudest clap of thunder she'd ever heard in her life.

Kerr-R-R-RACKKK!

Melanie lifted a hand to the side of her head, gave a brief shriek, and instinctively reached for her son with her free hand.

He wasn't the slightest bit frightened. Instead he was again clapping his hands in self-congratulation. "Make loud noise, Mommy. Chris make loud, *big* noise!"

"The biggest," she agreed, pulling him to her chest, hugging him tightly.

Melanie.

She whirled in surprise, feeling Teo so close in her mind that she'd felt sure he could touch her, as well. But he wasn't there.

What *was* there was one of the four men in the helmets. But this one didn't have his palm facing forward, nothing-up-my-sleeve style. This one had a very nasty-looking gun with an incredibly dark barrel pointed directly at her forehead.

"Game time's over," he called through the window. "All we want is the kid, ma'am. Just get out of the car. Real, real slow."

CHAPTER THIRTEEN

As they rounded yet another curve in the long, winding road leading the back way to Tierra Amarillo, Teo felt Melanie and Chris. He could almost see them. They were still inside the car, but in extreme danger.

"You find them yet?" Pablo asked, but Teo didn't answer.

I'm with you, Melanie, he projected.

He felt Chris first, a joyous, triumphant touch. *Made loud, LOUD noise. Teo! Come home now?*

Teo wanted to yell at him to be careful, wanted him to understand the gravity of the danger he and his mother were in. For, through the boy's vision, he could see a man in some kind of strange helmet standing at the window of their car, a large, dark weapon trained on Melanie's forehead. But he didn't want to frighten Chris. Not now.

And almost making his heart stop was the nearly casual reference Chris had made to *home*…Teo's home.

Can you make another noise, niño? Teo asked.

Juice all gone, Chris projected a little sadly.

Teo knew this was very likely so. Chris was only an infant in the world of telekinesis. Making a lightning bolt took a tremendous amount of energy at first. A fireball took even more. Almost the same amount as a full-scale healing did. It would be several minutes before Chris's "juice" was back up again.

Melanie…? Teo projected. And suddenly he was there. With her, in her mind, where he'd always longed to be. He could feel her terror, her frozen fear. And he felt her embrace, her knowledge that he was with her. Her block was still somewhat there, wasn't totally eradicated, but it had been lowered enough for him to break through, to hold her to his thoughts, to wrap his mind around hers.

Tears came to his eyes as she returned the embrace, and he stretched to meet the familiar-unfamiliar patterns that comprised her mind.

He felt a jolt of terror rock her, and knew with sudden horror that the terror she was feeling was not for herself, not even for Chris, but for him. Her mind started to close, to thrust him out again, block him from knowing the dangers she and Chris faced...still trying to protect him from the PRI's intent.

Don't shut me out! he demanded furiously, desperately. If she closed to him now, all he would have to rely on would be Chris's less than accurate projections. Without her, he wouldn't be able to reach them in time, wouldn't be able to help.

They can't hurt me! he projected strongly. He felt her reel with the impact of the fierce thought, felt her shock, her negation ripple like an after-wave back at him.

He rapid-fired images at her, images from his days at the PRI, his time alone, his destruction of the PRI wing, the reasons for his absolute seclusion. The PRI could not stop him. There was nothing they, or their kind, could ever do to him. Nothing.

Slowly, hesitantly, the guard around her mind slipped, quivered, yet held.

Teo suddenly remembered one of the projections Chris had sent him when he'd asked about Melanie's closed mind. *Rapunzel's castle.* Instinctively he projected the image at her, then frantically called to her, making certain she saw the rope ladder he'd added to the picture, the ladder dangling from the window high, high above.

I'm coming, he sent.

And felt her accept, and finally acknowledge.

And once up that ladder, mentally embracing her, taking her into his arms, he projected his proximity, his determination to help them. And his love of her, the nights they'd shared, the understanding he now had of himself, of her. Of what she'd done for him, for his sake.

He felt her acceptance of the images he sent, marveled at her honey-rich tone, her brandied flavor. And despite the danger, almost as though negating it, she returned the subtleties of their time together, the mystery, the intrigue and the incredible fascination she had for him. That she would always have for him.

Better hurry, she sent, her mental voice tinged with irony, dusted with longing and hunger. He couldn't help but smile.

"I found them," he told Pablo. "Step on it."

"Why don't you fly us there?" Pablo asked in all seriousness.

"This is no time for games," Teo snapped.

"Señor El Rayo...if there was ever a time for games, this is it."

Teo thought of Chris's innocent joy in making the "LOUD" noise and Melanie's sacrifice for his sake.

He had been so long without connection with another that he was almost surprised when Melanie and Chris both stretched their thoughts across his, hearing Pablo through him, and now augmenting Pablo's statement, expressing their approval. Their urgency.

For Teo, it was like hearing a family at dinner, all talking at once, smells from the stove mingling with laughter, with approbation, a nearly cacophonous harmony. But this was no innocent evening at home; this was danger of the worst kind. The life and death kind.

Help you came Chris's loud yell.

Stay away came Melanie's deeper, softer voice.

But Teo hesitated. If he lifted Pablo's old Chevy and

made it fly through the air, even rearranged the mountains, scaring the pants off the PRI men in their ridiculous helmets, they would still believe they only had Teo to fear, not Chris, not his mother.

They had to know that in dealing with Melanie and Chris, they had more than they'd bargained for. They had to know they had another Teo Sandoval on their hands. And they, and all the perverted minds like them, had to know, once and for all, that the piper had to be paid sometime. And he wanted them to know that today was that time.

He took a deep breath and projected what he wanted Chris to do, what he needed Melanie to do. And then he promised them he would be there.

I promise you, he told Melanie as he felt her withdrawing to obey his strange commands. *I'll be there for you.*

Melanie knew Teo was right, knew that the only way the people from the PRI and people like them were ever going to leave Chris alone was for Chris to clearly demonstrate that he would never be trainable, usable. That he was already too far advanced for them to ever attempt to bend him to their perverted ways of thinking.

But the notion of fighting them, relying on Teo to help them do so, was utterly, completely terrifying. It would require a totally open mind with Teo, a complete lowering of all mental and physical guards. She would literally become one with him, in body and spirit, for his thoughts would be directing her actions.

And, too, she could clearly see the reality of what she'd projected to Teo. The gun trained on her was less than three inches from her head, not miles away, a shadowy image in someone else's mind. And she could see the grim face of the man holding it, the narrowness of his eyes, the gritted teeth.

"Come on, lady! Unlock the door. We don't want any trouble."

Ready, Chris? she projected. Her heart was pounding so uncomfortably, she was halfway certain she would die of a cardiac before the battle even began.

Please hurry, she sent to Teo, perhaps to the universe. Don't let him be too late, she begged. She felt his warm assurance brush her thoughts, interweave with her soul. But she could also feel his tension, his worry, his fear.

She knew the fear he felt was directed at them—*for* them—but she couldn't shake the sense of danger she felt surrounding him, as well. She had left the security of his home so that he might be safe, and despite his assurance that the PRI men couldn't do a thing to him, she didn't believe it. She knew this to be incorrect.

Whatever Teo might have projected to her about Pablo Sandoval's motives, his reasons for telling her that Teo would be in danger if she stayed with him, she knew they were still valid. She knew, as Teo refused to see, that if he tried to interfere with the PRI's determined plans to take Chris now, they would simply kill him.

In coming to their rescue, he would be coming to his death. Everything in her cried out in negation of this, screamed a denial. And though Teo's mental voice sent a multilayered blanket of reassurance, she couldn't rid herself of the feeling that things were far, far from well.

But did they have any alternatives now? Chris's energies were spent; the men in the helmets were blocked to her, and if Chris could understand them, he wasn't letting on. And Teo was still miles away, and the closer he got, the worse it would be for him.

She turned her head to look at the other three men, standing in front of their cars now, each holding a weapon of some kind. Unlike their cohort, they apparently weren't willing to risk another stroll across the highway, another attempt to remove them from the car.

She felt Teo in her mind, not vibrantly like before, just a touch, nothing more. His touch. But in it she could feel the emotion he carried for her, the depth of desire, a measure of sorrow, a surge of joy. Love.

How strange, she thought as she slowly unfastened her seatbelt, that both of them would come to know they loved the other just when things were at their worst. All her life she had believed that when love came, everything would simply fall into place. Life would pulsate with happiness, and all would forever be well after that.

It wasn't true. She loved Teo and Chris more than life itself, but that hadn't made the danger disappear. And now she knew Teo loved her. But that didn't make the man with the gun lower the weapon, tell her "Sorry, my mistake."

She felt a shaft of pure despair and knew that the only stronger emotion than knowing and sharing true love, was knowing it could be destroyed at any moment.

Slowly, numbly, looking every bit as frightened as the man outside might have wished her to do, she pulled up on the door lock and motioned for Chris to come into her arms. With a sense of destiny reasserting itself, she watched as the last thing Chris picked up before settling onto her lap was his red ball.

If dreams could come true...so could nightmares.

Please...please, she asked, but wasn't even sure what she was pleading for. Just please.

"Lady—"

"Get away from the car," she called, interrupting him. "I'm not coming out unless you stand back."

"Lady, you're not calling the shots around here."

They won't hurt you while you have Chris in your arms, Teo projected. He couldn't know how it went against the grain to use her three-year-old as a shield, even though she knew that holding him close to her was as much for his protection as for hers. Without her, he would be snatched up by the PRI men and whisked away.

I'd find him, Teo's thoughts came through, solid, concrete. Fierce. *But I need you, too.*

Melanie didn't reach for the door handle until the man holding the gun on them had stepped back two full paces. The sound of the handle locking into place, the slow swing of the door, were both preternaturally loud in her ears, seemed to echo throughout infinity. To Melanie, they sounded like a death knell.

"Go home now," Chris said fretfully. His red ball was cold and clammy against her throat. She stretched her legs from the car and was almost amazed to find they still worked.

"Nice and slow," the man with the gun said.

Melanie did as he asked, stood up very slowly, turning her head in the direction of the other three men.

Are you ready? Teo's mental voice asked her, undoubtedly asking Chris, as well.

Before she could answer, she saw something white out of the corner of her eye and as she turned to see what it was, she caught a glint of sunlight striking metal that shot straight into her eyes, blinding her for half a second.

"Mommy!" Chris called even as Melanie felt something sting her cheek. One moment she felt Teo in her mind, the next he was slipping away. In fact, as a sudden weakness overcame her, Melanie realized that the whole world seemed to be slipping away, blurring. She couldn't feel Chris in her arms anymore, but as she slumped to the asphalt highway, she saw the little red ball bouncing toward a clearing to the side of the highway.

"M-o-m-m-y!" she heard Chris scream, but the sound came from far, far away.

* * *

One second she had been with him, then suddenly, abruptly, the connection he'd felt with her was broken. He could hear Chris, but the messages were too frantic, too disjointed.

Something had happened to Melanie.

Melanie! he screamed mentally. *Chris!*

But he heard nothing from Melanie, felt nothing. She was gone. Not blocked, she hadn't shut him out, she was simply gone. And now some of Chris's imagery began to make sense. Melanie had been shot, she was lying on the ground. Her eyes were open. Dead plant, dead plant, dead plant.

Dear God, Melanie was hurt…maybe dead. Chris was alone with those men. And he, invincible king of the mountain where he lived, was too late to save them. Too late to save his family.

"No!" he yelled, and the old Chevy rocked with the force of the rage sweeping through him. He let loose another yell, and this time tasted the fear on his own tongue, the sour, coppery taste of blood.

But it wasn't his. Though no longer able to hear Melanie, he knew, from the taste, from the complete blankness of their minds, that the taste came from her. *He was too late.*

"Oh, *Dios!*" Pablo cried beside him, and pressed his foot even harder on the gas pedal.

He couldn't be too late. Fate couldn't be this cruel, this evil. Gathering his forces, Teo pulled them in like a normal man might marshal his strength in preparation for a battle. He ignored Pablo's wild-eyed look of fear, the dizzying need to expel the already excess electricity building too rapidly, too furiously within him.

Chris. I'm coming. Now. Don't be frightened. I'm coming. I'm coming for you.

Galvanized by fear, by a raw protective instinct, Teo leaned forward, laying both palms flat against the old, cracked dashboard. The Chevy shuddered, the motor sang a sharp, whining protest, then shot forward, taking the curves as though on some invisible electrical track.

His plan with Melanie and Chris had been simple, almost incredibly simple. Together, they would project what they were seeing, draw the energy from him and he would create a disturbance, a distraction. This way the PRI would automatically assume Melanie and Chris had been the ones to do such amazing feats, and the tables would be turned, the PRI henchmen would be the ones captured.

And it would have worked. But something had gone awry, it was already too late.

Melanie couldn't be dead. She couldn't be dead. The phrase chased its tail in his thoughts, around and around, making him feel sick with dread, despairing. She couldn't be gone. Not now. Not when he finally understood what life could be, what love really meant.

Teo? He felt a timid voice touch his mind. A baby voice. Chris. The hysterics, the panic, were fading, but the voice was small, frightened. Alone.

Teo?

I'm coming, son. Wait for me.

Mommy... Chris's mental voice was so subdued, so lost. *Need toys. Dance toys...*

Teo felt despair mingling with a dark, deep rage. No child should ever have to face such a thing, no child of three should have a built-in escape from reality.

And no man of thirty-five should have to grapple with the emotions that threatened to choke him now, swamped him with thick, unshakable pain. Those bastards! He'd kill every last one of them! He'd tear them to bits, bury them and sow the ground with salt! He'd fly to Pennsylvania, raze the entire PRI structure to the ground! He'd chase down every single person who had ever contributed a cent to that dastardly foundation and make certain they never felt like being charitable—or curious—again!

Make toys dance, now....

Chris! he projected, his heart nearly exploding with anguish, with need. He fed some of his own anger into Chris's mind, sending crystal-clear images of what he wanted the boy to do. What he needed him to do.

They rounded another curve, the final curve, seemingly taking it on two wheels. Pablo had ceased to have any control over the Chevy and was busy crossing himself, saying a prayer through nearly blue lips.

Teo's heart lurched as he took in the scene at a glance. Melanie lay upon the ground, her hand outstretched toward the swiftly approaching Chevy, as though seeking him even in death.

Chris stood beside her, his face white with fear, with confusion.

Four men in strange helmets and three-piece suits stood around Melanie and Chris, three farther back than the one. All looked afraid, but all carried a look of triumph, of victory.

At the screech of the Chevy's tires, as though marionettes controlled by the same puppeteer, they all looked up simultaneously. Their guns raised automatically when the Chevy skidded to a halt.

Teo! Chris cried in relief, in fear.

I'm here. And underscoring his meaning, his reality, his determination, he held his bare hand outside the Chevy's window and released a bolt of blue lightning from his fingertips. It danced across the sky, shot over Chris's head, hung for a moment in splendid fury, then smacked the ground in front of the three men on the far side of Melanie and Chris.

The ground shook with the impact and the thunder coming from it, before it, after it, made the universe sound as if the last cell door on planet earth had been flung wide.

From the corner of his eye, he saw something white

flicker to his left and sent a shaft of lightning at it without waiting to see what it was. He heard a man scream, heard a rapid volley of gunfire.

Drop to the ground, he commanded Chris.

Chris didn't obey him. Instead he whirled to his left and screamed, "Bad man! Dead plant!"

No, Chris! Teo shouted at the boy mentally. Whatever else happened on this darkest of days, the boy couldn't add killing to it. No matter how murderous his own thoughts might be, Teo couldn't allow the boy to assume that kind of guilt, that depth of rage.

He whirled to his left, to see what he'd sent the bolt of lightning after, to see who Chris was so focused on. It was one of the scientists, complete with white lab coat. On a treacherous mountain road in northern New Mexico, on an even more treacherous mission, the idiot was wearing his lab coat. And, as might have been expected, in his hand was a dart gun. A gun filled with drug-filled needles.

One thought, one burning, terrible thought, and the gun in the man's hand burst into flame. With a scream, the scientist threw it from him and bent double.

Another thought and the guns of the others followed suit. But this thought hadn't been Teo's. Chris had done it. All by himself.

When the four men started running for their cars, Teo directed the cars to crush in upon themselves. These boys weren't going anywhere.

Make men dance? Chris asked.

Make them dance, Teo allowed, and watched as the four men lifted into the air...propelled there by the small child they'd thought to capture, the boy they'd imagined they could control.

The four men were joined by the scientist, still screaming, and soon all were spinning in a mockery of the innocent bobbing Chris usually performed with his toys. A bobbing they themselves had taught him.

Teo didn't want to take his eyes from the spectacle of the five men. Because if he did, he would have to look at Melanie. He would have to finally, truly look at her still form, her hand curled outward, her hair covering her face, her ashen face. And he would have to understand that she would never smile at him again, that she would never open her arms to him again, that she would never, ever open her thoughts to him.

"*¡Madre de Dios!*" Pablo swore, dropping to his knees beside Melanie. He felt for her throat, held it there, seeking her pulse, turned his face to the sky, then slowly, he pulled his hand away. Even more slowly, he crossed himself again, and Teo could see the tears upon his uncle's face.

"Forgive me, Teo," the older man said. Sobbed. "Forgive me. I didn't know this would happen."

Teo looked at his uncle for several seconds, seconds that spun endlessly in his mind, in his numbed heart. He didn't understand the words for a moment, didn't see the necessity of translating them into any cohesiveness. But he nodded, nonetheless, understanding them finally. What was Pablo's foolishness in the wake of his own inability to have trusted Melanie before now? What was Pablo's betrayal of fifteen years ago but a human error?

"It doesn't matter," he said, and he spoke the unvarnished truth. Nothing mattered now. Just one little boy without a mother, left to the care of one broken man who would never be whole again.

He stepped closer, feeling as though his legs were wooden. He could no longer hear the cries of the PRI men, couldn't feel the sting of the cool October morning. He was anesthetized, leaden. His heart had died. His soul was shriveled and broken.

When he finally reached her side, he knew what it was

to die. It was the urge to stop living, the urge to simply lay down and say, "This is it, I've had enough."

"I am so sorry," Pablo said. "I didn't know. Oh, God, I didn't know they would shoot her."

As if his uncle's words broke some spell that had been keeping Teo erect, his knees suddenly buckled and he dropped to the pavement. He didn't feel the sharp impact, didn't feel the graveled surface against his knuckles as he reached beneath her and drew her into his arms.

Slowly, gently, he stroked the hair from her face, remembering all too clearly how he'd touched it that first day he'd seen her, how she'd held him in her arms as he'd reeled from his healing of Demo Aguilar. He had told her that day she should leave. If she had...would she now be alive? If she had listened to him...would she be somewhere smiling, loving Chris? Or had this entire episode been a capitulation of her destiny, and his?

No, this was his fault. He should have seen, should have known. If he had let her know his strengths, his weaknesses, if he had ever opened up to her, talked to her, truly let her know how much she had affected him, she would never have left this morning. She would still be alive.

Gripped with agony, he saw himself at the source of her pain, the cause of her death. He felt he'd been running twenty miles, gasping for air, her blood on his hands, vainly calling her name.

But he couldn't reach her. Would never do so again.

"Melanie!" he yelled, but he only heard the echo of his own voice, the stillness of the forest.

He rocked her as if she were a child he was lulling to sleep, though it was really himself he was trying to comfort. He knew there was no comfort, no joy left on earth.

"I'll watch Chris for you, Melanie," he said. "I'll take care of him as if he were my own. Nothing will ever harm him. I promise, *querida*. You have my word."

But what joy would he bring the child? He would have none left inside him. It was all gone. And he'd never once, except through brief mental touch, told her that he loved her. He'd cheated her of hearing the words. Cheated himself of having said them. They were all that mattered in life, and he'd never spoken them.

"I love you," he said now, knowing it was too late, but needing to feel them upon his lips, needing to know they had at least been made concrete. "Melanie... Oh, God, Melanie...I loved you so."

And without warning, the storm in him broke, and for the first time in fifteen years, Teo began to cry. As he rocked her, and cried, he found some huge, horrible darkness beginning to melt inside him, a darkness that had been there for as long as he could remember, that had crystallized when the PRI worked its madness on him fifteen years ago, a darkness that had sharpened when he'd understood that it was his beloved uncle who had taken him to them, and that had finally become encrusted with bitterness when the first villager had called his child to his side lest the evil eye of El Rayo strike the boy dead.

Teo.

He stiffened, hearing her rich touch in his mind, feeling her thoughts weave around his. *Teo.*

He wanted to lower her from his fearful hold, look at her, but didn't dare risk the hope that flared wild and hot within him.

Melanie.

I can share that darkness with you, she projected. Stronger this time, deeper.

His heart pounding so loudly, so fiercely, that he was certain the entire mountains rocked with it, he dared to lower her, dared to look into her eyes.

And he saw everything he could ever have wished for.

And more. And knew, from the clarity of her thoughts, that she did, as well. She was alive.

I hear a siren, she projected. And as if her thoughts had conjured one, Teo heard it, too. But he didn't bother to look for it. He didn't want to look away from her, didn't trust her not to slip from his grasp again.

"I won't," she whispered. "It's time to renegotiate our bargain."

For the first time since he'd pulled into the terrible scene, the tight fist around his heart relaxed a single notch and he dared look away from her.

The five men literally dancing in the air, hovering some six feet above the ground in a bizarre parody of a square dance, were silent, all eyes upon the small force that held them in place.

"Chris?" Teo said softly. *Chris! Put the men down now. You'll scare the sheriff.* He transferred the flicker of amusement he felt at the thought.

His own body tensed as the scream of the siren intensified.

You don't have to leave, this time, Melanie projected. *Somebody has to stop things like this from ever happening again. We can tell the sheriff. He will tell someone else. And they will tell someone. And soon—*

And soon, Washington will have congressional hearings to set up watchdog committees, Teo finished for her. With her.

And we'll start a school for children like Chris, Melanie offered. Her tone was somewhat wistful.

"And we'll start a school here in New Mexico for children like Chris, for the brothers and sisters we'll give him. After you marry me," he said. The siren was getting closer.

After we go home.

"To share the darkness?" he asked.

"No," she whispered, her voice a thread, her thoughts a rainbow.

"To share the light."

* * * * *

Silhouette® —

where love comes alive—online...

eHARLEQUIN.com

your romantic life

—Romance 101—
♥ **Guides to romance, dating and flirting.**

—Dr. Romance —
♥ **Get romance advice and tips from our expert, Dr. Romance.**

—Recipes for Romance —
♥ **How to plan romantic meals for you and your sweetie.**

—Daily Love Dose—
♥ **Tips on how to keep the romance alive every day.**

—Tales from the Heart—
♥ **Discuss romantic dilemmas with other members in our Tales from the Heart message board.**

TRUEBLOOD, TEXAS

In October 2001 look for

A FATHER'S VOW

by Tina Leonard

Lost

One twin. Ben Mulholland
desperately needs a bone marrow
donor to save his little girl, Lucy.
The brother Ben never knew he
had is her best, maybe only, chance.
If he can just track him down…

Found

The miracle of hope. Caroline St. Clair
has loved Ben forever and she'll do
whatever it takes to ensure he doesn't lose his precious
daughter. In the process, old wounds are healed and flames
of passion reignited. But the future is far from secure.

Finders Keepers: bringing families together

HARLEQUIN®
Makes any time special®

Conveniently Yours

THE BRAVO
BILLIONAIRE

As a child, Jonas Bravo saw his baby brother kidnapped before his very eyes—and life, as he knew it, would never be the same. Now, with another child's well-being at stake, he was determined to fight the good fight. But to hold on to *this* baby, he would have to marry her guardian. And though he didn't trust her as far as he could throw her, Jonas knew he had to let lovely Emma Hewitt into his life. For was it possible that this woman, and this child, were about to bring back everything he'd lost that long-ago winter night...and thought he would never see again?

THE BRAVO BILLIONAIRE, by Christine Rimmer:
On sale in September 2001, only from Silhouette.

And coming in October, the missing Bravo baby is
alive and well...and all grown up. Find him in
THE MARRIAGE CONSPIRACY by **Christine Rimmer**
(SE #1423)—on sale in October 2001,
only from Silhouette Special Edition.

Available wherever Silhouette books are sold.

Silhouette®
Where, love comes alive™